I saw that something was taped on the wall . . .

. . . an article from the Manchester *Union-Leader* about the discovery of the body of Denise Mochaud. Next to it was a color photograph, a Polaroid.

It showed the body of a woman sprawled on her back on a pile of fallen leaves. Her mouth was taped shut, her eyes open and glazed. Her arms were hidden beneath her. Her throat had been torn side to side in a gaping half-moon.

I swayed and closed my eyes and clamped my hands over my mouth.

Tied just above the cut in the woman's throat was a green ribbon, in a jaunty butterfly bow.

The critics love OUT OF THE DARKNESS.

"Thought-provoking . . . a gritty, bittersweet story [with] added depth and dimension." (Starred review)
—*Publishers Weekly*

"Susan Kelly creates a murder mystery which is nothing short of sensational . . . The action is swift; the story hard to put down."
—*The Bookwatch*

"Liz Connors is one of the most believable as well as likable of the new breed of women sleuths. She is both tough and feminine, a classy, caring lady with a good brain and a good sense of humor."
—*Grounds for Murder*

SUSAN KELLY

OUT OF THE DARKNESS

ZEBRA BOOKS
KENSINGTON PUBLISHING CORP.

ONE

I was standing at the window of Jack's office on the third floor of the police station, looking out at the Central Square rooftops and waiting for Jack to return from interviewing the witness to a murder in Cambridgeport. I hoped he'd be back soon. I had some bad news I wanted to unload on him, and it didn't improve with age.

The weather matched the news. A fine icy January rain needled down on Central Square, turning the snow that had fallen three days earlier into leaden slush. The storm drains had backed up and Green Street was a fjord. The intersection of Massachusetts and Western avenues was the lake the fjord fed.

The forecasters were predicting that tonight the temperature would drop well below freezing, which meant that by dawn tomorrow the entire city of Cambridge would have gone from swimming pool to skating rink.

Beautiful.

My name is Elizabeth Connors. I'm a free-lance crime writer. At least, that was what I'd been when I'd gotten up this morning. Now I was wondering if I ought to enroll in bartending school.

Jack is Lieutenant John Lingemann, a detective with the Criminal Investigation Division of the Cambridge Police Department. He probably wasn't thinking about going to bartender school. Crime solving is a growth industry in Cambridge. So is crime. Writing about crime and crime solving, on the other hand, seemed to be losing ground fast.

I left the window—I was getting sick of contemplating the Division of Employment Security building on the other side of Green Street—and parked myself in the chair behind Jack's desk. There was a copy of the *Globe* on the blotter. Maybe I should consult the help wanted section. Why not? I had nothing else to do. I picked up the paper, checked the index on the front page, and turned to the classifieds. Then I settled back to do some semi-serious job-hunting.

There were several ads for bartending school.

I was mulling over the possibility of carving out a niche for myself in used-carpeting sales when the office door opened and Jack came in. I refolded the paper and tossed it back on the desk, setting aside for the minute any fantasy of becoming the empress of recycled broadloom.

"Hi, sweetie," I said. "How'd your interview go?"

"Okay." Jack shrugged out of his trenchcoat. "She *may* stick." He glanced at me sharply. "How about you?"

I shook my head and made a thumbs-down gesture with both hands.

"Swell," he said flatly. He hung up his coat on the hook behind the office door. I got up to let him have his own seat. He came over to me and gave me a single-armed hug, a gesture of comfort and support. I rested my head against his shoulder.

"Look at the bright side," I said. "I'll have more free time now. I can take up a hobby. Botany. Thai cooking. Meditation. Embroidery."

He smiled briefly. "Yeah, right." He released me and gave my back a quick pat. Then he sat down behind the desk and I perched on a corner of it.

"You kind of suspected this was coming," he said.

I nodded. "But not quite so fast."

At nine o'clock that morning, I'd gotten a phone call from Brandon Peters, the publisher and editor of *Cambridge Monthly*. He wanted to see me in his office at ten. He wouldn't tell me why. He didn't have to; I'd already guessed the reason from his tone of voice. I finished dressing and sloshed through the rain to the magazine's office in Kendall Square.

I was right on time for the appointment. Peters was waiting for me in the reception area. So were three other staff writers for the magazine, the two contributing editors, the circulation director, and the advertising manager.

By five past ten, we had confirmed what we all already knew—that we were all out of a job. And *Cambridge Monthly* itself was out of business at the end of the month. Peters looked ready to cry.

We hung around the office for another half hour or so. Mostly we were consoling Peters. The receptionist offered to run down to Au Bon Pain and get coffee for everyone. Nobody was interested.

At a quarter to eleven the meeting broke up. The staff writers and contributing editors decided to move the wake to the nearest bar. They asked me to join them, but I declined with thanks. Instead, I said goodbye to Peters and he to me—a little emotionally on both sides—and shook hands with my ex-colleagues. We all swore to keep in touch. Then I trudged through the slush to the police station. I'd promised Jack I'd tell him the worst as soon as it materialized.

I don't like to drink in the morning, anyway.

"So," Jack said. He leaned back in his chair and clasped his hands behind his head. "What exactly happened?"

I sighed. "Well, according to Peters, advertising for the magazine dropped badly in the past year. I noticed that myself, but ... I guess I didn't realize quite how severe the situation was. And circulation's gone down. A lot." I sighed again.

"Couldn't Peters find a buyer or a backer or whatever?"

"He sure tried. He said he's been scrambling around looking for some kind of angel since last summer."

"And no luck?"

"Nope."

"So no more *Cambridge Monthly.*"

"Nope."

We were silent for a few moments. Both of us knew exactly what the folding of *Cambridge Monthly* meant to me—the loss of about ten thousand dollars a year in income. Which represented a third of my total annual take.

There was an additional complication.

If *Cambridge Monthly* had been the only magazine I wrote for that was going belly-up, maybe I'd have been less depressed and worried. But I'd heard some pretty substantial rumors that *New England Chronicle,* a monthly for which I did a regular crime column, was also on the brink of death. If it did croak, I was out yet another ten grand.

Magazines were like restaurants. For every ten that

opened, one survived. And that was in *good* economic times. In a recession, the odds were even worse.

Maybe I really *should* give some serious consideration to bartender school.

"What are you doing this afternoon?" Jack said.

I'd been staring at my knees. I looked up at him. "I'm not sure. I know what I ought to do."

"What's that?"

"Retype my résumé. Start calling and writing to every editor I can think of. Come up with some article ideas no one will be able to resist."

Jack nodded. "I'll give you a ride home."

"Okay. Thanks."

He had parked his car in the garage beneath the station rather than in the Green Street lot, so we didn't have to swim to it. As we left the office, Jack gave me another pat on the back.

We went down the narrow front staircase that led to the garage. The walls were lined with yellow tile, making the well a perfect echo chamber. Just how perfect was now being demonstrated. A faint howling noise from below grew louder as we descended. By the time we reached the first-floor landing, it was bouncing off the ceiling.

The door off the landing led to the men's lockup. The howling was coming from there. I tilted my head at the door. "Who the hell's that?" I asked. "Wile E. Coyote?"

"Some drunk," Jack said. "Thinks he Pavarotti."

"Don't they all?" I replied, and we went down into the garage.

As we were getting into the car, Jack said, "Do you mind if we detour to the courthouse before I take you home?"

"No, of course not." I buckled my seat belt. "What's doing there?"

"I have to pick up a warrant."

"Fine. I always enjoy a little trip to the courthouse."

We drove out of the garage and onto Western Avenue. The rain beat a small persistent tattoo on the roof and windshield of the car.

"One good thing about this weather," I said. "The bad guys'll be staying in tonight."

"Some of them." Jack looped the car around the traffic island and onto Franklin Street, on the other side of Western. Aside from a new and fairly flossy condo development on the corner of Essex, the east stretch of Franklin was industrial and shabby residential. It looked better in the rain than it did in the sun.

As we were riding past a vacant lot that, a few years before, some MIT students had tried to claim as a tent city for the homeless, Jack said, "Liz?"

"Yes?"

He cleared his throat. "You know, if you find yourself in any financial difficulty, uh . . . well, it goes without saying, doesn't it?"

"Yes," I said. "It does." I reached over and lightly squeezed his arm. "Thank you very much, honey. It won't come to that."

"But if it does."

"You'll be the first to know."

"Good. Hold that thought."

We didn't speak again for the rest of the drive to the courthouse, through a maze of streets lined with warehouses and condemned tenements.

I thought some more about *Cambridge Monthly*.

Brandon Peters had started the magazine thirteen years ago, when the city was on the verge of becoming not just the academic capital of the U.S. but a major force in high technology as well. *CM* had begun as a fifteen-page compilation of puff pieces on local celebrities, folksy little notes on community doings, breathless pieces on such topics of import as where to buy the best chocolate chip cookies and fresh pasta, and a lot of small ads for small businesses like dry cleaners and florists. The only thing that distinguished the magazine from a giveaway was that it had a cover price of seventy-five cents.

CM nearly went under about six times in its first two years. Each time Peters had managed to resuscitate it. That he kept the magazine alive at all was a testament not only to his business acumen but to his firm conviction that *CM* would not only take hold but take off.

In 1983, it did. By the time I was writing for *CM,* two years later, it had become a 250-page book. Its advertising revenues put it in the top twenty of the nation's regional monthlies. And it was attracting some of the big writing talent in the greater Boston area, of which there was a good deal. Peters had hooked and reeled in this talent with a nearly irresistible lure: high pay and creative freedom. All he demanded was your best work. I had considered myself lucky to be one of his people.

When I was taking my toddler steps as a free-lancer, I'd done one or two pieces a year for the magazine on spec. From there, I'd gotten commissions for five or six articles annually. And finally I'd graduated to major features, cover stuff.

Now all that was over.

Jack found a place to leave the car on the corner of Charles Street and Third, two blocks behind the courthouse. We walked past a fleet of Middlesex County Sheriff's Department vans and into the courthouse through a rear entrance reserved for law-enforcement personnel. Just inside the door a fat middle-aged guy in a deputy's uniform was doing security-guard duty. He was also eating a Snickers bar and reading the sports page of the *Herald*. He said hi to Jack and nodded at me.

In detective novels, cops are always routing judges out of bed in the middle of the night to sign warrants. In my experience, cops go to the courthouse in the middle of the day and stand at a long desk in a big room. When you've gotten her attention, a twenty-three-year-old woman with big hair, a dress one size too small, sheer black pantyhose, white ankle socks, and Reeboks types up a form for you. You joke with her awhile. Then eventually a short tubby guy in an Anderson-Little suit wanders over and scrawls an illegible signature at the bottom of the form. You joke with him awhile. Then you take the form and leave the courthouse empowered to arrest Mr. Murderer or Mr. Rapist or Mr. Mugger or whomever.

Maybe the official procedure is more exotic in the cities where they film the cops shows and movies. In Cambridge, it's pretty damn banal.

A Somerville cop came in on the same mission as Jack. He leaned over the counter and kissed the big-haired woman. Hard to imagine him doing that to a cranky judge at 3:00 A.M. Jack and I left the courthouse. The security guard had finished his Snickers and was engrossed in the *Herald* gossip column. I hoped there weren't any terrorists in the vicinity. He wouldn't notice them attacking.

As we walked to the car, I said, "What's on for you this afternoon?"

"Usual crap," Jack said. He tapped his chest, over the

spot where the warrant lay tucked in his inside suit-coat pocket to protect it from the wet. "Make the arrest for this."

"Not a dangerous arrest, I hope?"

He shrugged. The shrug meant "Probably not, but you never can tell." Jack and I have known each other long enough to carry out some parts of our day-by-day conversations in a combination of mutual shorthand and body language. Like most married couples. Except we're not married.

"If it's interesting," Jack added, "I'll tell you about it tonight over dinner. You pick the restaurant."

"Italian."

"You're on."

We got in the car, and he drove me back to my place.

My apartment was three rooms on the second floor of a remodeled frame Victorian on a small, comma-shaped street. Off the kitchen was a little deck with a staircase that led down to an enclosed backyard. Very convenient for when I didn't feel like walking the dog at night or in bad weather.

I collected my mail from the table in the foyer and went up to the apartment. When I unlocked the door, Lucy, my undersized chocolate Lab/Weimaraner cross, was standing just inside it, tail churning. She hoisted herself up on her hind legs and put her forepaws on my thighs. I scratched her behind the ears and said, "I'm glad to see you, too."

I tossed my shoulder bag on the couch and sorted through the mail. It was mostly bills (just what I needed) and circulars from the Star Market and Johnny's Foodmaster. One letter. I didn't recognize the name of the sender above the return address. I slit open the envelope.

The letter was an invitation from a cadre of local amateur mystery writers who wanted me to come and speak about techniques of crime reporting at their next meeting. I grinned to myself at the image of me lecturing to a flock of junior Chandlers and Christies on how to interview press-hating cops. Or I could hold forth on the zesty challenge of devising ways to afford your own quarterly Blue Cross/Blue Shield payments. Maybe one of the Chandlers or Christies would make me the heroine of a novel.

Maybe they'd give me a free meal.

I put the mail on the coffee table and hung my jacket in the closet. The green light on my answering machine was blinking furiously. I pushed the message-retrieval button.

The first message was from another free-lancer who wanted to do a postmortem on the death of *Cambridge Monthly.* The second message was from a friend wanting to get together for lunch soon.

The third message was from Griffin Marcus.

It was short. He—or his voice—introduced himself and went on to say: "I'd like very much to talk with you about working with me on a project. If you could get back to me at 213-555-2679 sometime in the next few days, I'd appreciate it. Thanks. Goodbye."

I stared at the machine. Then I replayed the message. It still said the same thing. I scribbled the phone number down on the envelope of a Visa bill.

I walked to my wall-to-ceiling bookcase and scanned the shelves. On the fourth were three hardbound books grouped together. On the spine of each was the name Griffin Marcus.

The same one who'd just left the message on my machine? *Nah.*

I pulled one of the books from the shelf and read the back flap of the dust jacket. It contained some brief biographical information about Marcus. He lived in Los Angeles. I looked at the phone number I'd taken down on the credit-card bill. Two-one-three was the Los Angeles area code.

It had to be the same Griffin Marcus.

But why was he calling me?

Griffin Marcus was one of the most famous true-crime writers in the country. A celebrity. Hell, Barbara Walters had interviewed him, and if that's not famous, what is?

So what did he want with *me?*

There was clearly only one way to find out. Imagination can only take you so far. I glanced at my watch. It was one-thirty. That made it ten-thirty in L.A. He must have called here while Jack and I were at the courthouse.

I picked up the phone and dialed the 213 number. After three rings, a man's voice answered.

"Hello," I said. "This is Elizabeth Connors. May I please speak to Griffin Marcus?"

"This is he. Thanks for calling back so quick." His tone was brisk, assertive; the accent, New York. "Listen, I'm going to be up in your neck of the woods next week, and I was wondering if we could get together. The reason is, as I think I probably said on the message I left you, that I have a project I'm starting and I'll need help with it. That's what I'd like to talk over."

"Uh," I said, flustered. "Well, sure. I mean, yes, I'd like to meet with you.

"Great. Okay. Let me lay it out for you in short form.

I'm going to be doing a book about some murders up in New Hampshire and Massachusetts. I'm anticipating about, oh, say, six months of intensive on-site research. What I need is someone to work with me, someone who knows the area."

"I see," I said.

"Somebody recommended you to me as a good person."

"I see," I repeated.

"You're a real good writer, you know that?"

I almost dropped the receiver. "Thank you. Thank you very much." Had I heard correctly? *He* was telling me *I* was *good?*

"Well, okay, terrific. I should be getting into Boston a week from today. How about I give you a call then and we can work out the details?"

"That sounds fine."

"Catch you then," Marcus said. "Nice to talk with you."

"Wait a second," I said hurriedly.

"Yes?"

"You've read things I've written?"

"Oh, sure. The guy who gave me your name sent me some of your clips."

"Who was that?"

"Brandon Peters."

"Oh my God," I said. "What a sweetheart."

"Excuse me?"

"Oh—uh, nothing. Thanks, Mr. Marcus. I'll look forward to meeting you."

"Griffin," he said. "Call me Griffin."

I set the phone receiver back in its cradle and flopped down on the couch. I shook my head hard and blinked.

Jack wouldn't be the only one with an interesting story to tell over dinner tonight.

I spent the rest of the afternoon composing a note to Brandon Peters expressing my gratitude. I had it delivered to his home in Newton, along with a bottle of twelve-year-old single malt.

TWO

During the next week, I reread the three Griffin Marcus books I owned and borrowed the four I didn't from the library. They were all terrific, but the one I liked best was *Nightcrawler,* about the Richard Ramirez case. I don't scare easily—I couldn't and do what I do—but *Nightcrawler* had given me a genuine case of the creeps.

Jack had read five of the books and liked them. *His* favorite was the collection of interviews Marcus had done with cops nationwide.

By way of preparing to meet the man, I found out as much as I could about him. The bio material on his book jackets, in addition to saying that he lived in L.A., mentioned that he had a wife, a son, and a daughter. He had grown up in Brooklyn and gone to CCNY, then to the Columbia School of Journalism. He was forty-eight years old, ten years my senior.

Of his seven books, two had been made into theatrical movies and two into mini-series. There had been plans at one time to produce a weekly television show about him. Not *hosted* by him. Not based on one of his books. About *him*—a series whose hero was an Intrepid

Investigative Reporter. The show had never gotten to
the pilot stage, although I figured Marcus must have
picked up some nice option money for the right to his
life story.

All his books had been bestsellers.

As the date to meet Marcus approached, I started to
get nervous. Jack laughed at me.

"What're you antsy about?" he asked. "You're just as
good a writer as he is. Just not as famous. Yet."

No wonder I loved the guy.

Zero hour arrived.

I was to join Marcus at six o'clock in the lobby of the
Charles Hotel, just outside Harvard Square. When I got
there I didn't have any trouble recognizing him; I'd seen
too many photographs of the man to make that possible.
Anyhow, he was the only person in the lobby other than
the concierge and the woman behind the registration
desk.

I didn't go right up to him. Instead, I stood outside
the hotel gift shop and looked at him for a few minutes.
He didn't notice me; he was watching the main doors.

I was surprised at how tall he was—close to six-five,
it appeared. (Jack was six-three). He had very dark,
curly hair and a long, narrow face. He seemed to be on
the thin side, but that was difficult to tell given the bulk
of the three-quarter-length down coat he was wearing.

So much for the long-distance vantage point. I
walked toward him, and as I approached, he happened
to turn and see me. I smiled at him and he smiled back.
Surprise, surprise, my knees didn't buckle.

Up close, I could see there was a fair sprinkling of
gray in his hair. His eyebrows were black, finely drawn,

and slanted up slightly at the ends. His eyes were hazel. The cheekbones were high, Slavic.

"Liz Connors?" he said.

"Griffin Marcus?" I held out my hand and he took it. "Nice to meet you."

"You're easy to spot."

I laughed. "Yes, well, wherever I go, I'm usually the only five-foot-ten-inch redhead on the premises."

"You ought to try Copenhagen. There's a lot of them there." Marcus glanced once more at the hotel entrance. It was starting to snow. Small flakes drifted lazily down outside the glass doors.

"Nice," he said. "Reminds me of why I moved to L.A." He looked back at me. "Well—would you like to get a drink?"

"Love to."

"Okay. This is your town. What's a good place?" He frowned thoughtfully. "I have an idea. What about the Casablanca?"

I shook my head. "Gone."

The frown changed to a scowl. "What do you mean, *gone?*"

"It went the way of the wrecking ball about two years ago."

He had unusually mobile features. What they registered now was appalled disbelief. 'The Casa B? You're kidding."

"I wish I were."

"That place was a historical landmark."

"I know."

"What's there now?"

"Well, they built a replacement Casa B, but it's just not the same."

Marcus let out an exasperated breath. "Well, what do you suggest?"

"The bar upstairs isn't bad."

"Let's try it."

We went up a wide flight of oak stairs to something called the Quiet Bar. It had a lot of couches and easy chairs and looked out on a courtyard. We took a table for four by the window. Marcus slid out of his parka and dumped it on one of the empty chairs. I threw my coat on top of his.

We got settled, and a waitress came by to take our drink orders. Marcus looked at me questioningly.

"Vodka martini," I said. "Rocks. Twist."

"The same," Marcus said. He dug in the pocket of his Harris tweed sportcoat and pulled out a pack of Marlboro Lights. "Mind?" he said.

"Not at all. Go ahead."

He lit a cigarette. "I can tell this will be a good partnership."

"How so?"

He pointed the cigarette at me. "A, you drink martinis. B, you're not a health Nazi."

"Be warned," I said. "Everybody's not nearly as tolerant as I am. There are places here where they'll kill you if you light up. Kill you for your own good. And for God's sake, I don't know if you own any clothing with fur on it, but if you do, *don't* wear it into Harvard Square unless you want to have somebody throw blood on it and chase you down the street screaming that you're a murderer."

"Just like California," he said.

The waitress brought the drinks.

Marcus took a sip of his and leaned back in his chair. "Tell me about yourself."

All I could think of was Ted Baxter's line about it all starting out in a small five-thousand-watt radio station. "Not much to tell. I've been writing for about eight years now."

"And before that?"

"Taught college English."

"Really. You have a doctorate?"

I nodded. "I'm a medievalist by training."

"No kidding." Marcus set his glass down on the round marble-topped table between us. " 'Whan that Aprill with his shoures soote' . . . I forget the rest."

"Yes, most people do the second the exam is over. I didn't do Chaucer, anyway. I was, uh, a specialist in the Arthurian tradition." Why did saying that make me feel like a horse's ass?

Marcus said, "That must have been interesting."

"Yes, it was. What I was doing was sort of a combination of history, literature, and archaeology. I had fun writing my dissertation. And the scholarly articles afterward."

"So if it was so much fun, why didn't you stay in it? College teaching, I mean."

I made a face. "I said the research and writing were fun. I didn't say anything about the teaching."

"That bad?"

I shrugged. "I *thought* I'd be lecturing on great works to a bunch of interested, intelligent young men and women. What I ended up doing was teaching grammar to a pack of bored, illiterate morons. It got to the point where I thought if I had to grade one more freshman composition where the kid couldn't write a five-word sentence that didn't have six spelling errors, I'd start screaming at the top of my lungs."

Marcus smiled sympathetically. "Maybe you just weren't temperamentally suited to the work."

"Maybe. Although I don't know who could be, other than a Demerol addict. I like teaching adults, though. *Real* adults. They're polite and they're interested and they do the work and they have something worthwhile to say. Most kids generally don't." I took a deep breath; I hadn't meant to launch into a diatribe.

"You also taught in a police academy, didn't you?" Marcus asked.

I wondered how he knew, and then realized that Brandon Peters must have told him. "Yes. The one right here in Cambridge."

"How was that?"

"Fine. I liked it. I taught report writing. I always had the feeling that what I was doing in the academy was important."

"And now you're a crime writer."

"Uh-huh." I paused and sipped my drink. "That was always what I really wanted to do—write. And now I am."

"Why *crime* writing, though?"

I raised my eyebrows. "You ought to know the answer to that."

Marcus smiled. "I guess I do." He drained his glass. "Well. How about getting something to eat?"

"Sure."

"All right, what's a good restaurant hereabouts?"

I deliberated a moment. Then I said, "What do you know of Cambridge?"

Marcus shrugged. "Harvard. Harvard Square."

"Then you don't know much. How about a walk on the wild side?"

"The which?"

"East Cambridge," I said.

"Do I need to bring my Uzi or what?"

I smiled. "Stick with me and you'll be perfectly safe."

THREE

Marcus signed the check for the drinks. Then we put on our coats and went down to the lobby. The doorman hailed us a cab. Marcus tipped him, and we climbed into the taxi. "Seven-twenty-three Cambridge Street," I said to the driver. He nodded, and we hurtled out onto Bennett Street.

"Where are we going? Marcus asked. "Or is it a secret?"

"Have you ever had Portuguese food?"

"In Lisbon, yes."

"Oh. Well, this'll be something to compare it to."

The snow was coming down more heavily now, and beginning to stick. Marcus looked out the car window at it. He seemed to shiver and huddled more deeply into his coat. "East Cambridge,' he said. "The wild side of the city, huh?"

I laughed. "I was teasing you. It's not wild at all. It has a very low street crime rate. It does have its share of bad guys, though. Some real scum. But basically they only kill and maim each other, so it's like intramural pest control. What I meant abut E.C. is that it's the total opposite of Harvard Square, which is all most people think Cambridge is."

Marcus put his hands in his pockets and hunched his shoulders slightly. "Tell me about it."

"E.C.? Blue-collar, with a contingent of yuppies who couldn't quite afford town houses in the Back Bay, plus a few holdovers from the sixties who work in the financial district now but still have these fantasies about organizing the working class. Which of course hates their guts."

Marcus snickered.

"Be that as it may," I continued, "the Yankees settled East Cambridge. They owned all the mills and the glass-blowing factories. Then when the Yankees moved out, the Irish came in. After them, the Italians. Then the Poles. After that, the Portuguese. And in recent years, some Salvadorians and Haitians."

"Quite a stew."

"Yeah, and occasionally the pot boils over. What's interesting is that East Cambridge is one of the two biggest Portuguese communities in the U.S."

"What's the other?"

"Fall River. Also right here in Mass."

"Uh-huh."

We were zipping through Inman Square now. Marcus squinted out the cab windows. "This looks sort of familiar," he said. "Aren't there a bunch of jazz clubs around here?"

"Used to be. There's only one left. Ryle's on Hampshire Street, across from the fire station."

"What happened to the others?"

"They went out of business."

"What's there now?"

"Chic eateries."

Marcus grunted.

The cab made an extremely dangerous U-turn at the intersection of Cardinal Medeiros Avenue and Cambridge Street and lurched to a halt in front of Portugalia. Marcus paid the driver and we disembarked. The cab screeched off into the snowy night.

Marcus looked up at the sign over the restaurant. "This looks nice," he said. "Guess you really were kidding me about walks on the wild side."

"Actually, there's a place a block down that I wouldn't set foot in without a platoon of marines and a SWAT team," I said. "But you're entirely correct. It's fine here. Anyway, *I* have a gun."

Marcus stared at me. "You do?"

"Well, not with me. But yes. I *do* own a gun. And have the permit to carry it."

"May I ask why?"

"A couple of people tried to kill me a year or so ago. They didn't like what I'd written about them."

Marcus laughed and opened the restaurant door for me. The hostess showed us to a table in the smoking section. When the waitress appeared, Marcus and I ordered another vodka martini apiece.

I already knew what I was going to have for dinner. Marcus had to consult the menu. He asked me for suggestions. "Try the paella," I said. "If you're really hungry." He took my advice. I guess he was hungry.

"Connors is an Irish name," Marcus said. "Are you from East Cambridge originally?"

I laughed. "No. I was born in New York. Just like you."

"Brooklyn?"

"Nope."

"Manhattan."

"No, I'm not an uptown girl, either. Staten Island."

"Ah yes," Marcus said. "Where they used to have the hog-calling contests, I believe."

I wrinkled my nose, and laughed.

"Tell me more about yourself," he said.

"What do you want to know?"

"You married?"

I shook my head.

"Ever?"

I shook my head again.

"You live with anyone?"

This man wasn't shy about asking personal questions. Of course, that was how he'd gotten to be what he was. Or a factor in it.

"No," I said. "I have a—um, a companion. We've been together about eight years."

The waitress brought our drinks, along with a bowl of pickled vegetables and black olives and a basket of bread.

"And you live apart?" Marcus said.

I stiffened. "It's the way we both like it."

Marcus didn't hear the coolness in my voice. Or if he did, it didn't bother him.

I decided to swing the interrogatory Gatling on him. If he could dish it out, he could take it. "And you," I said. "You're married, right?"

"Separated.' He ate a black olive.

"I'm sorry."

He shrugged. "It happens. Maybe we'll work things out."

"You have two kids."

He smiled quite broadly. "Yeah. My son, who's twenty-two, and my daughter. She'll be eighteen in June."

I made a come-along gesture with my hand. "Tell me about them."

"Andy's a senior at Cal Tech. Leah's graduating from a private school in L.A. this spring. She's been accepted at Yale. Early admission. They're both great. I look at them sometimes and I wonder how the hell they turned out so well with me as their father." He swished the vodka and vermouth around in his glass with the little plastic stirrer.

"Obviously, you did something right with them. And your wife did, too."

"Pretty to think so," he said.

Something about his tone made me decide to change the subject. *"Your* name is interesting."

He looked at me curiously.

"Griffin," I said. "That's Welsh."

"My mother was."

"But Marcus isn't. Welsh, I mean."

"No. It was originally Marcovich. My father was a Russian Jew." Marcus grinned. "My grandparents got their name changed for them at Ellis Island."

"Were you raised as a Jew?"

He finished his martini. "No, I wasn't brought up anything. My mother was a nonpracticing Catholic. My father was a . . . sort of half-assed socialist, I guess. If he had a religion, that was it."

"I can dig that," I said.

"Why?"

"My mother's a Protestant who hates organized religion, and my father believes in reincarnation."

Marcus laughed and ate a piece of pickled cauliflower. "And you have an Irish Catholic last name?"

"Hard to believe, isn't it? If you handed me a communion wafer, I'd probably stand around waiting for you to offer me the Brie to put on it."

"You're probably a closet Episcopalian, then."

I reached for a black olive. "I'm going to turn the question you asked me before around to you. How did *you* get involved in crime writing?"

"Don't know," he said. "I always thought it might have to do with the fact that my father was murdered."

I drew a sharp breath and pulled back slightly in my chair. "My God."

"It's okay. It happened thirty years ago."

"Still ... My God. What ... Do you mind my asking what happened?"

Marcus shrugged. "A mugging. He was on his way home from the garment district one night. He was a labor organizer. Somebody stomped him and robbed him. For three bucks."

"It *was* a mugging?"

Marcus had his arms folded on the tabletop. He gazed at me steadily. "The police said so."

I was quiet for a moment. Then I said, "Is that what *you* think?"

"Who knows? He was mixed up in some pretty rough union stuff."

I bit my lower lip. "I'm sorry."

He made a dismissive gesture with his right hand. "It's a long time past."

The waitress brought our food. Marcus ordered some wine to go with it, a *vinho verde*.

"Look," he said. "I'm going to tell you all about the case I'm doing the book on. But let's wait till the coffee comes, okay?"

"Sure."

My *grelhada mista* with *batatas* was chunks of beef,

pork, chicken, and linguiça barbecued in a light glaze. Marcus's paella was rice with littlenecks, squid, shrimp, mussels, and linguiça thrown in, along with peas and carrots. We ate in silence. And drank the wine. I had two glasses. Marcus had four. It had no visible effect on him.

The waitress cleared the dishes and brought us each a cappuccino. Marcus lit a cigarette. "Okay," he said. "Here's the deal. I have a contract to do a book on some serial murders. They're not solved, not officially, but I know who did them."

I nodded.

"All right." He leaned across the table. "Between 1986 and 1990, seven women were murdered in the same way, by the same means. They all lived in southern New Hampshire and northeastern Massachusetts."

I widened my eyes. "Of course. The Merrimack Valley killings."

"Right." Marcus crushed his cigarette stub in the ashtray.

"You know who committed them?"

"I think so. I'm sure I do."

"I'm familiar with the case. But go on and tell me what you know about it that the cops don't."

He shook his head. "No. I'll give you a copy of the proposal for the book. Read it. Then give me your reaction."

I set my cup back in the saucer. "Fair enough. And after that?"

"On the basis of what you read, see if you want to work with me for the next two or three months. Help me with the research and interviewing."

"Uh-huh."

"I need someone who knows this area. Who has contacts up here I don't. Who knows how to investigate."

"And I'm it?"

"I can pay a thousand dollars a week."

I snatched my cup and brought it up to my face so he wouldn't see my jaw drop. What kind of advance and expenses was he getting for this book? Two zillion dollars? Yes, he probably was.

Marcus lit another cigarette. "Interested?"

"Give me the proposal," I said. "I'll get back to you tomorrow."

FOUR

Jack was sitting on the couch in my living room reading this week's *U.S. News & World Report* when I got back from my dinner with Marcus. There was a subdued blaze in the fireplace. Lucy was curled up on the couch next to Jack, her head in his lap.

He looked up from the magazine as I shut the door behind me.

"How'd it go?" he said.

"Fine," I replied. I took off my coat. "He wants to pay me a grand a week for the next two or three months to be his research assistant."

Jack let the magazine fall into his lap, onto Lucy's muzzle. She raised her head and stared at him, affronted.

"Way to go," Jack said. "Sit down and tell me about it."

I hung up my coat. "Of course. Want a cup of tea?"

"Okay."

Jack followed me to the kitchen. As I was filling the kettle, he said, "What's Marcus like?"

I smiled at him. "He seemed quite nice. Not at all pretentious or arrogant or any of the other celebrity crap. He's very intense. I suspect somewhat volatile. Smokes too much. Probably drinks too much, too, although you and I are no slouches in that department."

"That's true."

I set the kettle on the stove and turned on the burner beneath it. "In fact, I think you'd probably like Marcus. I'll introduce you. I'm sure he'd like to meet you, too."

Jack nodded and smiled. "So you're going to take the job?"

"I'm supposed to read his proposal and let him know tomorrow. But"—I sighed—"yes, I will. What else can I do? I need the damn money."

"Liz, if you need—"

I walked over to him and placed my index finger on his mouth. "I know, I know. But in addition to everything else, this is a fantastic opportunity for me."

"Then go for it."

"I knew you'd say that." I draped my arms around his neck and pulled his head down to mine."

The kiss got a little more serious than I'd initially intended.

I remembered to kill the flame beneath the kettle before the seriousness got completely out of hand.

The next morning after breakfast, I took a second cup of coffee into the living room and plunked down in an easy chair to read Marcus's proposal. It was about fifteen word-processed pages long and was entitled *Out of the Darkness*. This is how it went:

Early in the evening of January 21, 1990, Cheryl Timmons, a seventeen-year-old high school senior from Haverhill, Massachusetts, made a decision that would end her life.

To go shopping for a birthday gift for her mother.

She asked her best friend, Jennifer Belliveau, if Jennifer would like to come with her. But Jennifer had a date, so Cheryl went alone. She drove from her family's home to Plaistow, just over the New Hampshire border.

Route 125 in Plaistow is a commercial strip, lined with discount department stores, discount clothing stores, supermarkets, auto-parts outlets, and fast-food joints. It is unattractive but relatively safe. Nevertheless Cheryl, the younger sister of a police officer and the cousin of an assistant district attorney, took the safety precautions that are second nature to any child of a law-enforcement family. She parked her white Toyota in a well-lit area of the lot as close to Red's Shoe Barn as possible. She carried her keys in her hand along with her package when she left the store shortly after nine.

Cheryl's Toyota was found abandoned in the parking lot at eight the next morning by the manager of the Shoe Barn. The keys were in the ignition. Her handbag was on the front seat. The birthday gift for her mother, a pair of brown leather pumps, lay undisturbed on the rear seat.

Two days later, Cheryl's body was found in a wooded area on the banks of the Merrimack River in Plaistow.

She was fully clothed and had not been sexually assaulted.

She had been stabbed twenty-seven times in the chest and throat.

The killing had begun almost four years before, in another part of the state.

Carolyn Bragg was twenty-eight years old, an English teacher and drama coach at the St. Ignatius School in Concord, New Hampshire. On the evening of March 31, 1986, she directed a rehearsal of the senior class play, *Our Town*, in the school auditorium. The rehearsal ended at nine. Other than the custodian, Robert St. Jean, Carolyn was the last person to leave the school building.

Carolyn was unmarried, although she had a male friend whom she dated fairly regularly. She rented a small house in nearby Pembroke.

Carolyn's car, a red Nissan Stanza, was found in the high school parking lot the next morning.

Her body was discovered on the banks of the Merrimack River just outside Concord on April 3.

She was fully clothed and had not been sexually assaulted.

She had been stabbed thirty-two times in the chest and throat.

Denise Michaud was a thirty-three-year-old divorced mother of two, a seven-year-old girl and a five-year-old boy. She worked as a loan officer at the Bank of New Hampshire in Nashua, New Hampshire. She lived with her two children in a two-family house in the same city. Her parents and younger brother occupied the other half of the house.

On the night of November 2, 1986, Denise left her two children in the care of their grandparents and went shopping. Alyssa, her daughter, needed a new winter coat. There was a sale on such items at the Marshalls in the Royal Ridge Mall in Nashua, and Denise wanted to take advantage of it.

She never came home. Her parents, Mr. and Mrs. Michael Grogan, called the police at 11:00 P.M. that night and reported their daughter missing.

Denise's car, a blue Dodge Dart, was found by the loading dock behind Marshalls the next morning.

On November 15, Denise's body was found on the banks of the Merrimack River just over the Massachusetts border in Tyngsboro.

She was fully clothed and had not been sexually assaulted.

She had been stabbed twenty-two times in the chest and throat.

Diane Lamonica was twenty-one years old. She lived with her parents in Lowell, Massachusetts, and was a nursing student at Lowell General Hospital. She had a special interest in pediatric care.

On the night of February 13, 1987, Diane was supposed to meet a high school friend, Laurie Gutowski, for dinner and a movie afterward. Laurie got to the restaurant a little before seven. At seven-thirty, Diane, a normally punctual young woman, still hadn't appeared. Laurie called her friend's home and was told by Diane's mother that Diane had left the house in her father's car at 6:45. It should have taken her no more than fifteen minutes to reach the restaurant.

Laurie waited another half hour in the restaurant bar and then went home, puzzled and more than a little worried.

Two hours later, Diane's father called the police.

Diane's car was found in the parking lot behind a restored textile mill by the canal that runs through Lowell.

Seven days later, Diane's body was discovered lying in a wooded area on the banks of the Merrimack outside Dracut, a small town situated on the north side of the river from Lowell.

She was fully clothed and had not been sexually assaulted.

She had been stabbed nineteen times in the chest and throat.

Twenty-five-year-old Margaret Letourneau, known as Peggy, lived in Salem, New Hampshire, and worked in Lawrence, Massachusetts, as an aide at the Mary Immaculate Nursing Home. At the time of her death, she had been married for three years to Robert Letourneau, a salesman for Digital Equipment.

Lawrence, twenty-some miles north of Boston, was once one of the centers of the New England textile industry. Today it is one of the centers of the New England drug trade. Despite the efforts of urban renewers, there is little prosperity and less hope for many of the inhabitants of this city of 75,000.

Peggy, who worked the evening shift, was well aware that Lawrence was dangerous after dark. And Mary Immaculate was not located in one of the better neighborhoods of the city, of which there are only a few. Visitors to and employees of the nursing home had been mugged in the parking lot, some in broad daylight. Still, Peggy herself had never had a problem. She was always very careful, her husband said later, to park her car as near to the nursing home entrance as possible and in as well lit an area of the lot as possible. She would also wait to leave the building until she could do so with a group of coworkers. Failing that, she'd ask someone to escort her to her car.

On the night of October 25, 1988, she apparently didn't. Why she deviated from her normal cautious routine has never been explained.

Her gray Honda was still in the nursing home parking lot the next morning.

Three days later, Peggy's body was found on the banks of the Merrimack River in Andover, an affluent suburb of Lawrence.

She was fully clothed and had not been sexually assaulted.

She had been stabbed twenty-nine times in the chest and throat.

She was two months' pregnant when she died.

Lisa Goodenough was thirty-seven years old and a part-time lecturer in history at Merrimack College in North Andover, Massachusetts. She lived in the same town, with her husband, Thomas an executive with Western Electric, and their thirteen-year-old daughter, Sarah.

On April 1, 1989, Lisa left the college at five P.M., having taught two classes and held office hours. She drove a mile from the campus to the North Andover Mall to do some grocery shopping at Demoulas, the supermarket there.

She had told Sarah that she would be home no later than six o'clock.

She wasn't.

At seven P.M., Thomas Goodenough returned home from work. Finding Sarah alone, he called his wife's office at the college. The phone rang unanswered. He waited another hour and then called the North Andover police.

Lisa's blue Ford Taurus was found in the parking lot outside the Demoulas at ten that night.

Four days later, Lisa's body was found on the banks of the Merrimack River, just off Route 110 in Methuen, Massachusetts.

She was fully clothed and had not been sexually assaulted.

She had been stabbed in the chest and throat thirty-four times.

Linda Tessier, a thirty-three–year-old native and resident of Methuen, worked as a buyer in women's clothing for Jordan Marsh, a department store in the Methuen Mall. She was unmarried and had recently bought a condo in a pleasant, hilly section of the city very near the Presentation of Mary Academy. She had no special boyfriend but dated occasionally.

On December 8, 1989, she didn't show up for work. Nor did she call in sick, an omission completely out of character for this responsible business-woman. When they hadn't heard from her by noon, Linda's coworkers became concerned. One of them telephoned her at home. Linda's answering machine picked up the call.

At five o'clock that afternoon, Linda's car was found abandoned in the parking lot of the Nevins Memorial Library.

A week later, Linda's body was discovered just five hundred yards from the spot where Lisa Goodenough's corpse had been found.

Linda was fully clothed and had not been sexually assaulted.

She had been stabbed in the chest and throat thirty-one times.

In November 1990, the Boston cops were looking for a killer—one whose victims were prostitutes. The murderer had so far racked up two. The police weren't eager for the body count to climb.

Both victims had had their throats slashed.

The two prostitutes had patrolled the Combat Zone,

a small area between Chinatown and the theater district. Although many of the strip joints, peep shows, adult bookstores, and shops peddling handcuffs and leather panties that once flourished along lower Washington Street have fallen before a wave of gentrification, the Zone remains Boston's center for vice—in legend if not in actual fact. It still caters to every sexual taste.

The girls of the Zone go about their business with freedom and a head-tossing insouciance. Stop for a traffic light in the Zone, and if you're male, you're almost guaranteed that at least one woman of any imaginable race, racial mixture, or age will sashay up to the driver's window and offer you the sexual treat of your wildest fantasy.

Henry Kmiec, a thirty-one-year-old unemployed machinist from Manchester, New Hampshire, was trawling the Zone on the afternoon of November 20 when the cops stopped him for a moving violation.

In Boston City Hospital on that same day, a twenty-two-year-old prostitute named Keisha Madison was recovering from knife wounds to the chest and upper right arm she'd received from a john she'd picked up on lower Washington Street three nights earlier.

According to Keisha, her attacker had been driving a red Chevy pickup truck with New Hampshire plates and a badly rusted body.

That description fit the truck Henry Kmiec was driving when the police stopped him.

Also according to Keisha, her attacker had been a white man, aged twenty-five to thirty, with stringy shoulder-length dark blond hair, a straggly mustache, and pitted skin. He was somewhere between five-foot-ten and six feet tall and weighed about 160 or so.

That description fit Henry Kmiec.

In the bed and cab of the truck, police would find physical evidence—bloodstains, clothing fibers, fingerprints, and hairs—that would link Kmiec to the deaths of the two prostitutes, Carla Whitlow and Maria Acosta, and to the attack on Keisha Madison.

Keisha Madison picked Kmiec out of a lineup as the man who'd tried to kill her. She also said that Kmiec had boasted to her of killing Whitlow and Acosta.

Kmiec was charged with two counts of first-degree murder and one count of assault with intent to commit murder.

At his arraignment he hummed to himself, smiled at nothing in particular, made faces at the court officers, and drummed his fingers on his knees.

He giggled when the list of charges against him was read.

He pleaded guilty to all three.

On April 10, 1991, Henry Kmiec was sentenced to life in prison without parole. The sentence would be served at MCI Cedar Junction in Walpole, Massachusetts.

I am convinced that Henry Kmiec murdered not only Carla Whitlow and Maria Acosta but Carolyn Bragg, Denise Michaud, Diane Lamonica, Peggy Letourneau, Lisa Goodenough, Linda Tessier, and Cheryl Timmons as well.

There are, in the first place, no other solid suspects in the deaths of the seven women from northeastern Massachusetts and southern New Hampshire. But even if there were a dozen, Kmiec would stand out among them.

He has a well-documented history of violence against women. At the age of twelve, he attacked his mother with a hammer when she refused to buy him an air rifle. Mrs. Kmiec ran from the house to escape her son, who was later restrained by a neighbor. Four years later, when Kmiec was a sophomore at Manchester High School, he stabbed a fellow student. The student, a girl who sat in front of Kmiec in homeroom and whom he wanted to date, had rejected his advances. Kmiec lay in wait for her after school and attacked her as she left the building.

The victim, fortunately not badly injured, recovered from the physical effects of the assault fairly quickly. Kmiec spent the next six months in a juvenile detention facility.

When Kmiec went after the girl who refused to date him, he tried to knife her in the chest and throat. Eleven years later, he would slit the throats of Carla Whitlow and Maria Acosta. He would attempt to do the same to Keisha Madison, but would only manage to slash her arm and shoulder.

Carolyn Bragg, Denise Michaud, Diane Lamonica, Peggy Letourneau, Lisa Goodenough, Linda Tessier, and Cheryl Timmons of course died of multiple stab wounds to the neck and chest. The instrument that cut them was very similar, if not identical, to the double-edged hunting knife found in the glove compartment of Kmiec's truck—the knife he had used on Whitlow, Acosta, and Madison.

The body of Carla Whitlow, discarded by Kmiec in Tyngsboro, was found on the banks of the Merrimack

River, not far from the spot where Denise Michaud had been dumped.

A rusted red pickup truck had been seen in the vicinity of the Royal Ridge Mall the night Michaud disappeared from there. The same vehicle, or one very like it, was spotted parked near the administration building of Merrimack College the night Lisa Goodenough vanished. Its right headlight was missing.

Three days later, Henry Kmiec had the right headlight replaced on his truck.

There is one final piece of evidence that points more directly than any other to Kmiec as the murderer of nine women.

When the police searched his Manchester apartment after his arrest in Boston, they found a manila envelope full of newspaper clippings. All related to the deaths of Carolyn Bragg, Denise Michaud, Diane Lamonica, Peggy Letourneau, Lisa Goodenough, Linda Tessier, and Cheryl Timmons.

On the margin of the clip that described the discovery of Cheryl Timmons's body, Kmiec had scrawled: "I will do this agen [sic] soon."

I reread the proposal two more times. Then I put it on the coffee table, got up, and went to the phone. I dialed the Charles Hotel and asked to be connected with Griffin Marcus's room. He picked up on the second ring.

"I'm in," I said.

FIVE

The following morning I met Marcus in his suite at the Charles Hotel for a working breakfast. The room-service waiter and I showed up at the suite door simultaneously. Marcus answered it with the telephone in his other hand, the receiver tucked between his chin and shoulder. He gave me a distracted smile and stepped back from the door so the waiter could push the cart over the threshold. I followed the waiter. Actually, what I was following was the smell of the coffee in the silver pot on the top tier of the rolling tray. I'd had a quick glass of orange juice before I'd left home and nothing else. That coffeepot looked to me like the holy grail.

The waiter put the cart in the center of the room and fussed with the dishes and utensils. Marcus snapped something at whoever he was talking to and hung up the phone. "Dipshit," he said, and put the phone back on the desk. He signed the check the waiter offered him, and the waiter backed out of the room.

Marcus raked a hand through his hair and shook his head slightly. "Hi."

"Morning."

He glanced around the room in the manner of someone just becoming aware of his surroundings. "Throw your coat someplace and let's get started. Help yourself to the food." He motioned at the rolling cart.

Underneath their silver lids the dishes held scrambled eggs, melon slices, sausages, and bacon. There was an assortment of rolls and bread in a basket. Fat city. I took some eggs, cantaloupe, and a corn muffin. And coffee. Of course coffee.

I nibbled on a chunk of cantaloupe and surveyed the room. On the desk, next to the phone, was a laptop computer. One of the chairs was heaped with ratty-looking manila folders. An open cardboard box on the floor next to the television was stuffed with newspaper clippings, original and photocopied. Editions of today's *Globe, Herald, New York Times, L.A. Times,* and *Wall Street Journal* were strewn about the place. All in all, a familiar kind of mess.

"All right," Marcus said. "What did you think of the proposal?"

I put down my corn muffin, half eaten. "I thought you made a good case for Kmiec being the murderer."

He nodded.

"The guy sounds like a total wacko."

"Believe me, he is."

I had prepared for this meeting by going to the library and backtracking through the newspaper files for articles on the Merrimack Valley killings. And I'd taken copious notes on what I'd read. I took them from my handbag. "One thing," I said. "I know the cops were eyeing Kmiec for a while as a good suspect in the killings of those women. But then they seem to have dropped him. Why was that, do you know?"

Marcus poured himself more coffee. He gestured at me with the pot. "Sure," I said. "Thanks."

Marcus filled my cup and set the pot back on the cart. "The police didn't think they had enough evidence to make a case against Kmiec—I mean physical evidence, like hair or fibers or bloodstains. Plus nobody could place Kmiec himself near any of the crime scenes. Just a truck that looked a lot like his. And that was only in two cases."

"What about the message Kmiec scribbled on the border of the newspaper story about Cheryl Timmons's murder? 'I will do this again.' "

Marcus shrugged. "A good defense lawyer—hell, any defense lawyer—would have said that Kmiec was just fantasizing. Or identifying with the real murderer, because that's exactly the sort of thing a looney-toons like Kmiec would do. And that sort of thing does happen. I've seen it."

I nodded, then smiled. "You're doing a good job of poking holes in your own hypothesis, you know."

Marcus returned the smile. "Well, I have some other goods on Kmiec, stuff I didn't put in the proposal, that reinforces it."

I took another bite of my corn muffin and swallowed. "What's that?"

"The first thing is that Kmiec had a connection with at least three of the other victims."

"Really?"

"He graduated from high school in Manchester two years after Carolyn Bragg did. I think they were even in a few classes together. So they must have at least known about each other."

"God," I said. "She wasn't the girl he attacked because she wouldn't go out with him, was she?"

"No, no, that was a kid named Annemarie Mullaney."

"I see."

"At one time," Marcus continued, "Kmiec lived a few houses down the street from Denise Michaud. This was when he was about ten. His family moved shortly after that. Still—he could have known Denise by sight, at the least, wouldn't you say?"

"Possible."

"All right, the week before Peggy Letourneau died, Kmiec was in Lawrence, ostensibly looking for work."

"Hmmm," I said. "You may be pushing it there. Lawrence is a good-size town with a fair amount of industry. Two people being there at the same time might be more of a coincidence that anything else."

"And maybe he was stalking her." Marcus was sitting on the couch. He leaned back and stretched out his legs. "Even if it's all coincidence, though, I have more on Kmiec."

"What?"

"The killer of the first seven women obviously had some kind of weird attachment to the Merrimack River. Why else would he have dumped all the bodies on or near the banks? Particularly since there were better places to stash the corpses."

"He probably wanted them to be found."

"Then why not just leave them alongside the highway? Or in a Dumpster?"

It was my turn to shrug.

"And," Marcus said, "Carla Whitlow, the prostitute Kmiec confessed to killing—he drove all the hell the way from Boston to Tyngsboro just so he could throw *her* down by the river."

"Why do you suppose he didn't do the same with Maria Acosta, then?"

"Maybe something prevented him. Maybe he was afraid he'd be seen." There was a pack of Marlboro

Lights on the coffee table. Marcus took one and lit it. "I don't know."

"Okay," I said. "So let's say Kmiec has this thing for the Merrimack River. What's at the root of it?"

"That, I can't tell you. What I *can* tell you is that it goes way back in his past history. When he was nine, he drowned a puppy in the river. Threw it off the bridge. Apparently just for the hell of it."

"*Oh,*" I said, recoiling.

"You know," Marcus said, "a lot of serial murderers start out by torturing and killing animals. They get older, they progress to humans."

"I know. I've read a lot about serial killers." I coughed. "I met one once. He even asked me to go out with him."

Marcus stared at me. "You're just full of little surprises, aren't you? First I find you carry a gun, then I . . ." He waved a hand. "Tell me about it."

"He wasn't at all like Kmiec. More like Ted Bundy."

"Handsome? Intelligent? Charming? Sincere? Sensitive?"

"All those. He was also a psychiatric social worker."

"Figures." Marcus leaned forward and stubbed out his cigarette in the ashtray on the coffee table. "How'd you get hooked up with him?"

"Three women had been murdered right here in town. Jack was investigating the case. I was writing about it. Anyway, I interviewed the guy. He worked with one of the victims. Turned out he killed her and the other two. Plus some more out in Indiana."

"Where is he now?"

"Bridgewater. The state hospital for the criminally insane."

"I know about Bridgewater."

"Of course."

Marcus had drunk three cups of black coffee but eaten no breakfast. Now he took a blueberry muffin from the basket, split it, and put it on a plate.

"Let's get back to Kmiec," he said.

"There's more?"

"Oh, sure. He had a big collection of snuff videos. And slasher movies."

"The kind where fourteen adolescents get hacked up by a guy in a hockey mask?"

"Uh-huh." Marcus took a bite of the blueberry muffin. "Kmiec was a big aficionado."

"What a beautiful human being."

"A prince."

I flipped though my copy of the book proposal. "Griffin?"

"Yes?"

I glanced again at the papers in my lap. "There's something you don't mention in your proposal."

"What'd I miss?"

"I thought the Merrimack Valley Killer had eight victims, not just seven. Number eight being a woman from Andover named Sheila Gavin."

Marcus shook his head. "No, I'm pretty sure Kmiec didn't do Gavin. In fact, almost positive."

I frowned. "But . . . how can you be sure?" I checked my notes again. "Sheila Gavin died on . . . let's see . . . March 12, 1988, about five months after Linda Tessier. She lived a mile from the river. She was also stabbed, with a weapon similar to that used on the other seven, twenty-one times in the chest and throat. Sounds an awful lot to me like the same m.o. And"—I took a deep breath—"the killer seems to have averaged about two murders per year. But there's a big break, twenty

months, between Diane Lamonica and Peggy Letourneau. Sheila Gavin falls into that gap. Into the earlier
part of it, anyway."

"You're right," Marcus said. "You're absolutely right
in what you're saying. There's only one thing wrong
with it."

"What's that?"

Marcus lit another cigarette. "Gavin was murdered by
her husband."

I looked at Marcus quizzically. "I never heard he was
arrested."

"That's because he wasn't. Again, the police couldn't
make a case. *But*—the Gavins had been having big mar-
ital problems. Gavin—his first name's Timothy—had
been involved with another woman. He and Sheila had
separated a few times."

"So why didn't they just get a divorce?"

"Gavin has big bucks. He owns a computer company
in North Andover. D-Star, it's called. Anyway, he was
afraid Sheila might take him for huge alimony and child
support."

"How do you know?"

"Two people swore he'd said that very thing to
them."

"Oh. Well, still, it's a big jump from worrying about
whether your wife will take you to the cleaners to killing her."

"It's a jump a lot of men have been willing to take."

"True," I said. "True."

"Besides, Sheila's body wasn't found *by* the Merrimack River. She was left in her car, in the driveway of
her and Timothy's house. Their sixteen-year-old son
found her that night when he got home from band prac-
tice."

I winced. "Yes. I'd forgotten that little detail. And where was Timothy at the time?"

"In Washington on a business trip. He had a great alibi. He was in meetings all that day up till eleven P.M. the night Sheila died. He was never out of the sight of at least six people."

"Except when he went to the men's room, I suppose."

"That wouldn't have given him time to get to National airport, fly to Boston, drive the thirty or so miles to Andover, kill Sheila, and get back to the Hay-Adams."

"So he hired someone to do if for him. And told whoever it was he hired to make the murder look like the ones of Carolyn Bragg, Denise Michaud, and Diane Lamonica. Which of course had gotten pretty good press coverage."

"Either that or the killer came up on his own with the idea of doing an imitation."

"So," I argued. "Why didn't he do a *complete* imitation and leave the body on the riverbank?"

"Don't know. Maybe he was pressed for time. Anyway, the cops buy Gavin for having Sheila offed."

I nodded. "Okay. But doesn't that big break between the murders of Diane Lamonica and Peggy Letourneau still need to be explained?"

"I can do that."

"Oh?"

"Kmiec was in prison in New Hampshire from July 1987 to July 1988. He did one year on a breaking-and-entering-in-the-nighttime charge. Tried to rip off a video rental store in Manchester."

I snorted. "What was he trying to steal, more snuff flicks?"

Marcus laughed. "No, the cash."

"How was he in prison?" I asked. "His behavior? Anybody notice any unusual tendencies about him there? Did he talk about using violence against women? Killing them?"

Marcus looked at me a moment. "You're sharp," he said. "You really are. Actually, Kmiec was a model prisoner. Except for one little quirk."

"What was that?"

"In his cell he kept a collection of pictures of women that had been ripped from magazines."

"And?"

"The pictures were all stuck through with little pen and pencil holes. In the chest and throat area."

I tossed the book proposal and my notes onto the coffee table. "I think you've sold me," I said. I leaned forward and put my elbows on my knees. "There's only one last thing that puzzles me. If Kmiec was, is, such an obvious suspect for the Merrimack Valley killings, why did the police cross him off their list?"

"They didn't."

"But you said . . ."

Marcus shook his head. "No, I said they couldn't make a case against him. I never said they didn't think he was the killer. They do. The ones I've talked to, anyway, down here and in New Hampshire."

"And you feel we can?"

"Can what?"

"Make the case the cops couldn't."

Marcus held out his right hand, palm turned upward. "We can try. We damn well better. I don't want to give back the advance."

This man didn't lack confidence. I shook my head slightly and smiled. "Well . . . I'm game."

"All *right.*"

"High five," I said, laughing, and slapped his still outstretched palm. "Okay. Where do I start?"

"You want to go through the material I've accumulated?" He pointed at the manila files. "See if I've missed anything?"

"Sure."

"Great. I have a few phone calls to make."

The first file was labeled "Carolyn Bragg." I was just about to open it and begin reading when Marcus said, "Liz?"

I looked up at him. He was standing by the desk, one hand on the telephone. "Yes?"

"Keep in mind one thing."

"What's that?"

"The killings stopped as soon as Kmiec was arrested. Have any women in the Merrimack Valley been hacked to death since then?"

"Not to my knowledge."

"So isn't that a good clincher?"

"Yes," I said. "It is."

SIX

The phone calls Marcus was making were to the Massachusetts Corrections Commission. He had apparently written to the administration several times and received either no response or a vague one. What he wanted was permission to interview Henry Kmiec in the state prison at Walpole.

"Keep trying," I told him. "Somebody, somewhere, eventually in the bureaucracy will *have* to take it under advisement."

"Assholes," Marcus muttered.

"They're state employees," I said. "What do you expect?"

"And another thing," Marcus said. "Why do you people give your maximum-security slammers such silly goddam names? Cedar Junction? MCI Cedar Junction at Walpole? Like, excuse me?"

"It was changed a few years ago. Used to be MCI Walpole at Walpole. The town fathers didn't like the fair name of the town of Walpole being besmirched by the association."

"But . . . Cedar Junction? It sounds like a time-share

at a resort in the Poconos." Marcus disappeared into the suite's bedroom.

I glanced up from the Denise Michaud file. "Is Dannemora any better?" I yelled after him. "That sounds like a song title. 'How Are Things in Dannemora?' And Alcatraz? Means 'lily' in Spanish. Your nose is out of joint—no pun intended—just 'cause the corrections commission isn't treating you with the respect you feel is due you."

I heard him laugh.

I was pleased he could take a joke. He was going to be easy to work with. Thank God.

By three o'clock I'd finished combing and recombing the material Marcus had amassed on the nine murder victims. I set the last folder aside and rubbed my eyes. Then I mumbled, "Shit." I dug in my purse for my compact, opened it, and inspected my face. Sure enough, in rubbing my eyes I'd smeared my mascara a little. I always did that. Oh well. I was here to work, not to be gorgeous.

Marcus came out of the bedroom. He'd been using the phone in there so as not to disturb me. I appreciated the consideration, since he did a lot of yelling.

He said, "Well?"

The room-service breakfast cart had been taken and replaced an hour ago with more coffee and a plate of sandwiches. By the end of this gig I was going to weigh two hundred pounds if Marcus didn't stop feeding me. The coffee was still hot. I poured myself a cup.

"There's only one discrepancy that leaps out at me," I said. "Actually, it was in your proposal as well as in your files."

"What's that?"

I stood up so I could stretch. "The two prostitutes had their throats slit. The other seven women died of multiple stab wounds. There's a difference there. Why wouldn't the killer have done to Acosta and Whitlow what he did to the rest? Why the deviation?"

"It's not a huge deviation."

"Well, I don't know. A quick slash as opposed to the repeat stuff? It seems ... less angry, somehow. More impulsive and less compulsive. Another thing—don't serial killers usually develop an m.o. and stick to it? Isn't that ritual aspect one of the hallmarks of serial slayings?"

Marcus was leaning on the jamb of the bedroom doorway. "Sure. But the pattern can vary. Look at Bundy when he went on that rampage in the Florida sorority house. Completely different from the way he operated with his previous victims."

I nodded. "But he was breaking down then. Cracking up. That's one reason why the police were able to catch him."

"Everything you just said can apply to Kmiec, too. Maybe he started to go after prostitutes because they were the easiest targets. And kill them quicker for the same reason—it was easier. He didn't have the time and the capacity any longer to be methodical. He was breaking down, losing it. When the police finally got him, he was a giggling idiot. Remember this is the guy who chuckled to himself while the judge was pronouncing sentence."

"Right. Yeah, I suppose."

Marcus pushed himself away from the doorjamb and glanced at his watch. It was a Patek Philippe, I'd noticed. Mine was a Timex.

"Why don't we call it quits for today?" he said.

"Whatever. Are we meeting again tomorrow morning?"

"Is eight okay?"

"It's ghastly," I said. "But I'll manage. Here?"

"I'll pick you up."

"You have a car?"

"Rented one."

"Gotcha."

He held my coat for me. "Got any plans for tonight?"

"Spending it with Jack."

He smiled. "Have a nice time."

"We will. We usually do."

We did.

I left the Charles Hotel at three-thirty and strolled up through Harvard Square. Strolling was possible; it was about thirty-five degrees and not sleeting or raining or snowing. I stopped at Wordsworth and the Booksmith to check out the newest books. Then I walked to the police station. I got there at four forty-five, fifteen minutes before the official detective quitting time.

Jack was at his desk, going over some reports. He looked up as I walked into the office and grinned.

"Hey," he said. "How does it feel to be gainfully employed?"

I dropped into the visitor's chair. "It feels divine."

He tossed the pen he'd been holding onto the desk blotter. "I bet it does. Think you'll be able to work with Marcus?"

"So far," I replied. "He put up very gracefully with all my bullshit today."

"Man must be bucking for a sainthood," Jack remarked. He pushed back his chair and rose. "Let's escape from this zoo while we can, shall we?"

"Sure," I said. "Want me to sneak you out under my coat past the captain?"

"The captain's at City Hall," Jack said, "arguing with the city manager about the budget. Anyway, it's Charlene I'm scared of."

Charlene was the C.I.D. secretary. She had a habit of pouncing on Jack with a handful of pink message slips, all marked URGENT, at 4:59 P.M.

I poked my head out the office door. Charlene wasn't at her desk. The outer office was empty but for the intern from the criminal justice program at Northeastern University. He was working the computer.

"Coast's clear," I announced.

"Good," Jack said. "Let's move." He grabbed his coat from the hook behind the door and we moved. Out of the C.I.D. and down the wrought-iron staircase on the Green Street side of the building. It was littered with cigarette butts. City ordinance had declared the C.P.D. building a nonsmoking area years ago. The ruling didn't seem to be enforced very vigorously.

Outside the chief's office on the second floor we were waylaid by one of the other detectives. It sounded like the cop wanted to have a private conversation with Jack. I drifted away from them and ended up standing alongside the Dutch door of the Crime Analysis Bureau.

I leaned against the cinder-block wall (the C.P.D. building was a real showplace) and watched Jack. He was listening very intently to the other detective and nodding occasionally.

Jack was an extremely handsome man—or at least, he defined my concept of a good-looking man, which absolutely precluded any trace of the beautiful or pretty. I'm a feminist who believes in certain rigid sex distinctions. One of them is that long eyelashes, full red lips, and downy cheeks are the exclusive purview of women, and look like hell on men. (The appeal of Warren Beatty is totally lost on me.) Jack's face was long and hard-boned. His ancestry was German and Scots, but in certain lights—and moods—he looked as if one of his progenitors had been a Plains Indian. It was something about the structure of the bones around and beneath his eyes. Mongol heritage, probably. What added weight to that supposition was that he tanned to the shade of teak in the summer. So does my mother, who is half German. I take after the Celtic side of the family, skin-wise. I don't even freckle.

Jack's eyes were brown, his hair the same color, with a sprinkling of gray. The rest of him was long and lean and well built, which is exactly how I like my men. Of course he'd been the only one in my life for the past eight years, so I was beginning to lose my sense of comparison.

I have a taste for good-looking men. But I also want them to be smart and have a strong ironic bent. And read books and be articulate. In fact, I insist on it.

Jack is and does.

He's also tough, solid, and ethical.

So he likes to spend Sunday afternoon glued to the tube watching whatever jerks are pasting each other on a football field somewhere. So what? I can read or go for a walk or work on one of my articles. Which is exactly what I do, since I can't stand football.

Jack finished up with the other detective and smiled at me. I joined him and together we went down the rest of the stairs.

"What do you want to do tonight?" he asked.

"Did you have anything in mind?"

"I've been thinking about Chinese food all day."

Boy, Portuguese one night and Chinese the next. My digestive system could take a seat on the U.N. Security Council. "Do you want to go get some?"

We walked out of the building onto Green Street.

"I don't feel like going to a restaurant," he said. "We could order something in."

"Perfect," I said. I had only eaten one of the room-service sandwiches for lunch, so I figured a bit of mu shu pork and Hunan beef wouldn't turn me into a blob overnight. "Your place?"

"Sure."

We drove to my apartment to pick up Lucy and my overnight bag and then to his. Jack and I have this great arrangement. I cook dinner for him and me, and he buys dinner for me and him. I like to cook; he doesn't. I don't like to clean up afterward; he doesn't mind. He makes more money than I do, so he's better able to pick up the restaurant tabs. Is that fair or what?

Jack's apartment was larger than mine, and in a "nicer" part of the city. (Again, a consequence of his greater income.) He'd lived there a long time. Even when he was married. His wife had died—run down by a drunk driver on Garden Street—three years before I'd met him.

The Chinese meal eaten and the cartons in which it had been delivered disposed of, the three of us sat on the floor before the fireplace. Lucy had preempted the choice spot, nearest the screen. I was telling Jack about the day I'd spent with Griffin Marcus. I was especially telling him about Henry Kmiec.

"Kmiec I know of," Jack said. "More than just what I read in the papers, I mean."

I had been lying on my stomach. I rolled over onto my side and stared at him. "Really? Was he ever arrested for anything in Cambridge?"

Jack shook his head. "No, not that I ever heard. And I would have heard if he had been. No, this is just stuff I've gotten from listening to other cops, from Boston and New Hampshire. A bunch of guys getting together and having drinks and blowing smoke. Sooner or later you start talking about your cases. And your bad guys."

"And Kmiec comes up in the conversation a lot?"

"Sure. He's one of the lengendary dirtballs. Not exactly in the same league as the Boston Strangler, but . . . up there."

I rolled back onto my stomach, reached out, and patted Lucy's head. "Marcus is convinced Kmiec is the Merrimack Valley Killer."

"Marcus is probably right," Jack said. "From what I've been told."

"He thinks he and I, working together, can prove that Kmiec is guilty."

Jack smiled at me. The firelight brought out that Indian look in his face. "Best of luck to you both, babe," he said. "Best of luck."

SEVEN

Jack dropped me and the dog off at my place the next morning at seven forty-five. I took Lucy up to the apartment and got her settled in with a bowl of water and a new beef neck bone. Slurping the marrow out of the bone could be her project for the day. My landlord's mother would let her out at noon for her midday backyard reconnaissance.

I unpacked my overnight case. Then I packed my shoulder bag with a notebook, fresh pens and pencils, and my miniature portable tape recorder. Marcus hadn't told me what he and I would be doing today, so it seemed wise to prepare for any eventuality.

My gun I left home, in its usual place, handcuffed through the cylinder frame to the drainpipe of the kitchen sink.

I went down to the street a little before eight. A gray Ford Explorer was idling at the curb. Marcus was at the wheel. I gave him points for not renting a BMW or a Saab. Then again, maybe he assumed that you couldn't navigate in the winter in New England without a four-wheel-drive vehicle. I'd have to assure him that yes, we *did* plow and sand our roads when it snowed.

I climbed up into the car and said, "Morning."

Marcus had a road map unfolded on the steering wheel. He glanced up and said, "Hi." Then he looked back at the map. "Tell me—how the hell do you get from here to Route 93?"

"Easily. I'll show you."

He nodded. "Well, you gave me great directions here from the hotel."

"I'm good at that," I said. "Surprisingly so, in view of I don't drive."

He was dumbfounded. Coming from L.A., he probably thought that not driving was like not breathing. "You *don't?* Why not?"

"Long story. I'll bore you with it some other time. Now, the best way to get from here to 93 is . . ."

Ten minutes later we were on the highway heading north.

"So," Marcus said. "Did you have a nice time with your friend last night?"

"Fine, thank you," I said. Then I added, "And this morning, too."

He smiled.

The commuter traffic going south to Boston was very heavy. It was only slightly less so northbound.

"Is this the high-tech strip?" Marcus asked.

"No," I said. "That's Route 128, west of Boston. It's our Silicon Valley. Only it hasn't been doing so well lately. We're coming to the entrance to 128 now, in fact. It's usually a mess at drive time."

It was. A jackknifed tractor-trailer on one of the off-ramps brought us to a standstill for a quarter of an hour. To pass the intermission, I asked Marcus what our destination was.

"Manchester," he said. "We're going to talk to Kmiec's mother. And his landlord and a guy he worked for."

"I brought my tape recorder," I said.

"So did I."

"Well, if one of them fails . . ."

We got through the traffic snarl and rolling again. It was a gorgeous day, blue-skied and about forty degrees. Perfect weather for interviewing the nearest and dearest of a homicidal maniac.

When we got to Andover, I said, "If you'll look to your left, you'll see the Raytheon plant."

"Where they make the Patriot missiles?"

"The very one."

"Interesting," Marcus said. "Sort of makes Andover the ideal target for a terrorist attack or a bomb, doesn't it?"

"I'm sure they've thought of that. And now guess what we're approaching?"

"Tell me."

"The Merrimack River."

Marcus said quickly, "Where's the Marriott?"

I was startled. "The . . . ? Oh. The hotel? Up here on the right. Why?"

"Can we get there from here?"

"Sure. Take the River Road exit."

Marcus put the car in the right-hand lane.

"What do we want with the Marriott?" I said. "You're unhappy with the service at the Charles?"

He didn't answer.

We drove into the Marriott lot, to the far end. Marcus stopped the car and killed the engine. Then he reached into his coat pocket and took out a folded piece of paper, which he opened and began to study. It looked like a hand-drawn map.

"Right," he said. He refolded the paper and put it on the dashboard. "Let's go."

He got out of the car and walked across the remainder of the parking lot to a field. I shrugged and followed him.

We hopped over the low fence that separated the asphalt from the brown and dry grass. In front of us were some woods.

"Down there," Marcus said, pointing. "That's where they found Peggy Letourneau."

"I see."

"Let's take a look."

We tramped across the field. The ground was soggy and a little springy underfoot. Like walking on a really large sponge.

The woods sloped away down to the bank of the Merrimack. Through the bare trees we could see the river, wide and blue and calm beneath the winter sun. It didn't look nearly as badly polluted as it was.

We came into a small clearing bisected by the trunk of a fallen birch.

"Here," Marcus said.

I stopped short.

There was of course no sign in the clearing that several years before, a nightmare had taken place in it.

"Was she killed here?" I asked. "Or somewhere else and brought here afterward?"

"Killed here," Marcus said. "That's what the forensic team from the state police concluded."

I nodded.

We stood for a few minutes in silence. Then we went back to the car.

We were riding on 93 again when I said, "If Peggy was kidnapped out of the nursing home parking lot and brought back there to be murdered, then Kmiec must have somehow subdued her."

"Hard to guess," Marcus said. "There wasn't any trauma to her skull, so Kmiec didn't knock her out. He didn't choke her till she blacked out—at least there wasn't any physical evidence he did. And he didn't somehow drug her, because they tested for that in the autopsy. Probably he jumped out at her and put the knife to her throat and said something like, 'Scream and you're dead.' And then he dragged her into his truck."

"Then she was probably conscious when he stabbed her."

"Probably."

"God."

"He must have wanted it that way," Marcus said. "For them all to be aware, up to the very last second, of what was happening to them."

"I'd like to kill the son of a bitch myself," I said.

Neither of us spoke again till we reached the Queen City Bridge exit into Manchester.

"I memorized the street atlas for this place this morning," Marcus said. "I think I'll really be able to find what we're looking for without getting hopelessly lost first."

"What *are* we looking for?"

"Freeling's Tow Service. Kmiec worked there just before the Cheryl Timmons murder."

I frowned. "I thought Kmiec was a machinist."

"He was, once. He got shit-canned from that job. He got shit-canned or laid off from a lot of jobs."

"Why?"

Marcus snorted. "You name it. Chronic unexcused absenteeism. Showing up for work drunk. Fighting. Stealing. Being, in a word, the schmuck that he is."

Freeling's Tow Service was on a street that mixed two-and three-decker frame residentials with small businesses. It was situated between a store that sold unfinished pine furniture and a pizza parlor. Freeling's was a one-story cinder-block construction painted white. It looked well kept, as did the tow trucks parked in serried ranks outside it.

Marcus found a space to dock the Explorer a block up, in front of a fishmonger's. The fish place was running a special on mussels—fifty-nine cents a pound. Why did I have such a great facility for picking up and absorbing that kind of inconsequential detail?

As we walked to the tow service, I said. "What do you want me to do?"

Marcus glanced at me in seeming surprise. "Whatever you want. You think of a question, ask it."

"Okay."

"I mean," Marcus added, "this *is* something you've done before. And very well, if I'm any judge."

"Thanks."

"So you do what you know how to do. That's why I hired you."

"Right."

Roger Freeling, owner of Freeling's Tow, was in his mid-fifties. He was a few inches shorter than I, about five-eight, and built square, like a child's wooden alphabet block. Just about as sturdy, too. He had a gray crewcut and hard, watchful eyes that took in everything and gave nothing away.

Cop eyes. Tough eyes. He had to be tough to run a successful trucking operation.

We sat down with him in a little cluttered office near

the rear of the building. Marcus had made this appointment the day before yesterday. It had not been difficult,
Marcus had told me, to get Freeling to agree to the interview. Since Freeling had in no way the manner of
someone loquacious, I wondered why it had been so
easy to get him to talk to us.

I found out quickly.

"Biggest mistake I ever made," Freeling said. "Hiring
that jerk Kmiec."

"What did he do here?" Griffin asked. "Drive a
truck?"

"Oh, Christ, no," Freeling said. He was wearing a red
plaid wool jacket, the kind that looks like a heavy shirt.
He reached into the breast pocket and pulled out a small
cigar. "Kmiec I wouldna let drive a go-cart. Nah, I hired
him to keep the trucks washed and vacuumed and this
place swept out." Freeling lit the cigar.

"You knew he had a criminal record when you took
him on," Marcus said.

Freeling shrugged. "Yeah, well, who else can you get
to do that kind of shitwork? Anyway, he did his time."

Marcus nodded. "How long was he working here?"

Freeling blew out a cloud of blue-gray smoke. "Three
weeks."

"And then you let him go."

Freeling took the cigar out of his mouth and made a
disgusted face. "You got that right."

"What happened?"

"I came in here one night"—Freeling cocked his head
to indicate the office—"and I found him right here with
his hands in the top drawer of the desk." Freeling
looked down at the scarred oak before him. "I kicked
his ass out and across the street. Told him if I ever saw

him around here again, he'd get worse than his ass kicked."

Marcus nodded.

"How did Kmiec get along with the other people who worked here?" I asked.

Freeling looked at me as if intrigued to learn that I had the power of coherent speech. "Kmiec was too goddam weird to get along with anybody. I'da fired the asshole anyway even if I hadn't caught him in here looking for something to lift."

"Weird in what way?" I said.

Freeling stamped out the cigar in a birdbath-size ashtray that had CONNOLLY'S PAINT AND SUPPLY stamped on it in gold. "Look," he said, not to me but to Marcus. "The guy was a wetbrain. He walked around here talking to himself. Plus, he'd do stupid shit like hide the tools. Christ only knows why. One of the guys would go looking for a jack or whatever and not be able to find it and get pissed, and Kmiec would stand there laughing like a retard." Freeling shook his head. " 'Course, he *was* a retard, so that's no big deal."

"He may have acted crazy. He was apparently smart enough to get away with murder for a long time," Marcus said. "Crazy doesn't mean stupid."

Freeling gave him a hard stare. "So what the hell's the difference?"

EIGHT

We spent another fifteen minutes with Freeling. What we learned was that Kmiec had not, in his three-week tenure at the tow shop, said or done anything that might indicate he had a violent enough hatred of women to go out and kill nine of them and try to kill a tenth. Freeling hadn't known anything about Kmiec's collection of slash and snuff movies. Freeling had also mentioned that it was a good thing for Kmiec that he, Freeling, hadn't known about Kmiec's hobby.

"He'da been out on his ass a lot quicker and a lot harder," Freeling said. "I don't go for that shit. I got two daughters."

As we walked back to the car, Marcus said to me, "Did that bother you?"

I looked at him curiously. "What?"

"Freeling treated you as if you weren't in the room."

I laughed. "Do you think that's the first time I've been treated that way? I can cope. If I couldn't, I'd have gone scuttling back to the groves of academe long before this."

"Well, you handled the situation very well."

"You mean I didn't stamp my little feminist foot and

threaten to punch Freeling out if he didn't treat me with respect?"

Marcus laughed reluctantly. "Something like that."

I stopped walking. "Griffin," I said. "Look at me."

He did.

"Do I look like someone who has to prove to a middle-aged trucker that she's tough? Do I?"

"No."

"So don't worry about it." I swung up into the passenger seat of the Explorer. "I don't."

We found a sandwich shop a mile away and went in for coffee. It was ten-thirty and I was in acute need of a post-breakfast dose of caffeine. Clearly Marcus was, too.

The restaurant had tile on the floor and posters of New Hampshire's scenic splendors on the walls. We sat down in a booth beneath a faded profile of the Old Man in the Mountain.

"Sorry it's not Ma Maison or Le Cirque," I said.

Marcus just looked at me and I laughed.

"Seriously," I said. "New Hampshire's beautiful. I hope before you leave you'll be able to see more of it than whatever hellholes Kmiec hung out in."

"I'll try."

The waitress brought us each a thick white china mug of coffee. It smelled wonderful.

"Where're we going next?" I asked.

"To visit Kmiec's mother."

"That ought to be exhilarating," I said, stirring artificial sweetener into my coffee.

"No doubt," Marcus replied. He held his cup under

his nose as if he were inhaling the steam to clear his nasal passages. "Liz?"

"Yes?"

"Today is just the prelims."

"I know," I said. "In a week or so we'll go back and hit Freeling again, and maybe some of the other guys in the tow place. See if they've remembered anything else about Kmiec in the meantime."

He smiled and drank some coffee. "I said *intensive on-site research*, didn't I?"

"I believe you did."

Edith Kmiec lived in a trailer plunked on a small scraggly plot of land on a winding country road just outside the Manchester city limits. The nearest residence to hers was an ultramodern multilevel redwood-and-plate-glass solar-heated marvel with decks thrusting off the various stories like pulled-out dresser drawers. New Hampshire had funny zoning laws. You were always finding meticulously restored early nineteenth-century farmhouses with manicured lawns, tennis courts, and swimming pools cheek-by-jowl with tarpaper shacks featuring the hulks of 1953 DeSotos rusting irrevocably in what passed as front yards.

Marcus pulled the Explorer into a weedy, potholed gravel drive that led up to the trailer.

"Isn't this delightful?" he remarked, gazing at a pile of used tires haphazardly pyramided at the head of the drive. "So country."

"I don't think this is the worst place either one of us has ever been in," I said. "Or will be."

As we walked up to the trailer, a scrawny dog that looked as if it might be part beagle came wandering out of the thicket that marked the property line between the redwood palace and the trailer. It inspected us for a bit, as if trying to decide whether we were worth the effort to bark at. Then it lay down and began gnawing urgently at its right hindquarters.

I thought fleetingly of Lucy, sleek and well fed, chomping away at the beef neck bone back in Cambridge.

A wooden crate served as the step leading up to the trailer. Marcus mounted it and knocked on the front door.

To the right of the door was a window hung with once-white eyelet curtains. One of the curtains fluttered.

The trailer door opened. A short woman in a shapeless flower-print dress peered out at us. Her bare legs were a bas relief of varicose veins. On her feet were fake-fur pink scuffs. Her white hair was pulled back into a short ponytail with a rubber band.

"Mrs. Kmiec?" marcus said. "I'm Griffin Marcus." He gestured at me. "This is Elizabeth Connors."

The woman stood still, affectless, in the doorway. Then she said, "You didn't tell me you was bringing nobody with you."

Marcus smiled. "Ms. Connors is my associate."

The woman nodded as if it didn't matter anyway. As if nothing did. She opened the door wider. Marcus and I stepped inside the trailer.

It was pretty awful, but not nearly as awful as I'd expected. Relatively clean, for one thing. The light was very dim, which perhaps made the atmosphere seem heavier and more depressed than it actually was.

We were in the living room space of the trailer. It was furnished with a maple rocker with an orange plaid cushion, a pea-green area rug, a black-and-white-tweed armchair, and a loveseat upholstered in maroon velour. A small color TV set stood on a maple end table in the far corner of the room. On the screen Sally Jessy Raphael was talking earnestly to a woman whose best friend had seduced her fifteen-year-old son.

"You can siddown," Mrs. Kmiec said. She was a small, thin woman, but she stood and moved as if she weighed three hundred pounds.

Marcus took the loveseat, I the rocker. Mrs. Kmiec simply remained in the middle of the room.

"I hope you'll sit down, too," Marcus said.

Mr. Kmiec looked around the room as if she didn't know it. Then she moved to the tweed armchair and placed herself there. Marcus glanced at me. I raised my eyebrows and shook my head very slightly. "You first," I mouthed.

"I want to thank you again for agreeing to speak with us," Marcus said. "I know this is a very difficult situation for you. Because it is, we appreciate your kindness all the more. And we'll be as quick as possible."

"I don't mind," Mrs. Kmiec said. I was sure she was telling the truth. Her time probably wasn't much more valuable to her than anything else.

"Can you tell us something about your son Henry?" Marcus asked. "About what he was like as a boy?"

"He was a good boy," Mrs. Kmiec said.

"Never in any trouble?"

Mrs. Kmiec canted her head side to side. "Oh no, he was a real good boy." Her voice, like her manner, was completely lacking in affect.

On the television, Sally Jessy Raphael was introducing the seductress.

Marcus said, very gently, "Mrs. Kmiec, he once attacked you with a hammer, didn't he? When he was a young kid."

The woman's hands had been lying flat in her lap. Now the right moved to cover the left. "Oh, that wasn't nothing. He was just a little mad at me, was all."

Marcus turned to me. I shrugged minutely. He looked back at Mrs. Kmiec. She had her head tilted at a forty-five-degree angle. Her face had the expression of someone overhearing a distant and barely audible but far more interesting conversation than the one going on in this room.

I reached over and snapped off the TV, terminating the seductress in the middle of explaining why she found true fulfillment in sexual congress with her college roommate's adolescent son.

The quiet in the room was profound. Whatever Mrs. Kmiec was listening to hadn't come from the television.

"I know what they say about Henry and those women," she recited. "It's not true. None of it. Henry wouldn't kill nobody. He's a good boy."

Marcus inhaled strongly. "Mrs. Kmiec," he began.

She smiled at him vaguely. "Henry's a good boy. He's away now. But he'll be back soon. He'll take care of me then. I know he will. He said. He said he'd take care of me."

Marcus drew another long breath. "I'm sure he did, Mrs. Kmiec." He rose. "Thank you for your help."

She gave him that novocaine smile.

"Liz?"

"Coming."

When we were outside the trailer, I said, "Are we going to hit *her* again next week?"

Marcus grimaced. "Jesus H. Christ. I had no idea she was that out of it."

"How old is she?"

"Sixty-one. Sixty-two maybe."

"God," I said. "That's all? I'd have guessed a hundred and seven. Does she have Alzheimer's or something?"

"I don't know." He glanced over his shoulder back at the trailer. "Maybe she's on Thorazine. She acts like it."

"But she seems to be able to function," I said. "That place was fairly neat. She seemed clean and put together, in a threadbare way."

"When I spoke to her on the phone, she seemed *compos mentis.*" We got into the Explorer. "Not what I'd call smart as a whip," Marcus continued, "but competent." He stared at the trailer through the windshield.

"Maybe she has good days and bad ones," I said. "This could be one of her bad ones."

"We'll find out," Marcus said. He started the car.

The apartment Kmiec had lived in at the time of his arrest was in a three-decker gray shingle-sided house on a trash-strewn side street in Manchester's industrial section. The house next to it was boarded up and had a CONDEMNED sign in one of the front windows. Kmiec's old place looked as if it was about one step up from that. Chunks of the concrete stoop had broken off and lay scattered about the ground. A plastic trash bag, splitting along the seams, sat on the porch.

"God," Marcus said. "What a sty."

"Where'd you expect somebody like Kmiec would be living? The Gold Coast?"

We got out of the Explorer.

"You know," I said, "when the cops have to go into

a place like this to question someone, they stand up the whole time."

Marcus arched his eyebrows questioningly.

"Sure," I said. "If you sit down, especially on an up-holstered chair or couch, a roach might crawl into your clothing." Marcus laughed. "I'm serious," I said.

"I believe you. Sounds like good advice."

We went gingerly up the decaying stoop.

"The landlord's name is DeWitt," Marcus said. He bent down and squinted at the collection of buzzers. Three of the six buttons had names written on tape beneath them. One was DeWitt's. Marcus pushed it.

A minute or so later we heard footsteps and the door creaked open about a foot. A male face that hadn't seen a razor so far today appeared in the space.

"Joseph DeWitt?" Marcus said. "I'm Griffin Marcus. This is Elizabeth Connors."

DeWitt looked blank.

"We spoke the other day," Marcus added.

Some of the blankness on DeWitt's face dissolved. "Oh, yeah," he said. "Right. Yeah. You're the one wants to talk about Kmiec."

"Yes. May we come in?"

"Huh? Oh, yeah, sure, come on in."

The air in the foyer was stale. DeWitt led us down a dark, narrow hall to another door. It opened into a kitchen.

Like Edith Kmiec's trailer, the place was better on the inside than on the outside. The kitchen appliances and fixtures were old, but they looked as if they worked. The linoleum and Formica countertops were worn almost through in spots, but they were clean. An old Kelvinator vibrated in one corner.

We sat at a round pine table with mismatched wooden

chairs. In the center of the table stood a milk-glass vase filled with pink plastic rosebuds.

DeWitt was around my height and skinny. He wore tan twill trousers and a gray sweatshirt with the sleeves cut off raggedly at the elbows. Underneath that was what appeared to be the top of a navy-blue union suit. His hair was brown and sparse. He could have been anywhere between forty and sixty.

"How long did Henry Kmiec live here?" I asked.

DeWitt ruminated. " 'Bout maybe a year and a half, I guess. Yeah. 'Bout that."

"Was he a good tenant?"

DeWitt shrugged. "He paid his rent. He didn't wreck the place or make no noise."

"What was he like otherwise?"

DeWitt looked at me as if I'd asked the question in Flemish.

"What kind of person was he?"

DeWitt shrugged again. "I never seen him that much. Okay, I guess."

"Which apartment did he live in?" Marcus asked.

DeWitt pointed his right thumb at the ceiling. "Second floor."

"Is anyone living there now?"

"Nope."

"May we see it?"

DeWitt sat still for a moment. Then he said, "Yeah, sure, I s'pose." He got up and felt around on top of the refrigerator till he found an iron ring of keys.

We trailed him back down the hall and up a flight of creaking wooden stairs. DeWitt unlocked a door opposite the second-floor landing. He gave a languid wave to indicate we could enter.

The apartment was two rooms, kitchen and bed-sitting room combined. The bathroom had a claw-foot tub. There was an iron bedstead with a naked mattress and a deal bureau on one side of the main room. On the opposite side were two vinyl armchairs flanking a Parsons table. The kitchen was a pullman, with an undercounter refrigerator and a two-burner hot plate. Marcus and I circled slowly around the place as if we were prospective home buyers checking out a good deal on a handyman's special. DeWitt watched incuriously from the doorway.

"Has anyone lived here since Kmiec?" I asked.

"Nope."

"Then it looks the way it did when he lived here."

"Police took out a lot of stuff."

"What kind of stuff?"

"Tapes. Magazines."

"What magazines?"

DeWitt made a pursuing movement with his mouth. "You know, Them ones."

"Dirty magazines?"

DeWitt nodded.

"Did Kmiec ever have any visitors?" Marcus asked.

DeWitt shrugged. It was his favorite reply. "Never seen any."

"How'd he spend his time when he was here, then?"

"Lookin' at them magazines, I guess. Watchin' them tapes on the VCR."

"When he went out," I said, "did he go and come back at odd hours?"

"You mean like late at night?"

"Yes."

"Yeah. The wife and I heard him come in sometimes maybe three, four in the morning."

"Where'd he go?"

DeWitt shrugged. What else?

"But he never caused a disturbance of any kind?"

"Nope."

Marcus nodded. "Okay, Mr. DeWitt, thanks. You've been a big help."

As we followed the landlord back down the stairs, I whispered to Marcus, "They have livelier bodies down at the morgue."

He grinned and whispered back, "Give the man credit. At least he's not a sexist."

We were heading south on 93, back to Cambridge, when I said, "What do you think we accomplished today?"

"I'm not sure," Marcus said. He scratched his chin thoughtfully. "We got a lot of good background stuff, good for the book."

"But nothing substantive."

"Well"—Marcus smiled at me—"this is only day one. What did you expect, that we'd dig up somebody who witnessed Kmiec committing all nine murders? And took notes and photos?"

"No," I said, laughing.

"Anyhow," Marcus said, "maybe we *did* learn something today. Only we won't realize what till later."

"That's always happening to me."

"It's the way the game works."

NINE

We got off Route 93 just over the Massachusetts border and got onto Route 110, so Marcus could scout out the location where Lisa Goodenough's body had been found. It was very much like the clearing in which Peggy Letourneau had died—a wooded area out of sight of the road. It told us nothing; whatever secrets it might have held were long gone. But I understood that Marcus wanted to get a feel for the scene, so he could reproduce it in the book.

When we were back in the car, he said, "We're in Methuen, right?"

I nodded.

"Where Lisa died and where Linda Tessier lived and worked and died. What kind of a town is it?"

"Basically the creation of three families named Searles, Tenney, and Nevins," I said. "There's some farming that still goes on, but mostly it's light industry—textiles and machinery. And of course the mall."

"Uh-huh."

"When we tour it—which we *are* going to do?"

"Yeah."

"Okay, well, when we ride around it, you'll see a lot

of stone walls and little fortressy-looking structures. They're all part of the old Searles estate. One of the Searles, I forget which one, decided to build himself a castle. The main buildings and grounds are a Catholic girls' school now."

"Sure, Linda Tessier lived right near there. The Presentation of Mary Academy."

"That's right." I thought for a moment. "I wonder if Kmiec had any previous association with Methuen."

"You mean because he was so active in it? It's something to find out."

We arrived in Cambridge at a quarter to five.

"Have a drink with me," Marcus said. "We can talk about what's next."

"All right."

He left the Explorer in the circular drive in front of the hotel for someone to put in the garage, and we went up to the bar. The table we'd had the night we'd met was free, so we took it.

"Maybe we can make this ours," Marcus said, shedding his parka.

"What a lovely thought," I said. "We can get them to screw a brass plaque to the tabletop with our names engraved."

After the waitress had served the drinks, I said, "Griffin?"

"Yes?"

"We haven't talked much about the victims yet."

He smiled at me over his glass. "You must be psychic. I was just about to say the same thing."

"I know you said before that you thought there was a possibility Kmiec might have been stalking Peggy Letourneau in Lawrence."

"Uh-huh."

"Well, what about the other six? Were they targets of opportunity, or do you think he zeroed in on each one and tracked her?"

"And then moved in for the kill? I'm not sure. I'm not even sure about Peggy Letourneau."

I bit the knuckle of my right hand and frowned. "What did all the first seven victims have in common?"

Marcus looked at me sharply. "What do *you* think they do?"

I let my hand fall to my lap. "If they were very similar in several significant ways, it would establish a pattern, wouldn't it? Which would strongly imply that Kmiec had chosen them precisely because they embodied those qualities."

"Let's see.," Marcus said. "They were all young."

"They all lived and worked near the river."

Marcus was ticking the item off on his fingers. "They were all educated, with professional training of some sort. Except for Cheryl. But she had college and career plans, so that put her in the same category."

"They were all white."

We fell silent for a moment. I sipped my drink.

"What else?" Marcus said finally. "Some were married, one was divorced, some were single, some were mothers, some weren't. No pattern there."

"And they didn't look alike, particularly," I added. "Not going by the pictures I've seen of them, anyway."

"Maybe when we dig further into their backgrounds something will turn up," Marcus said.

"Mmmm. You know, the prostitutes—Carla Whitlow, Maria Acosta, and Keisha Madison—have even less in common with the other seven than the seven do among themselves. They were young women, yes, but not educated, not living by the river, and Acosta was Hispanic and Whitlow and Madison were black."

"I know."

"Does that bother you?"

"Yes, it bothers the hell out of me that a scum like Kmiec could carve them up."

"Oh, Griffin—"

"I know what you mean. No, it doesn't bother me— for the reason I told you before. Kmiec was falling apart. I think he became completely possessed by his urge to kill. The prostitutes were the most convenient targets. That they happened to be non-white was incidental."

"Who was killed first?" I asked. "Maria Acosta or Carla Whitlow?"

Marcus lit a cigarette. "Carla Whitlow."

"That accords with your theory. He put Carla by the river. So at the time he murdered her, he was still functioning enough to be able to perform that part of the ritual. By the time he killed Maria Acosta . . ." I gestured with my hands. "He was too far gone to do that."

Marcus nodded. "And the third—or I should say the tenth—intended victim, Keisha, was even able to fight him off."

"Bully for her," I said. "If the cops didn't give her a medal, maybe you and I should."

Marcus smiled and finished his drink. He looked at my glass. "Would you like another?"

I hesitated. Then I said, "No. But thank you. I'm a little tired. Maybe I'll just go on home and prepare for whatever you have lined up for tomorrow. What *do* you have lined up for tomorrow?"

"I plan to spend the morning fighting with the corrections commission."

"Sounds like fun." I drained my glass. "You don't need me for that. *Oh*—you know what I could do?"

"What?"

"I have a friend who's a forensic psychiatrist. I could call her and see if she's got some time free to talk with me about serial killers. I'm sure she knows about Kmiec, too. Maybe she can come up with some kind of explanation for his river fixation."

"Now that," Marcus said, "is an excellent idea."

"Okay. That's what I'll do."

I stood up and so did he. He helped me with my coat.

"You and Jack getting together tonight?"

I shook my head. "No. He and a friend of his from the department are going to a Celtics game. I think I'll write down my impressions of what we heard and saw today and then just flop out."

"Sounds reasonable."

"Good night, Griffin. I'll see you tomorrow sometime."

"Sure. Midafternoon?"

"Fine."

We smiled at each other. As I left the bar, he was sitting down again and motioning to the waitress for another drink.

TEN

The following morning at ten-thirty I was sitting in the second-floor cafeteria of the Middlesex County Courthouse having coffee with Brenda Adams, M.D. I always thought her name and title together sounded like a comic-strip character's. She did, too. Having been born with the first and professionally required to use the second, she could do little about the situation but laugh at it.

As a black woman in a profession dominated by white men, she had to maintain a sense of humor anyway. She was a year or so older than I, divorced, with two kids. After the breakup of the marriage, she and the kids had moved into her widowed mother's house in Jamaica Plain. The grandmother was a vigorous woman in her mid-sixties who kept an eye on the kids and took them on outings when they weren't in school. It took a lot of the pressure off Brenda.

I had met her through David Epstein, another forensic psychiatrist. He'd steered me to her when I was researching an article on child abuse. Not a jolly note on which to begin a friendship, but we had.

Surrounded by cops, court officers, ADAs, victims,

defendants, witnesses, and jurors from the District and Superior courts on coffee break, we talked. Brenda was, as I'd assumed, fairly familiar with the Kmiec case. I filled her in on the bits and pieces of information Marcus and I had collected yesterday.

"It's the business with the river that gets me," I said. "Eight out of nine of the bodies were left by the river. Why? Explain that fetish to me."

One of the reasons I was so fond of Brenda was that she never spoke in psychobabble. And she didn't now.

"Obviously it has some special significance for him," she said. "But you're already aware of that. What the significance is ... you know there are universal symbols we all recognize the meaning of, at least in this culture. Like dawn symbolizing hope, spring symbolizing rebirth and renewal."

"Yeah," I said. "Like black equals evil and white equals good."

She nodded thoughtfully. "Yes, we frequently see that principle applied in day-to-day life, don't we?"

I looked at her and we both laughed.

"Brenda, I keep thinking of rivers and water as having something to do with a purification ritual. Am I off base there?"

Brenda rested her chin in her palm and smiled at me. "Water as a purification ritual," she repeated. "You literary types are all the same. Liz, what I was going to tell you about crazy people is that they don't share our symbolic code. They make up their own. The river could represent anything to Kmiec."

"I had a feeling you'd say that."

"Anyhow," Brenda continued. "I couldn't possibly begin to guess what the damn river meant to Kmiec unless I talked to him myself. Maybe even then I couldn't tell you."

"I had a feeling you'd say that, too. But no harm in asking. Okay, let me switch tracks. When the police cleared out Kmiec's apartment after he was arrested, they found a huge library of snuff and slash videos."

"Oh, *nice,*" Brenda said. "Are you going to ask me whether they inspired him to go out and kill women?"

"Well—did they?"

"My first question would be, When did he start collecting that shit?"

I shrugged. "I haven't found out yet."

Brenda pushed her empty Styrofoam coffee cup to the side. "There's a theory that men watching movies of men raping and dicing up women relieves them of their urge to do those same things in real life." She crossed her arms on the tabletop. "It's not a theory I subscribe to." Her voice was hard.

"Me neither," I said. "My feeling is that the sick are made sicker by those things. *And* that they get inspiration from them."

"You're right, on the basis of what I've seen." Brenda uncrossed her arms and seemed to relax slightly.

"Well, call me a deluded optimist, but I've always cherished the hope that the only men who truly enjoyed movies about women being tortured and killed were already degenerates to begin with."

"I think you have a point." Brenda looked away from me and out the window that overlooked Spring Street and an auto-body shop. "I hope you do. I certainly hope you do." She pushed back her chair. "Come on. I may have some offprints of articles in my office that might help you."

We threaded our way through the maze of tables. The

public-address system requested that attorney McCarron please report to Courtroom 9B.

Brenda's office was in the clinic on the first floor of the courthouse. I waited in the reception area while she went through her files.

She appeared with a handful of pamphlets. "Here," she said. "Some material on organized and disorganized killers."

"Thanks. Kmiec seems to have been both."

Her eyebrows went up.

"Is that unusual?" I said.

She sighed. "My take is, the more we learn about serial killers, the less we know about them. There are ones who change m.o.'s. Others don't. There *are* ones who go from organized to disorganized. Sometimes the organized ones have a few of the characteristics of the disorganized. And vice versa."

I was thinking about the conversation I'd had with Marcus on the same subject. "So it would be plausible for Kmiec to go from fairly organized to fairly disorganized?"

"It wouldn't be impossible. There are serial killers who change weapons with each murder. I recall reading about a case where a guy used a knife one time, a gun another, a meat hook the third time, then a garrote . . . as if he were experimenting to find the perfect technique. Or maybe he was using whatever was handy. Anyway, you get the point."

"Yeah. Thanks, Bren."

"Anytime." She thrust the pamphlets at me. "Read. If you have other questions, I'll be happy to answer them. If I can."

* * *

I took the elevator to the thirteenth floor, where the C.P.D.'s police prosecutor had his office. A police prosecutor isn't a prosecutor in the accepted sense of one who argues cases in court—he or she is the person who arranges for cops to show up at trial to testify. I'd agreed to meet Jack outside the office. He'd had to testify in a trial this morning.

He was leaning against the wall, talking to a woman from the Victim/Witness Assistance Bureau. Jack dresses very well, very Brooks Brothers. Today he was outstandingly natty in a gray suit, white shirt, and blue-and-gray diagonally striped tie.

I walked up to him, tugged his lapel, and said, "How did the women on the jury manage to restrain themselves from throwing their underwear at you?"

"Damned if I know," he said matter-of-factly.

The Vic/Wit woman grinned at me and said, "I was wondering the same thing myself." She winked at me and went back to her office.

"Someday," I said to Jack, "someday I'll say something to you that will make you blush."

We walked to the elevators.

"How'd your trial go?" I asked.

"Same as usual. The defense attorney and I each managed to imply that the other was the biggest sleazebag liar in the history of jurisprudence."

"Who was the defense attorney?"

"Roy Stewart."

I laughed. Stewart was someone Jack and I had known for a long time. We were even friendly with him. What the general public doesn't understand is that criminal trials are dog-and-pony shows, and whoever puts on the best act wins. Which is why after the show is over, the two sides can go out for a drink together and have a laugh.

Except in the worst cases.

The trial Jack had just testified in wasn't one of those. The defendant was accused of a string of burglaries. No one had been injured, no one had been threatened during them. The defendant would probably get convicted (even Stewart knew he was about 110 percent guilty) and probably receive a five-year sentence. He would serve a year and a half of it, at the most, at one of the medium-security prisons, and then be released to burglarize again. This wasn't his first time in court on the same charge. It wouldn't be his last.

So what could you do but laugh?

The elevator arrived and we rode it down to the Thorndike Street level.

"How about an early lunch?" Jack asked.

"That sounds good."

We walked two blocks down Third Street to the American Twine Company building, which had a delicatessen in its basement. I got a table while Jack went for the food. It was eleven forty-five and the place wasn't crowded. In thirty minutes half the courthouse would be here getting pasta salad to go.

Jack brought us each coffee and me my lunch of preference, a large vegetable salad. He had a sandwich.

"How was the game last night?" I asked.

"Very good." Jack paused for a moment, his sandwich halfway to his mouth. "You know what was the best part?"

"Larry Bird hit a scoop shot singing 'Un Bel Di.' What?"

"The crowd was so civilized." He put his sandwich

on the paper plate. "There were no fights." He sounded genuinely astonished.

"Amazing," I said. "Celtics fans must be behind the times. What's a sporting event without a little bloodshed?"

"Nice for a change." Jack picked up his sandwich. "What about you? What'd you and Marcus do yesterday?"

I told him. He listened very attentively, as he always did when I described the progress of my work to him.

"You have a long haul ahead of you," he commented when I finished.

"Well, if you can come up with any helpful hints, I'll be very appreciative."

"I'll do what I can."

We ate our lunch.

As we were walking back to the car, Jack said, "Where to now?"

"If it's no trouble, could you drop me at the Charles? I have to meet Marcus."

"Sure."

Jack's car was a yellow 1965 Mustang. Astoundingly, it had never been stolen—here, in the Grant Theft Auto capital of the universe. People were forever stopping him on the street and asking him if he'd sell it to them.

As we were going down Cambridge Street, Jack said, "Liz?"

"Yes?"

"The other night you told me something that's been bothering me a little."

I looked at him with concern. "What's that?"

"About Marcus being a heavy drinker."

"Well, he's not a *lush,* Jack."

"Yeah, okay. Be that as it may. Will you promise me something?"

"What?"

"If he has more than a few drinks, will you not drive anywhere with him?"

I was silent for a moment. Then I said, "Do you really think I'd get in a car with anyone I thought was incapable of operating it?"

"No. But promise me anyway."

"Jaaa-aack!"

"Humor me."

I sighed and raised my right hand. "I, Alice Elizabeth Connors, do solemnly promise. Happy?"

"I'm holding you to that."

"Oh, *really.*"

There wasn't one level surface in the living room of Marcus's suite that wasn't covered with paper. Marcus stood in the center of the room, beaming like someone who'd just won Megabucks and a date with this year's blonde.

"What's up?" I asked, peeling off my jacket.

"I get to see Kmiec next week."

"Far out," I said. "You finally made contact with a sentient being in the corrections commission. Congratulations."

He grinned. "It was only a matter of time."

"Well, that's great. Will they let you do a series of interviews with him?"

"It looks that way."

"Wonderful." I transferred a stack of manila folders from an easy chair to the floor. "Hotel housekeeping must love you," I said, sitting down.

"What'd you get from the psychiatrist?" Marcus asked.

I gave him a synopsis of my conversation with Brenda Adams. He nodded, rather absently. Clearly, his mind was on the upcoming meeting with Kmiec.

I reached into my bag and took out a wad of index cards. "Griffin?"

"Yes?"

I pointed at the array of folders and notebooks on the couch and coffee table. "I'm going to see if I can cross-index some of that stuff. Maybe some kind of pattern will emerge that wasn't visible before."

"Excellent," he said. "You want some coffee?"

"Sure." I picked up the Carolyn Bragg folder. "What are we going to do tomorrow?"

"Go to Lowell."

I raised my eyebrows.

"*I'm* going to talk to some cops. *You're* going to talk to Diane Lamonica's parents."

I inhaled sharply.

"What's the matter?" Marcus said.

"Oh—nothing. I'd have thought you'd want to interview them yourself, that's all."

"I will. Later."

I nodded. "They know I'm coming?"

"Yes."

"Was it difficult to get them to agree to this?"

He made a so-so gesture with his right hand.

"Okay," I said. "If they're ready for me, I'm ready for them."

For the next few hours, I cross-indexed until I was cross-eyed. The files on the individual victims were fairly easy. It was going to be a real thrill, by contrast, to classify the box of clippings on the murders from the

Globe, the *Herald,* the Manchester *Union-Leader,* the New Hampshire *Sunday News,* the Lowell *Sun,* the Nashua *Sunday Telegraph,* the Lawrence *Eagle-Tribune,* and the Haverhill *Gazette.* A thrill that could wait for another day. I shuffled the index cards together and slipped a rubber band around them.

Marcus had spent the afternoon in the bedroom, on the phone. He came into the living room as I was restacking the files. There was a clear space on the sofa now, and he dropped onto it. He put his feet on the coffee table and lit a cigarette. We smiled at each other.

"Griffin, something's bothering me," I said.

He frowned. "What's wrong?"

"Kmiec confessed very readily to killing Carla Whitlow and Maria Acosta and to attacking Keisha Madison, didn't he?"

"I told you that. It was in the book proposal."

"My question is, if Kmiec was so willing to admit responsibility for what happened to Whitlow and Acosta and Madison, why not for the other seven?"

Marcus stared at me for a moment. Then he shrugged. "Well, for one thing, the cops nailed him for Acosta and Whitlow with the forensic evidence. And they had a good eyewitness in Keisha Madison. They didn't have any of that for the other victims."

I nodded. "Still ... why didn't Kmiec just go for broke? He was already going to spend the rest of his life in prison."

"I see what you mean." Marcus paused and mashed out his cigarette in the end-table ashtray. "Maybe he's enjoying his little secret. Playing head games with the cops. Thwarting them."

"That's possible."

"Or maybe he's saving the story."

"For someone like you?"

"Why not? He *wants* to talk to me, according to the corrections commission. Maybe he wants to confess, too."

"Because you're famous, I bet," I said. "He thinks you'll make him famous, too."

"Well . . . I will, won't I?"

"I suppose you will." I shook my head. "Jesus! What a way to become a star. Griffin?"

"Yes?"

"This is a grotesque business we're in."

"Yeah," he said. "But it sure is fun, isn't it?"

ELEVEN

At nine the next morning, Marcus and I were on the road. We took Route 93 up to Route 128 and 128 to Route 3. The commuter traffic had abated somewhat but was still fairly heavy. A byproduct of flextime, maybe.

We were in the middle of a massive slowdown on 128 when Marcus said, "You're quiet this morning."

I shook my head. "Just psyching myself up for the Lamonicas."

He nodded. "That's always the worst, isn't it? Interviewing the relatives of the victims."

I looked out the window at the rolling parking lot around us. "It's better than what the cops have to do—*break* the news to the relatives of the victims."

"Has Jack had to do that often?"

"Often enough."

"You never get used to it, do you?"

"*He* hasn't."

The traffic got unstuck and we started to move a little faster, maybe thirty miles an hour.

"I got the lowdown on Kmiec's mother and his family background yesterday," Marcus said.

"Tell me."

"Henry was the fourth of seven children, six of whom survived infancy."

"What happened to the seventh?"

"Died at the age of three months. Cause of death was officially found to be SIDS, but I think they suspect the kid was smothered or suffocated, most likely by the father."

I screwed up my face and said, "God."

"Kmiec senior was a real loser. He drank, and when he drank, he got mean and he beat up on the wife and kids. The baby was probably screaming one night, and Paul—that was the father's name—got fed up and stuffed some rolled-up socks in the kid's mouth and then had a few more beers and forgot what he'd done and . . . no more baby."

I shivered. "I've heard so many of those stories . . . you'd think that I'd be, well, that I'd react to them less sharply. But always, it's like I'm hearing them for the first time."

"I know. Anyway, Paul, when he worked at all, which wasn't much, worked for the Manchester sanitation department. He disappeared in 1975. Ran off, probably. Nobody's seen him since. He may well be dead now."

"Go on."

"So Edith was left with the six kids, or should I say five—the oldest was in prison at that point, on an armed robbery charge. She got a job for a while on the assembly line of a tool-and-dye place, but then that folded. Ultimately she ended up on welfare."

"What are her circumstances now? Other than not good?"

"She's still on welfare. That tin can she lives in is a rental."

"And the state welfare agency considers her competent to be on her own? The Edith Kmiec you and I met, Griffin, was *not* playing with a full deck."

"I asked about that. Apparently a social worker makes a weekly visit. I guess she's not sufficiently crazy or senile for the DSS to step in and take custody of her, or whatever it is they do."

"She may be better off in her trailer than in state care anyway."

"That's what I thought. What she is, I guess, is just a person who's been poor and abused her entire existence. That'll take its toll on your mind and spirit eventually."

"No kidding," I said. "All she has now is her delusion that Henry's a good boy who'll come back someday to take care of her. Maybe the delusion is what keeps her functional. She probably remembers Paul as a loving father and good husband, too. To the extent she remembers him at all, of course."

"Probably," Marcus said. "How could you look back on a lifetime in hell and then look forward to the future? Without rewriting your own past?"

We were quiet for a few minutes. Then I said, "What happened to the other Kmiec kids?"

"The oldest son died in prison. A fight. The next oldest son and one of the daughters imitated Daddy and just split one fine day. God knows where to or how *they* ended up. Another daughter died of an O.D. Another got married; she lives in Maine now, Damariscotta, I think. She's no prize package, either—she got arrested once on a felony child abuse charge."

"There's a surprise," I said. "What a swell family saga. You think Kmiec inherited his killer instinct?"

"Maybe."

* * *

Salvatore and Marie Lamonica lived in a raised ranch on a quiet street in the Upper Highlands section of Lowell. Everything looks shabby in January, but this house and its grounds were impeccably maintained. Shrubbery that couldn't survive the winter without protection had been neatly shrouded in burlap, and whoever had shoveled the snow off the front path seemed to have done so using a ruler to keep the edges even.

Marcus dropped me at the foot of the driveway. "I'll be back in two hours," he said. "Good luck."

"You too."

He drove off, and I walked up the pristine path to the front door. I rang the bell.

The door was opened by a small, slender woman with thick curly salt-and-pepper hair and a face that had once been pretty but was now dominated by dark pouches under the eyes. The flesh around the Roman nose and full mouth was pinched.

Diane had been dead for five years. It probably seemed like yesterday to Marie Lamonica. It probably always would.

I introduced myself. She nodded and said, "Please come in." She held the door wider, and I stepped over the threshold. Then we went up a short flight of stairs to a living room.

It wasn't a living room; it was a shrine to Diane. There were pictures of her everywhere—on the coffee table, on the end tables, on the walls, on the mantel.

"Let me take your coat," Marie Lamonica said.

"Thank you."

The dominant photograph of Diane was an eight-by-ten blowup of her high school yearbook photo—and I knew it was her high school yearbook photo because it was the stiltedly posed, overtinted, and badly airbrushed production typical of such things. Diane was wearing the idiotically pouty expression demanded of all female subjects by high school yearbook photographers; nevertheless, beneath the ersatz sultriness, her face glinted with verve and intelligence. The real girl was much better portrayed in the gallery of snapshots taken by family and friends, laughing and grinning and in one case crossing her eyes at the camera. I hoped the Lamonicas would let us have one of those photos to use in the book.

There were also pictures of Diane as a toddler, Diane as an elementary school pupil, and Diane in a frilly white dress and short veil—making her First Communion, I supposed.

A vague suggestion of an idea slid into my mind.

"Please sit down," Mrs. Lamonica said.

I lowered myself carefully onto a green-upholstered Mediterranean-style camelback sofa. The room—the shrine—was excruciatingly neat. So much so that I felt uncomfortable using the furniture, as if I were soiling it.

I heard footsteps and a short, heavyset man with wavy gray hair and thick dark eyebrows over a strong nose walked into the room.

"Oh, Sal," Mrs. Lamonica said. "This is Miss Connors."

I said, "How do you do?" and we shook hands across the coffee table. Next to a spotless crystal ashtray on the table, Diane, posing theatrically in a blue maillot, vamped good-humoredly at me.

The Lamonicas sat down in matching armchairs facing the sofa.

Marcus had told me he'd been having a terrible time getting the friends and relatives of the victims to sit for interviews. We both knew why. They were terrified that the lives of their daughters, sisters, nieces, best pals, whatever, might be dissected and distorted in print. That their memories and reputations might be at best trampled and at worst trashed. That the alchemy of publicity might transform the victims into villains, as it so often did.

That Carolyn, Denise, Diane, Peggy, Lisa, Linda, Cheryl, Carla, and Maria might ultimately be portrayed as co-conspirators in their own dreadful fates.

Why was she out alone at night shopping?

Why didn't she have dinner at home with her parents?

Why was she working and not home with her child?

Why was she out working late at night and not home with her husband?

And finally . . .

She asked for it, didn't she?

The Lamonicas had been the only people so far who'd consented to be interviewed. And they'd been initially resistant.

Now they were watching me, silently and steadily and carefully, waiting for me to begin, making their own judgments, and still harboring reservations.

"The first thing," I said, "is that I want to thank you for seeing me. I know this is terrible for you. But I also want to tell you that Griffin Marcus's intention is to portray Diane as she was. He believes, as I do, that the victims of crimes are all too often ignored or just forgotten. We don't think of them as statistics. We want them to be remembered as real people."

The speech didn't say what I had hoped it would— hard to put that in words—but it must have communicated something to the Lamonicas. A look passed between them. Then Mrs. Lamonica nodded at me and smiled very slightly.

"We'll be happy to help you," she said.

"Thank you."

"Mr. Marcus wrote us a lovely letter. And we spoke to him on the phone. He seems like a very fine person."

I smiled.

"Let me show you Diane's room," Mrs. Lamonica said. She rose. Mr. Lamonica and I followed her down the hall and turned into the last open door on the right.

Another shrine. It looked as if the inhabitant had left it this morning and would be returning tonight. There was a Lowell High School pennant on the wall. The bed had a white eyelet spread. The curtains matched. A tape deck and speakers stood on a low table beneath the front window. There was a dressing table with a lace-edged white skirt. Photographs were tucked into the mirror frame. A bottle of Jontue, a brush, a comb, an earring tree, and a plastic stand holding makeup brushes, lipsticks, mascara wands, and little boxes of blush, eyeliner, and eye shadow were arrayed on the table. A desk held a neat pile of notebooks and texts in the center of the blotter. The throw pillows on the bed were the same shade of rose as the carpet. On the wall opposite the bed was a poster from a rock concert at the Lowell Memorial Auditorium.

I felt my throat constrict, and swallowed to unblock it.

Mrs. Lamonica went to the closet, opened it, and took down a cardboard box from the top shelf.

"Here are some of Diane's things," she said. "Would you like to look at them?"

"Oh, yes, very much."

We went back to the living room. Marie Lamonica put the box on the coffee table. "I'll make coffee," she said, and went to the kitchen. Mr. Lamonica remained in the living room, watching me as I sorted through the contents of the box.

Diane's report cards, arranged chronologically from kindergarten to senior year. She had been an A and B student. A lifesaving certificate from the Red Cross. A term paper on *Macbeth* that had earned her an A+. A poem she had written in the seventh grade. A blue ribbon for winning the fourth-grade spelling bee. The program for her senior prom—the theme of the dance had been "A Night in Camelot." Invitations to the weddings and baby showers of various friends and relatives. And a huge red cardboard-and-paper-lace valentine, dated the last Valentine's Day Diane would ever celebrate, inscribed, "To Dee-Dee, with all my love always, Mike."

Mrs. Lamonica returned to the living room carrying a tray with a coffee service and a small plate of cookies. I moved the box so she could place the tray on the table.

"Was Mike Diane's fiancé?" I asked.

Mrs. Lamonica nodded. "He was a senior at the university here. They were going to get married when he graduated." She offered me a cup of coffee.

"Do you think Mike would talk to me or Griffin Marcus?"

Mrs. Lamonica paused. "I could ask him. He still lives here in town." She sighed. "He got married a year ago." She looked away from me. "We were glad he was able to meet someone and be happy again." She handed me the plate of cookies. I took one. They were flavored with anise.

Mr. Lamonica spoke for the first time. "What do you want us to tell you about Dee-Dee?"

"Whatever you want," I said. "Whatever you can."

* * *

I finished up with the Lamonicas fifteen minutes early. Both showed me to the door. I thanked them for their help and mentioned that Marcus would be calling them again soon. Our goodbyes were subdued.

I didn't want to spend the next quarter-hour standing at the foot of the Lamonicas' driveway, so I went for a walk. I needed a little time to poke and prod at the idea I'd gotten earlier.

"How'd it go?" Marcus asked.

I clasped the seat belt around me. "I have a very good sense of Diane as her parents saw her. And a sense of Salvatore and Marie as well." I tapped my shoulder bag. "It's all in my notes for you. Did you know Diane— they called her Dee-Dee, by the way—did you know she'd been engaged when she died?"

"No."

"Well, she was. To a guy named Michael D'Alessio. They were high school sweethearts, I guess. I have his address and phone number for you."

"Great. Thanks."

"How'd it go with the Lowell cops? Did you learn anything?"

He shook his head. "Not really."

I looked at him. *"Nothing?"*

"Well, what *would* they tell me about an officially unsolved murder? I didn't expect information. I wanted to scope out the place, get a sense of how the cops here operate, what their investigative approaches might be."

I nodded. "Well, I certainly learned absolutely zip that would help clear the case in any way I can tell. But that wasn't my mission, was it?"

"Nope, you were supposed to get me background on the Lamonicas and Diane for the book."

"You got it."

He smiled at me. "I have no doubt of that. Would you like some lunch?"

"Sure."

"Okay. What's decent around here?"

"Let's go downtown. There are a bunch of restaurants in the restored area there."

"You mean where they have the brick sidewalks and the gaslights?"

"Yeah. Lowell got itself declared a national park about fifteen or so years back. Smart move. They got all that federal money to put toward sprucing up the mills and the old business district. In the summer now you can go for a romantic cruise on the canal, even. It's really very nice."

We found a restaurant with a wide-planked floor, dark paneling, and hanging plants. The menu leaned heavily toward tarted-up hamburgers, fancy salads, soups, and Mexicana.

Marcus didn't order a prelunch drink. I'd have to remember to tell that to Jack.

Over salad I said, "I got a weird idea today."

Marcus raised his eyebrows. "Oh?"

I put down my fork. "Well, it came to me when I was looking at the pictures of Diane. One of them was of her in her communion dress."

"Yes?"

"Well, it made something click in my mind. That perhaps all of the first seven victims had one other thing in common."

"Don't tell me," Marcus said. "Let me figure it out for myself." He rubbed his forehead with his forefinger and thumb, staring at the tabletop. I resumed eating my salad.

Marcus looked up at me slowly. "Goddam," he said, snapping his fingers. "That's right."

He clearly didn't need to have the pieces assembled for him, but I did so anyway. "Carolyn Bragg taught at a Catholic high school. So did Lisa Goodenough—Merrimack College is run by Augustinians. Linda Tessier lived near a Catholic girls' school. Peggy Letourneau worked at a Catholic nursing home. Diane Lamonica was raised Catholic. Denise Michaud's maiden name was Grogan—Irish and probably Catholic. The same for Cheryl Timmons. All the first seven victims were either raised in the same religion or strongly associated with it in some way."

"So what does that mean?" Marcus asked.

"I don't know."

TWELVE

After lunch we drove across the river to Dracut to find the spot where Diane's body had been left. Again, it was a small clearing in the woods, out of sight of the highway, within sight of the river. Marcus and I walked around it like a pair of surveyors. In a way we were. The snow cover was crusty and hard.

"I have some more phone calls to make," Marcus said.

"And I have some more cross-referencing to do."

We hiked up the riverbank to the car and drove back to Cambridge and the Charles Hotel.

Marcus went to the bedroom to make his phone calls. I stayed in the living room with the files and some fresh index cards.

The file on each victim contained a sketchy description of her. These I was going to break down into their components. I labeled the index cards accordingly: Hair Color; Skin Color; Eye Color; Height; Weight; Unusual Physical Characteristics (Scars, Tattoos, Birthmarks, Disfigurements, etc.). Then I began reading through the file descriptions and making notes. It took me about twenty minutes. Then I read over each card, looking for patterns.

Hair Color revealed nothing. Cheryl Timmons and Lisa Goodenough had been blondes, Denise Michaud a redhead. Peggy Letourneau's hair had been light brown. Carolyn Bragg and Linda Tessier had had medium-brown hair. Diane Lamonica's and Maria Acosta's had been very dark brown. Carla Whitlow's had been black.

Nor in Eye Color was any pattern disclosed. Brown for Diane, Maria, Carla, and Linda. Blue for Cheryl and Lisa. Hazel for Denise and Carolyn. Green for Peggy.

Skin Color was similarly eclectic. Olive for Diane and Maria. Fair for Cheryl, Lisa, Denise, and Peggy. Medium black for Carla. Medium for Carolyn.

Unusual Physical Characteristics yielded little. Peggy, of course, had been two months' pregnant (*two* victims in that murder). Diane had an appendectomy scar. Linda had a well-healed fracture of the right tibia. Carolyn had a small fading leaf-shaped scar on her right forearm, probably the result of a burn. Carla's nose had once been broken. Maria had a purple birthmark on the nape of her neck.

Things came together on the Height card—for the first seven victims, anyway. The tallest of them was five-foot-two. The shortest was four-eleven.

Maria Acosta had been five-foot-five; Carla Whitlow, five-foot-seven. Pretty big jump there.

I looked at the Weight card. The range for the first seven women was 95 pounds to 115.

Carolyn, Denise, Diane, Peggy, Lisa, Linda, and Cheryl: small, slender women all.

"Griffin," I yelled.

After a moment the bedroom door opened. He peered around it. "Is the place on fire or what?"

"We may have another pattern for the first seven women."

"What's that?"

I showed him.

He flopped down on the couch beside me. "You noticed that too, huh? Good."

"It's pretty obvious. No big deal."

He took a cigarette from the ever-present pack on the coffee table and lit it. "Why do you do that?"

"Do what?"

"Deprecate yourself. I pay you a compliment and you shrug it off. Why?"

I shrugged.

He stared at me a moment and then laughed, shaking his head.

"Actually," I said, "I'm really extremely vain. I just pretend to be modest and self-effacing."

"Oh, you do, do you?"

"Uh-huh."

Marcus nodded. Then he lunged forward and ground out his cigarette in the coffee-table ashtray. I blinked. I wasn't yet accustomed to his physical volatility, his sudden leaps from relaxation to abrupt, nervous motion. Jack was more level in his manifestations of strength and energy.

"Okay," Marcus said. "What we have here are seven young, educated, small, slim women who also lived and worked near the Merrimack River and were murdered near it, all of whom were either Catholic or somehow associated with Catholicism. What does that tell us?"

"Search me," I said. "Why don't you ask Henry Kmiec?"

* * *

Jack was coming to my place for dinner at seven. I left the Charles and hopped across town to pick up a pair of salmon steaks at the New Deal Fish Market on Cambridge Street in East Cambridge and then to the greengrocer across from the New Deal to grab some peapods and carrots. The greengrocer also had some divine-looking baking potatoes. No eyes and no slash marks from the harvesting machinery farmers use now. My father claims it's impossible to buy a decent potato since hand-digging them went the way of buggy whips and monaural record players. I think he's right.

The carrots were sliced, the pods were trimmed, the potatoes washed and pricked and in the oven, the fish ready to slide beneath the broiler, and I was on the living room couch, vodka martini in hand, when Jack showed up. He let himself into the apartment with the key I'd given him long ago.

"Yo, studmuffins," I said, and raised my glass to him.

"I don't know what it is," he replied, hanging up his coat, "but beautiful women are always saying that exact same thing to me. They even scream it out on the streets."

"And *still* you don't blush."

"Nah. I'm too used to it."

I laughed, set my glass on the end table, got up, went over to him, and kissed him. "Sit down. Give Lucy a pat. I'll get you a drink."

When I returned from the kitchen with Jack's bourbon on the rocks and a bowl of smokehouse almonds, the dog was lying in a Sphinx position before the fireplace. Jack was lounging on the sofa. I handed him his glass and put the dish of nuts on the coffee table. The dog looked from Jack to me and back to Jack again, very expectantly, very intently.

"Is she suggesting one of us should build a fire?" Jack asked.

"Yeah," I said. "You."

He laughed and pushed himself up off the couch. As he was laying the kindling on the grate, I said, "How's it going with you? Is your witness in the Cambridgeport murder still willing to testify in court?"

"So far." He arranged a split log on the kindling. "I think she's nervous about retaliation, though."

"Does she have reason to be?"

He set a match to the kindling. "Maybe. The guy who did the murder—excuse me, the *alleged* murder—is out on bail. He's not wrapped too tightly, either."

"A VM," I said.

"That's right."

VM meant "violent moron." It was our designation for about 40 percent of the bad guys Jack and the rest of the C.P.D. arrested, guys so affectless they didn't even breathe hard while stabbing or shooting or bludgeoning somebody. Murder for them was just another reflexive way of responding to a situation.

The kindling caught and flared up around the logs. Jack returned to the couch, and Lucy resumed her Sphinx position before the fireplace screen.

Jack picked up his drink and took a handful of the salted almonds. "So what did you do today?"

I told him.

"Interesting parallels" was his comment.

"And not coincidental ones, either, I don't think."

Jack ate an almond. "I wonder if Kmiec took souvenirs of the murders. And if he did, what kind."

"I was thinking that, too. In the case of Carla Whitlow and Maria Acosta, I have the feeling he didn't. With regard to the other seven victims, I don't know.

And I can't see a way to find out, at the moment. That's the kind of information the police investigators would keep to themselves." I looked sharply at Jack. "But *you* might be able to get it through your contacts in the state police here and in New Hampshire."

"I might." Jack pinched his lower lip between thumb and forefinger and tugged it. "I might even share the information with you."

"All *right.*"

"But not with Marcus."

"But. . ."

"No," Jack said. "N-O. You, I know I can trust with privileged information. Marcus, I know no such thing about. What would he do with the information?"

"Put it in the book, of course."

"Exactly. And suppose by the time the book goes to press, those seven murders aren't officially closed out yet? And information prejudicial to the possible solution of the cases—or their prosecution—is in the book? What happens then?"

I was silent for a moment. Then I said, "I'm not going to argue with you. I can't."

He nodded.

"But I'd rather not have the information if I can't transmit it to Marcus. Given that I work for the guy as an information gatherer, I'd feel pretty weird withholding it from him."

"Sure."

I sipped my drink. "You may be underestimating Marcus, though, honey. I truly don't think he's the kind of guy who'd deliberately screw up a major criminal case just so he could write a sensational best-selling book."

"I didn't say he'd do it *deliberately*. Or for personal gain."

"Yeah, I know. Well, it's silly to debate the issue. But you must understand that I'm in an awkward position here."

"I understand that perfectly."

I smiled and patted his thigh. "Okay. Let me go check on dinner. Want another drink?"

"A half one."

"Just a half?"

He smiled back at me. "Well, I might indulge in a brandy after dinner."

"Ah-hah," I said. "Am I to deduce from that that you plan to spend the night here?"

"That's a reasonable deduction. Why? You had other plans?"

"Nothing special. Just let me call Tom Berenger and Kevin Costner and cancel the threesome we had scheduled for midnight."

"You do that."

"Poor boys," I said. "They'll be awfully disappointed."

Jack grinned at me. "Maybe," he said. "But *you* won't."

THIRTEEN

The next day Marcus and I drove up to Concord, to the Saint Ignatius School, where Carolyn Bragg had taught until her death. Marcus had persuaded the nun who was head of the English Department to talk to us about Carolyn. What we learned from the interview was that Carolyn had been hardworking and dedicated to her profession and popular with her students and colleagues. She had also been bright, charming, and attractive. Her death had been a horrible tragedy for Saint Ignatius.

As we left the school building, I said to Marcus, "It's so hard to get the relatives or friends of a murder victim to admit that the victim had even one tiny little human flaw, isn't it? Like maybe the person was occasionally forgetful or addicted to peanut M&M's or hated to get out of bed in the morning—even something as trivial as that."

Marcus smiled. "They want to protect. It's natural. It's understandable. Helpful, no."

"And the funny thing is, you and I aren't trying to make the victims look bad. Just *real*."

"Yeah."

We drove to the clearing in the wood on the riverbank

outside the city where Carolyn's body had been found. Marcus had brought a Nikon with him and took a few pictures of the site.

"Will these go in the book?"

Marcus shook his head. "No, I'll bring a professional photographer up here at some point. He'll decide which sites will make the best images. I'm just doing idea shots now. For my own reference, and yours."

"Ferrante-Dege on Mass. Ave. in Harvard Square can make you up some contact sheets in a day."

"Good." He glanced at me over the camera. "Do you ever do any of your own photographic work?"

"Once in a while. There's an excellent woman in Boston I generally use. If she's not available, I'll do my own."

Marcus handed me the camera. "Here. You can do the Denise Michaud shots down in Nashua. And also, this afternoon while I'm talking to the Concord police, I'd like you to wander around the city and take a few shots of whatever looks interesting or representative of the place. Use your own judgment. I'd also like a shot of Saint Ignatius with the parking lot, where they found Carolyn's car, in the foreground."

"*Certainement, mon général,*" I said.

Late Thursday afternoon Marcus handed me my first paycheck. He would have handed it to me on the normal payday, Friday, except that he had to catch a 7:00 A.M. shuttle to New York for a meeting with his East Coast agent. The East Coast agent did his book deals. His West Coast agent handled the movie and television stuff. He also had agents in London, Paris, Berlin, and Tokyo to handle the foreign rights.

I hotfooted it to the Baybank Harvard Trust Company and deposited the check, feeling that warm-all-over glow you get when you know where your next meal is coming from.

Actually, my next meal came from Jack. We went to Capucino's, in Porter Square, and ate about a trough of linguine apiece. Then we went to Nightstage, outside of Kendall Square, and listened to some jazz. A nice way to open the weekend. Saturday we hung out.

Jack spent Sunday afternoon watching football. Lucy and I went for a long walk along the Charles.

I presented myself at Marcus's suite at nine on Monday morning. Today was his first interview with Kmiec. I knocked on the door. "It's open," he yelled.

He was vibrating with anticipation and doing a really lousy job of concealing it.

"Are you *sure* you want to go through with this?" I teased.

"God, I can't wait," he said.

"Gee, I never would have guessed. You're so blasé. Well, while you're off having all the fun, what am I supposed to be doing?"

"Would you mind continuing with the cross-indexing?"

"Oh, *really,*" I said in feigned disgust. "Next you'll be asking me to iron your shirts." I smiled. "Yes, of course I'll do the cross-indexing. For two-fifty a day, I can do cross-indexing. I'll even pick up the contact sheets from Ferrante-Dege."

"Perfect."

"I know," I said. "If Elizabeth weren't my middle name, Perfect would be."

He nodded. His mind was on Kmiec, and he wasn't truly listening. I probably could have undressed before him and he wouldn't have noticed.

"I'll be back around four, I think," he said. "You'll be here?"

"Are you kidding? I want to hear every single word of what Kmiec says to you and you say to him."

"Okay. Here's the room key." He tossed me a flat perforated plastic rectangle. "Have fun."

"You too."

He snatched up his coat and left.

I ordered a pot of coffee from room service and settled on the couch with the box of newspaper clippings. What excitement.

By eleven the thrill had become too much for me and I walked down the Ferrante-Dege to get the photographs. My shots of Concord had come out well. There was a real arty one of the State House taken from an odd angle that I thought especially nice. The ones of the Saint Ignatius parking lot were plain and stark. Marcus would probably find them more useful than a wide-angled slant on a golden dome.

I got a salad to go at one of the Square restaurants and trekked back to the hotel. Back in the suite, I spread the contact sheets out on the coffee table and studied them as I forked up spinach, romaine, green peppers, mushrooms, and chick-peas.

We had also taken shots of the places where the bodies of Carolyn Bragg, Denise Michaud, Lisa Goodenough, Peggy Letourneau, Diane Lamonica, and Linda Tessier had been left. And where, according to the forensic information we'd acquired, they'd been murdered. We hadn't yet gotten to Plaistow to examine the place where Cheryl Timmons had been dumped, nor had we checked the Tyngsboro location where Carla Whitlow had been found.

What struck me now, as I looked at each photograph, was how vividly similar all the sites appeared to be. They weren't *just* all clearings in the wood on a riverbank—they also seemed to be clearings of about the same size, perhaps twenty feet in diameter, and pretty much equidistant from the river.

Interesting. I'd have to suggest to Marcus that we return to each site and take some measurements.

The cops had surely done that, but it wasn't the kind of information they'd be likely to divulge.

I leaned back against the couch and gazed at the ceiling. I was trying in my own imagination to penetrate the mind of a killer who could so relentlessly, so meticulously, so patiently cruise up and down the path of a river till he found the seven perfect and matching spots in five cities and two states in which to commit his murders.

Marcus blew into the suite a little after four.

"How'd it go?" I said.

He stood just inside the door, his hands in his pocket, staring at me.

"Kmiec confessed," he said.

I sat very still, my hands in my lap. "What?" I said stupidly.

Marcus took two steps into the room. "At exactly eleven fifty-six this morning, Henry Kmiec told me that he killed Carolyn Bragg, Denise Michaud, Diane Lamonica, Peggy Letourneau, Lisa Goodenough, Linda

Tessier, and Cheryl Timmons. In explicit detail he told me."

"Holy God," I said.

Marcus ripped off his coat and dumped it on a chair. "Liz, Jesus, it was un-fucking-believable. I mean, I have talked to a lot of killers in my time—Richard Ramirez, Charles Manson, Ted Bundy, Henry Lee Lucas. But I have never talked to anyone like Henry Kmiec." He dropped down on the couch beside me and took a cigarette from the pack on the coffee table. He looked at me. "Remember those eyes that Manson had?"

I nodded. "In something you wrote about him once, you described them as 'polished chips of hardened lava.' "

Marcus lit the cigarette. "Yeah. Well, Manson has the eyes of a newborn in comparison to Kmiec. This guy is—" He broke off speaking and took a drag on the cigarette.

"He gave you details of the killings?" I asked. "Verifiable details?"

Marcus swung his feet up onto the coffee table. "He told me he'd taken a souvenir from each one of the seven victims."

"What?"

"A lock of her hair."

"Which he kept?"

"No, he said he scattered them all in the river afterward." Marcus stubbed out his cigarette, half-smoked, and sprang up from the couch. "Excuse me just a moment. I have to make a phone call."

I was limp with astonishment. Not that Kmiec had committed the murders, but that he'd blurted out the fact to Marcus. Maybe Marcus had been right, maybe Kmiec did see him as a ticket to fame.

Marcus came out of the bedroom.

"Explicit details?" I said.

"He gave me very graphic descriptions of how he killed each woman. It's all in my notes. You can read them later." Marcus glanced at me sideways. "How strong is your stomach?"

"Quite."

"Good. It'll have to be. I almost lost my lunch listening to him. *Me*. Can you believe that?"

The question didn't require an answer. "When are you seeing him again?"

"Wednesday."

"Is he going to tell the police what he told you?"

Marcus's expression went oddly blank, the first time I'd seen it do so. "I have no idea."

"What about you?"

"I don't know what the hell to do. That was all I thought about on the drive back here.You have any suggestions?"

I took a long breath. "I've never been in a situation like this. I don't know what to tell you."

"I can get a magazine article into print fairly quickly. But that won't do me any good if Kmiec decides to start chatting with one of the newspaper people. They'll get the story into print overnight."

I stared at Marcus. We'd been talking about two completely different things. "Griffin, what I meant was, are *you* going to tell the police?"

"Of course not."

"I see."

He looked at me quite hard. "Is that a problem for you?"

I hcsitated. "The book won't be published till what—a year and a half from now?"

"Give or take a few months."

"That's a long time for us to be sitting on that kind of information."

Marcus lit another cigarette. "So what? Kmiec's not going anywhere. He's done killing. And he won't be getting away with murder."

"No, I realize that."

"So what's the problem?"

"I guess . . . I don't know." I felt confused, as if my thought processes had muddied and tangled.

"You feel like an accessory after the fact?"

"Sort of."

"Well, you aren't. You're a writer. *Nothing* is more important than the story."

I could think of one or two things that might be, but I didn't mention them.

"I know you won't say anything about this to Jack."

I almost laughed. Now I understood why I was confused. The other night I'd had Jack telling me not to reveal crucial information to Marcus. Now Marcus was very politely warning me not to shoot off my mouth to Jack.

Cute.

"Gotta make another call," Marcus said.

Alone in the living room, I picked up the contact sheets and slid them into a manila envelope. Automatically I neatened up the stacks of file folders and note cards. Busywork for my hands while my mind was otherwise occupied.

I understood Marcus's position perfectly. If I were he, I'd want to keep as tight a lid on Kmiec's confession as possible. If we told the cops, every reporter in town would be all over the story tomorrow. And it was *our*—or at least Marcus's—story. On the other hand . . .

did he and I have some kind of moral obligation to reveal what we now knew?

Every crime writer of my acquaintance would side with Marcus. Some of them wouldn't feel too easy about it. Some of them might waver, feel guilty. But ultimately, they'd all agree with him. The story was the most important thing.

What really bothered me was how our silence might affect the families of the victims. Didn't they deserve to know that the killer of their loved ones had broken silence?

But they would find that out eventually. And certainly, Marcus and I weren't abetting Kmiec, allowing him to escape justice or roam free.

Didn't I owe loyalty to Marcus?

I could visualize myself debating this point with Jack. Jack. Oh, God.

For the past eight years I'd been discussing the details of my work with him and vice versa, with very few restraints on either side. We bounced ideas off each other. We traded facts like baseball cards. We helped each other. It felt . . . natural.

Now I was in the middle of the biggest case of my career and I couldn't say word one about it to him. That meant every time we were together I'd have to monitor every syllable I uttered. I could imagine our conversations:

He: So how'd it go today?

Me: Oh, fine.

He: Anything new?

Me: Not much.

In a way I was relieved I wasn't seeing him this evening. That way I'd have at least twenty-four hours to work up a suitable charade.

With luck I wouldn't have to maintain the act for long. Marcus would probably rush an abbreviated version of the story into print in a month or so. Then he'd go full-tilt at the book. And even with Kmiec's confession made public by him, and other writers trying to jump on the bandwagon, I didn't think Marcus had to worry about being preempted. He'd' blow any potential competitor out of the water because he had the clout and the financial backing of a huge, prestigious publishing house to do so. Plus, he had a head start on the research and writing for the book. And he might be able to persuade Kmiec to give him exclusive access. Mr. or Ms. Unknown or Less Well Known Crime Writer wouldn't have a chance against those kinds of odds.

So in a month, say, what was troubling me now would be academic.

I could live with that, I supposed.

I would damn well have to.

The bedroom door opened. Marcus looked out at me and said, "Are you free tonight?"

So absorbed was I in brooding that I jumped at the sound of his voice. "What?"

"I said, are you free tonight?"

I peered back at him, a little startled. "Uh—oh, I guess so. Jack and I don't have any plans. Why? You want to continue working?"

"God, no. I was going to ask if you'd have dinner with me."

"Oh."

"I'm all keyed up."

"I noticed."

"I need two drinks, minimum, food, and pleasant company."

My first reaction was to make an excuse. Beg off.

Take a raincheck. Then, as I thought about it, the idea began to seem better to me. Was there anything to be gained from going home, sitting alone in my apartment, and weighing the ethical pros and cons of keeping secrets? Especially since the problem seemed to be one I'd have to accommodate myself to rather than solve? Would a few hours *not* spent fretting about it help?

Maybe.

"Sure," I said. "I'll have dinner with you."

He smiled. "I'm glad."

It sounded as if Marcus needed distraction as badly as I did.

"I have to go home first and let my dog out and feed her." I plucked at my black Middlesex County D.A.'s office sweatshirt with the Day-Glo green lettering (IF YOU CAN'T DO THE TIME, THEN DON'T DO THE CRIME). "I'd also like to change."

"I'll drive you. I'd like to see where you live, anyway."

"Be warned," I said. "It's not Holmby Hills."

"Good," he said. "I hate Holmby Hills."

"It's very nice," he said, looking around at my living room.

"Thank you."

Lucy was sniffing energetically around Marcus's shoes. He reached down and scratched her behind the ears. "What kind of dog is this? I've never seen one like her."

I explained Lucy's pedigree. "Would you like a drink while you're waiting for me?"

"That would be great."

"Okay. Sit down. Be with you in a sec."

I let Lucy out to run around in the backyard and put a bowl of food on the kitchen floor for her. Then I made Marcus a vodka martini and brought it to the living room.

I left my bedroom door ajar so we could yell conversation back and forth at each other while I dressed. I wondered what to wear. I settled on an Italian-designed black wool jersey dress I'd bought a few years ago, when I'd been able to afford expensive clothes (on sale). To that I added some black-and-gold beads and earrings. I combed out my hair and repaired my makeup.

When I came out of the bedroom, Marcus had finished his drink. He rose as I entered the living room, and said, "Well, you look *very* nice."

"Thanks."

I took his empty glass to the kitchen. Lucy was chomping away at her dinner. I shut and deadbolted the back door. "Behave yourself," I said to her.

"Where shall we go?" Marcus asked.

I looked at him, my head cocked. "You're a visiting celebrity. Would you like to go where the visiting celebrities go when they come to Cambridge?"

He shrugged. "Whatever you like."

"Okay, the Harvest. Maybe we'll see somebody as famous as you."

He grimaced.

We didn't have a reservation, so we didn't get a table in the restaurant right away.

"All to the good," I said. "It's fun to sit in the bar and watch the mating dances."

"The what?"

"The Harvest bar is also where all the local trendies

hang out looking for a soulmate. Or at least a decent one-night stand."

Marcus raised one eyebrow.

"You know," I said, "when you do that, you look like Mr. Spock."

"Fascinating," Marcus replied, and I snickered.

We got a table for two in a corner of the bar. A waitress fought her way to us through a mob of well-dressed people standing around in cocktail-party poses and took our orders for drinks.

"Griffin?"

"Yes?"

Keeping my voice low, I said, "How did it feel when you first realized Kmiec was going to spill the beans to you?"

He glanced around the bar. Then he leaned across the table toward me. "Like the biggest hard-on of my life," he hissed.

I laughed into my drink and spattered vodka and vermouth all over my dress front. I set down the glass and brushed ineffectually at the spilled liquor. I was shaking my head and giggling uncontrollably.

"Sorry," Marcus said.

"That's all right." I gasped.

"You gotta admit," he continued, "writing about crime may be better than sex."

I was still laughing. "I know what you mean."

"Although," he mused, "I could be exaggerating there."

"Perhaps." I had restored myself to order.

"What's the food like here?" Marcus asked.

"Expensive."

He nodded and looked idly around the room. I followed his look. "You were right," he said. "Trendy. Very trendy."

"But no celebrities tonight, other than you."

"Will you knock off that celebrity bullshit?"

"Sure, if you'll answer one last question."

"What's that?"

"Did Barbara Walters ask you what kind of a tree you'd be if you were a tree? I must have missed that part of her interview with you. Anyway, I'd love to hear. A mighty oak? Or a birch that bends with the wind yet springs back into place the moment the storm has passed?"

He studied me. "You're obnoxious, you know that?"

I smiled. "I know. If I weren't so adorable, I'd be impossible."

The waitress asked us if we wanted another drink.

"Desperately," Marcus said. "In fact, bring an extra so I can"——he pointed at me—"pour it over her head."

After dinner we walked back to the hotel, where we'd left the car. It was a lovely night, very clear and not too cold. Harvard Square looked active. The only time it wasn't, really, was after midnight. And sometimes not even then.

"I'm expecting some messages," Marcus said. "You mind if I check for them before I take you home?"

"Of course not."

There were indeed several messages for him at the desk. He flipped through them as we rode the elevator up to the suite. "I have to make a phone call," Marcus said. "I think I can still get this one guy at his office."

It was nine. "He keeps late hours."

"His office is in L.A."

"Oh."

I shucked my coat and wandered around the living room while Marcus made his call from the bedroom. I pulled back the curtains that covered the big window facing south. Before me, past the Kennedy School, was a panoramic spread of the Charles River, the Harvard Business School, and, beyond them, Allston Brighton. I loved looking at the nightscape of a city.

Marcus made his call from the bedroom. I could hear him moving around, shuffling through papers.

"Was the guy in his office?" I asked.

"Hmmmm? Oh. Yes. I got him."

"That's nice."

I heard him come up behind me. I was just ready to say something about the view when he put his hands on my shoulders. My eyes widened. Then I went very stiff. I felt his breath ruffle my hair. And then I felt his mouth on the side of my neck.

Oh, no, I thought. Oh, shit. How do I handle this?

He turned me around to face him. As he did, I caught a glimpse of the king-size bed in the adjoining room.

He slid his hands down my back and drew me toward him. If I was going to put a stop to what was happening, it would have to be right now.

Stay cool. And good-humored.

I put my hands against his chest and canted my head away from his. "What *is* this?" I said lightly. "Are you trying to start something?"

"Yeah," he said. "That's exactly what I'm doing. Trying to start something."

His mouth came closer to mine. I jerked my head farther away from his. With his right hand, very gently but very firmly, he brought my face back up to his.

"No," I said. In that moment I wasn't cool any longer

and I shoved at him. He stepped back immediately and let his arms fall to his sides.

"Okay," he said, and smiled slightly.

He went over to the couch, sat down, and picked up the manila folder atop the pile on the coffee table. He began thumbing through it.

I stood at the window staring at him. He looked perfectly relaxed, concentrated on his reading. Pretense? I rubbed my left forearm nervously.

In my shock I blurted out the first thought that came to my mind.

"Do you still want us to work together?"

"Hmmm?" Maybe he really was that involved in reading. At any rate, it seemed to take a few beats before my words fully registered with him. If he was acting, he was magnificent at it. Finally he raised his head and said, "What?" in bemused tones.

I repeated the question.

He was fully focused on me now. He shook his head as if in astonishment. "Of course I want us to keep working together. Why wouldn't I?"

"I can think of one good reason."

He tossed the folder onto the coffee table and leaned back against the couch cushions, still staring at me. "Let me get this straight," he said. "You think I'm going to fire you because you wouldn't screw me?"

I shrugged. "It happens."

"Well, it's not happening here. Jesus." He got up, crossed the room, and stopped about four feet away from me, his hands resting on his hips. "Yes," he said, sounding weary, "I want you, Elizabeth Connors, to continue working with me, with no strings attached. All right? Got that?"

"Yup," I said flatly. "Got it."

"Good." He glanced at his watch. "It's getting late, Come on, I'll take you home."

"You don't have to do that."

He made an important gesture. "I want to, okay? Now, where's your coat?"

"Over there." I pointed to the chair in the corner, where I'd tossed it earlier. He handed it to me. He didn't offer to help me into it. I was glad.

As we were riding down in the elevator, he said, "I hope you understand I didn't plan this evening. What happened up there . . . just happened."

I nodded.

"I like you. I think you're beautiful. I would love to go to bed with you."

I sighed. "Griffin, you know I've been with Jack for the past eight years. It's monogamous—on both sides." God, that sounded priggish. A weird age we lived in, when a simple statement of fidelity was a thing you felt gawky and almost laughably naive making. Nevertheless, I continued doggedly, "I don't fool around."

"Yeah, I know. Sorry. Forget it. If it's not going to happen, it's not going to happen. I can live with that."

There wasn't much conversation between us during the ride back to my place. The atmosphere in the car was less strained than restrained. It was as if we'd settled one way of behaving with each other but not come up with a replacement mode. And we both had to tread a little carefully till we did.

Marcus stopped the car in front of my building.

"I'll wait till I see you're inside," he said.

"Okay." I opened the car door. "Thank you for the dinner."

"You're welcome. See you tomorrow."

"Good night."

" 'Night."

Alone in my apartment, safely enclosed in the cocoon of my solitary habitat, I poured myself a little glass of brandy and huddled up on the sofa. Lucy rested her head on my thigh. I stroked her ears absently.

I was shaken.

I wasn't especially bothered by what Marcus had done. Other men had done the same thing, and I'd brushed off it *and* them.

What bothered me was what I'd felt while Marcus was doing it.

Why not? was what I'd felt.

It was just a little needle of response, but it had pierced quite deeply.

I hadn't had a feeling like that about any man but Jack in so long ... it was impossible to remember when.

That was what shook me.

FOURTEEN

By breakfast I had managed to rationalize the whole episode. Marcus had been flying high on the wings of Kmiec's confession. The kind of exhilaration he'd felt was something it's impossible to understand unless you're a crime writer (or a cop; I'd seen Jack in similar states of exultation when he'd made a really great arrest). Marcus and I had shared that exhilaration, a unique intimacy that few people ever experience. He'd also had a fair amount to drink, although you'd not have known it to look at or listen to him. And there had been that sexual note to our conversation. I'd even introduced it, talking as I had about mating dances. And one-night stands.

Okay, so that explained Marcus's behavior in the hotel.

What about my internal response to it?

I hadn't been drunk—that takes a lot more than a couple of martinis and a glass or two of Pouilly-Fuissé.

It wasn't the direction of the conversation. I had a number of male buddies with whom I joked. Often the humor had a sexual content. Big deal. The jokes never had an aphrodisiacal effect on me. Certainly not enough to make me throw myself into the arms of the guys who told them.

I wasn't bored with Jack.

The hell with it, I thought finally. Marcus is very attractive. You like men, especially the good-looking, smart, intense, funny, interesting ones. You'd just spent a nice evening with a premier representative of the species. So you felt a little pull toward him when he made a move at you. So what? you didn't act on the impulse. Big deal. You can't control your impulses. Or your hormones. You *can* control your actions.

It wouldn't happen again, anyway.

The real irony was that I'd thought an evening out would distract me from one crisis of conscience. Instead, it had presented me with a second.

Rather than find a new way of dealing with each other, Marcus and I went back to the old one. When I showed up at his suite, it was as if last night had never happened. I took my cue from him.

"I checked the orbits of the victims," he said.

"Oh, yeah?"

He was sitting on the couch with the files open and spread around him. "Cheryl Timmons, Linda Tessier, Denise Michaud, Peggy Letourneau, Maria Acosta, and obviously Diane Lamonica were given Catholic funerals."

I nodded. "That confirms for those six what we were almost sure of anyway."

"Carolyn Bragg was a Lutheran and Lisa Goodenough a Congregationalist, or at least they were buried as such. But Kmiec may have figured that since they both worked at Catholic schools, that was what they were."

"Okay," I dragged the desk chair over to the coffee table and sat down facing Marcus. "Then we do have a pattern, probably very deliberate, of religious similarity. This is too much coincidence for me."

"And I can't tell you what the pattern means. I also can't ask Kmiec, as you suggested the other day."

"I wasn't being serious when I said that, Griffin."

He smiled. "I know. Just kidding. I wish I *could* ask him. But I can't put words in his mouth or ideas in his head. He has to tell me *what* he wants, *when* he wants, how *much* he wants, the *way* he wants."

"Sure." Here was one of the most frustrating aspects of interviewing, for reporters and cops alike. *You did not lead the witness.* Or the suspect. You could ask all the questions you wanted. But they couldn't be loaded ones. You couldn't give the interviewees clues to the information you wanted them to provide, even if you were dead positive they possessed it. Even if you were desperate. Even if you knew you were being toyed with, jerked around by someone charmed by the notion of keeping you twisting in the wind.

That was the rule. The witnesses and the suspects were under no obligation to play fair. You were.

Of course, the rule got broken. The temptation was always there—to ask that killer question, the one that would provide all the answers. Sometimes the temptation was nearly irresistible. I knew of cops and writers who had succumbed to it.

Thirty-five years ago, in pre-Miranda days, there'd been a series of murders—two in Boston, one in Arlington, one in Somerville, and one in Cambridge. For a variety of compelling reasons, the cops figured they were the work of the same man. One suspect looked especially good to them, and he was taken into custody and interrogated.

The cops wanted to solve this case very badly. There'd been a lot of negative publicity about the fact that it had dragged on for two years and no arrest had been made.

The interrogation was supervised by a lieutenant from the state police, who was also coordinating the murder investigation. Detectives from the Boston, Somerville, Arlington, and Cambridge police departments were also present. But the state police lieutenant asked by far the most questions.

The Cambridge cop, a sergeant named Struneski, now long since retired, had described to me the proceedings—and his disgust at how they were conducted and how he'd finally walked out of the interrogation long before it had ended.

Struneski had shaken his head at the memory, still mad after all these years. "Liz, you know how you're supposed to question a suspect? You're supposed to say, like, 'What was Mary Smith wearing when you killed her?' Like that, you know?"

I had indicated my agreement.

"Well, this lieutenant, he was saying to this guy, 'Now, Joe, Mary Smith was wearing a blue skirt and a white blouse when you killed her, wasn't she?' The whole interrogation was just like that. 'Joe, you hit Jane Jones six times on the back of the head with a ball-peen hammer, isn't that right, Joe?' Or 'Joe, when you pushed Mary Smith against the kitchen door, you broke her wrist, didn't you, Joe?' Shit."

I would never forget that conversation with Struneski. Or what it had taught me as a novice crime writer.

"Joe" had gotten convicted. As far as I knew, he was still in prison.

"Is there any coffee?" I asked.

Marcus was reading one of the files. Without looking up from it, he said, "Pot and cups over there on the desk."

"You want some?"

"No, thanks."

I poured myself some coffee and returned to the chair.

"Griffin, have you interviewed Keisha Madison yet?"

This time he did glance up from his reading. "Yeah. Twice. Once by phone and once in person."

"Hmmm." I sipped the coffee. "What did she tell you about Kmiec? She was the only woman to survive an attack by the guy. That makes her an incredible source."

Marcus shut the folder and set it aside. "It was hard to get her to open up at first."

"I can understand that. Why would she want to relive the kind of experience she'd had?" I hitched my chair a little closer to the coffee table. "But she did eventually talk?"

"Oh, yes, yes." Marcus leaned back against the couch cushions. "Once she got rolling, in fact, it was hard to stop her."

"Okay." I set my cup down on one of the few uncluttered spots on the coffee table. "The sequence of events was that she was . . . what?"

"Standing in the Combat Zone, on the corner of Washington and Essex streets, a little after eight, when a guy in a red pickup truck with New Hampshire plates pulled up beside the curb. He leaned over and rolled down the passenger window. She asked him if he was looking to party, honey, and he said, yeah, he was. She got into the truck. He drove off down Washington, and they negotiated the price of a blow job. She directed him to an alley in Chinatown she uses a lot. So they went there, he stopped the truck, and she was ready to get down to business when he pulled a hunting knife out of the inside of his coat. Then he told her he was going to do to her what he'd done to 'them other two whores.' He got off two quick slashes at her. There was some kind of struggle. Anyway, Keisha kicked out at him and then managed to get the door open on her side and she rolled out of the truck. She hit the pavement, and Kmiec took off."

"God." I drew a long breath. "She was lucky."

"Lucky and strong," Marcus said. "She's a big, solid woman." He eyed me. "A little shorter than you, but she must weigh around one seventy. And it's not fat."

"What did she say about Kmiec himself? How did he seem to her—I mean, before he went after her with the knife."

"At first no more peculiar than the rest of her johns. She said he had funny eyes, which is for damn sure true. But. . ." Marcus shrugged. "I guess a lot of the guys that hang out in the Zone have funny eyes."

"Did he say anything to her?"

"Nothing besides the whore comment."

"Was that unusual—I mean, by her standards? Was it unusual that he didn't want to speak at all to her after they struck their deal?"

"She didn't think about it. She said some of her johns want to recite their whole life story. Some won't talk at all. She said she didn't give a shit either way, as long as she got paid up front."

"Too bad," I said. "I mean, too bad Kmiec had to be one of the taciturn ones."

Marcus smiled wryly. "Wouldn't it have been great if he'd told her *why* he was doing what he was doing?"

I scratched my head. "Or made a reference to rivers or Catholicism or *something* helpful. Where's Keisha now? Still working the streets?"

"South Carolina."

"Oh?"

"She has family there. She went back to them about a year ago."

"Don't blame her," I said. "Is she still—?"

"Hooking? No. She got into some kind of job-training program."

"I'm glad. Jesus! Isn't it nice to have at least one potentially happy ending out of all of this?"

"They're in short supply," Marcus said. He got up and stretched, then stood looking down at me. "How good are you at writing letters?"

"What?" I reared back in my chair and squinted up at him. "You are the prince of non sequiturs. What kind of letters?"

"What I'd like you to do today is write to the families of the victims—except the Lamonicas, since we already have them—and ask again if they'd be willing to be interviewed. I'm not having a hell of a lot of luck with that. As I've told you before."

I slung one arm over the back of the chair and smiled up at him. "Oh," I said. "*Oh.* I get it. You think I can put a different spin on the request than you?"

"I don't know. You're a woman. Maybe they'll respond better to an inquiry from a woman than from a man."

"I don't know about that, either."

"It's worth trying. Would you?"

"Sure. That's what you're paying me for."

"Good. Thanks."

"Do you have copies of the letters *you* wrote?"

"Yeah. They're in one of these folders."

"Okay. I'd like to read them first. I don't want to repeat your phrasing."

"Right, good idea."

"Your letters were typed?"

"Yes."

"Okay," I said briskly. "I'll handwrite mine. On nice paper."

"The personal touch."

"Hey," I said, "It works." I got up. "Excuse me. I have to go down to Bob Slate in Harvard Square and buy some decent stationery."

Marcus reached for his hip pocket. "Let me give you some money."

I waved my right hand. "Put it on my account."

Jack picked me up in front of the Charles at five-thirty. As I slid into the front passenger seat of the Mustang, he grinned and said, "Cracked the case yet, honey?"

I knew he was teasing me. His words nevertheless gave me a jolt. I hid it by busying myself with the seat belt. Then I glanced at him. There was nothing in his face but good humor. He hadn't turned psychic.

"Right," I said. I bent sideways and kissed him on the cheek. "The case is all wrapped up, a done deal. Tomorrow Marcus and I are going to take on another big one."

"Oh, really?" Jack pulled the car out onto Bennett Street. "What would that be?"

"Well, Marcus has a theory that it wasn't really John

Wilkes Booth in Ford's Theater that night but a renegade CIA agent and . . ."

Jack laughed. "Hey, sounds good. But why a CIA agent? Isn't that a little old hat? Why not Bigfoot?"

"Now *there's* a theory. I'll mention it to Marcus."

"And when you do, don't forget the part about the space aliens. They were controlling Bigfoot."

"Well, naturally. And if we can figure out a way to drag Elvis into the plot, we'll have the biggest bestseller in human history."

"Damn straight," Jack said. "Stephen King, eat your heart out." He smiled at me. "What would you like to do tonight?"

I thought for a moment. "I don't know. First, go home and feed the dog and let her outside, of course. I don't know after that. What are you in the mood for?"

He smiled at me again, this time a bit wider.

"Other than *that,*" I said. "I've seldom seen you not in the mood for *that.*"

He threw me a look of comically exaggerated surprise. "Oh, you were asking about *dinner? Dinner?* Sorry."

I rolled my eyes and shook my head slowly. "What are you going to call your memoirs? *The Sensuous Detective? Sex and the Single Lieutenant?*"

"Those would be excellent titles for the first two volumes."

"Oh, God," I said. "I suppose you'll want me to help you write these masterpieces?"

"No," he replied thoughtfully. "Just rehearse the good parts with me."

* * *

We ended up going to a seafood restaurant in Kendall Square and were back at my place by nine. As soon as Jack had shut and dead-bolted the apartment door behind him, I was all over him like a typhoon.

Afterward, lying in the bed in which we'd eventually landed, Jack said, "Don't take this as a complaint, because it's about as far from a complaint as it could be, but"—he propped himself up on an elbow and stared at me—"what got into you tonight?"

"To the best of my recollection it was you, dear."

"Let me rephrase the question. What came over you tonight?"

I rolled my head left on the pillow to look back at him. "Did I do or say something odd?"

He smiled and put a hand on my right breast. I reached up and covered his hand with one of mine. "Let's put it this way—you usually wait for me to take off my coat before you assault me."

I made circles on the back of his hand with my fingertips. "I don't know," I said lightly, languidly. "I just got carried away. It's your fault for being so cute. And—"

"What?"

"You shouldn't take me to seafood restaurants. You *know* how I get after I've eaten broiled haddock. Completely out of control."

"I thought it was oysters that did that."

"Men," I said, continuing to stroke his hand. "It's men that go wild after they've eaten oysters. For women, it's haddock."

He laughed and kissed me. "I'll keep that in mind."

I hugged him. "I think you should go to sleep now. Get some rest. You want to be fresh for tomorrow morning."

"Will I need to be?"

"You never can tell," I said. "The effects of broiled haddock on women have been known to last as long as twelve hours."

He went to sleep. I didn't. I lay awake for the next hour. Finally, I slid out of bed, being very careful not to disturb him, and got into my robe. I shut the bedroom door behind me very quietly and tiptoed into the kitchen. I made a cup of tea and sat down with it at the table.

I let the tea grow cool as I thought. I didn't have to think long or hard. I knew exactly why I'd done what I'd done tonight. What had come over me, as Jack had put it.

Guilt.

FIFTEEN

Wednesday Marcus went for his second interview with Kmiec. I wrote the two letters—to the Timmons and the Goodenough families—I hadn't finished yesterday and spent a few hours cross-indexing. Then I walked to the main branch of the public library on Broadway and did some research on Concord, Manchester, Nashau, Lowell, Dracut, Andover, North Andover, Methuen, Haverhill, and Plaistow. Marcus wanted basic statistical information on each of the cities and towns where the first seven victims had lived and died: population, industry, median income, geography, and ethnic mix. I put it all on five-by eight index cards for easy reference. By the time I was finished, I could have written chamber of commerce brochures for each town.

I deliberately refrained from thinking about what had gone on between Jack and me the night before. And this morning.

Marcus and I arrived back at the hotel simultaneously. He was coming through the main entrance as I was coming through the side doors. We converged in the lobby.

"How'd it go?" I asked.

"Incredible. Come on. I'll buy you a drink and tell you about it."

We went up to the Quiet Bar. The table we'd occupied the previous times we'd been here was again free. There must have been a magic circle around it penetrable only by tall New York–born true-crime writers who drank vodka martinis.

We shucked our coats and dumped them on one of the spare chairs and sat down. I leaned forward and put my elbows on the table and my chin in my hands. "Tell, tell," I said.

"Jesus, where to being," he said, lighting a cigarette.

The waitress appeared and Marcus gave her our order.

"Griffin," I said. "Describe Kmiec to me. I know he's around five-foot-ten, that he has longish stringy dirty blond hair and acne scars. Oh, yes, and eyes from the bottom circle of hell. I've seen the newspaper photos of him. But what's he *like*—up close and in person?"

Marcus hesitated a moment, as if trying to find the right words. Then he said, "Totally without affect. That's the thing about him that hits you the hardest."

I raised my eyebrows.

"If he has any emotions at all," Marcus continued, "I've never seen an indication of it." He made a circular motion with the hand holding the cigarette. "He didn't even get excited when he was telling me about the killings. Often, guys like him do, you know. It's like they're getting off on the memory."

"I know."

The waitress brought our drinks.

"But not Kmiec. He explains to me exactly how he stuck the knife in Peggy Letourneau and he sounds as if he's reading from the phone book. He talks in a mono-tone. It never varies."

"Uh-huh."

"I've never seen a detachment quite like that. It's as if"—Marcus shook his head—"he's divorced himself from himself. You understand what I'm saying?"

"Vividly." I thought of the kind of criminal Jack and I had labeled VMs—violent morons. "I've seen—and heard—guys like that."

"Not like Kmiec, you haven't. This guy is from an-other dimension, believe me." Marcus picked up his drink. "God. You're with him for five minutes and you want to take a bath in Lysol."

He fell silent for a moment, frowning at his drink. Half his mind, or maybe even three quarters, was still back in the state prison with Henry Kmiec. I knew that condition, knew how hard it was sometimes to reenter your own level of reality when you'd been immersed so totally in someone else's. You could get lost in another person's life if you were writing about it. The trick was to resume your own.

"I think I may be starting to get a handle on the Cath-olic connection," Marcus said.

"Really? What?"

"Well, Mama Edith was a Catholic. Papa Paul may have been raised as one—who knows? Anyhow, Edith did attend church off and on while Henry and the other kids were growing up. *When* Pual would allow her, which I gather wasn't any too frequently. He wouldn't permit her to have the kids baptized or to take them to mass with her. Finally, he forbade her to go altogether."

"Thereby taking away from her what was probably her one solace in life," I said. "Nice guy, Paul."

"Yeah, a real humanitarian."

"Did Henry tell you this?"

Marcus nodded and took a sip of his drink.

"How'd you get it out of him?"

Marcus shrugged. "Asked him what religion he was. I figured that wasn't a leading question."

"No," I agreed. "So then what?"

"He told me he hated Catholics."

"*Really.*" I leaned forward slightly. "Why?"

"They made trouble for him."

"Griffin, I'm on the edge of my chair. What kind of trouble?"

"He tried to break into a rectory when he was thirteen. A priest caught him and called the police. The cops picked him up, took him to the police station, and later released him to Paul's custody. And Paul beat the shit out of him that night. Not because he cared about Henry breaking into church property, but for getting into trouble with the law."

I took a deep breath and sat back in my chair. "Did Henry tell you anything else after that? Something that might . . ."

"No." Marcus shook his head vigorously. "And I didn't want to press him just yet."

"Sure. Well, what else did you learn?"

The nearest occupied table to us was about ten feet away. I couldn't hear the conversation going on there, so presumably the three men couldn't overhear us. Nevertheless, Marcus lowered his voice. I had to lean over the table again to make out what he was saying.

"He gave me another detail of the murders."

I stared at Marcus. "What?"

"He told me he tied a green ribbon, very loosely, around each victim's neck after he killed her."

"My God."

"Yeah."

"Did he say why?"

"Nope. Couldn't get that out of him."

"Yet."

"Yet."

I bit my lip. "Is there some way we can get this verified?"

Marcus looked away from me, out the window at the courtyard. "I don't know. I'm working on it. There's a guy named Tucker, an investigator with the New Hampshire State Police. I've gotten sort of friendly with him. He's been pretty cooperative so far. Maybe . . ."

"He'll leak something?" I shook my head dubiously. "I don't know about that, Griffin."

Marcus lit another cigarette. "Well, I'll work on it. I'll figure out something. Or"—he smiled at me—"you will."

I smiled back at him, a little abstractedly, and drank some of my martini.

Jack could find out about the green ribbons.

Sure, and then he'd swear me to secrecy.

I wiped that thought out of my mind and replaced it with another. "Griffin?"

"Mm-hmm?"

"Did Kmiec say he put a ribbon around the necks of Maria and Carla?"

"No. Just the first seven women."

"He explain why not?"

"He said he didn't have the chance with Maria. And he forgot the ribbon the night he went out hunting and caught Carla."

"I see." I set my glass on the table and gazed at it for a moment. "Did he say what significance the green ribbon had?"

"No. He shut right up after that. And I didn't want to push too hard."

My hand closed hard around the glass. "That son of a bitch," I said. "He's really enjoying dragging this out, isn't he? Feeding you stuff in bits and pieces. He's playing with you."

"Of course he is. Hasn't that ever happened to you?"

I sighed. "All the time."

Marcus reached across the table and touched my hand. "Let go of the glass," he said. "You'll break it and cut yourself."

I nodded and loosened my death grip on the martini. Marcus smiled and said, "Better. If you hurt your hand, who'll finish the cross-indexing?"

I laughed reluctantly. "God forbid something should call a halt to that." I made a conscious effort to relax. "Tell me about this Tucker. You haven't mentioned him before. Nice guy? Good cop?"

"Seems so." Marcus stubbed out his cigarette. "His first name is Daniel. Dan. He's around my age, I guess, maybe a few years older. Divorced. Has one kid, who lives with the ex-wife. Actually, Tucker was one of the first people I got in touch with when I got the idea for this project. He's heading up the task force that's investigating the New Hampshire murders—Carolyn, Denise, and Cheryl."

"And he's been helpful to you."

"Yeah." Marcus lifted one shoulder in a half shrug. "Well, you know, helpful within limits. Those guys never tell you everything they know. But Tucker was the one who gave me the stuff about Paul Kmiec disappearing and what happened to the other kids in the family and about Edith's present situation."

"And does Tucker think Henry is it? The Merrimack Valley Killer?"

"Yup."

"And he's been on the case from the beginning, so he'll know if the seven bodies really *did* have green ribbons tied around their necks."

"Uh-huh."

"Good luck trying to pry that confirmation out of him."

"I'll need it. That's one of those details the cops like to keep secret."

"Can you blame them? That's how they distinguish the true confessions from the phony ones."

Marcus finished his drink and glanced at my nearly empty glass. "Another?"

I pursed my lips. "Oh—all right. Thank you. Then I'm going to run."

"Fine." He raised a hand to get the waitress's attention. When he had, he smiled at her and made a circling motion with his index finger over the table. She nodded.

"What do we have on for tomorrow?" I asked.

"I have to go to New York again," he said. "Thursday and Friday."

"So I'm on my own. What do you want me to do?"

"Whatever you think needs to be done." He groped in his sport coat pocket. "Here. An extra key to the room."

He tossed it across the table and I caught it. The waitress delivered our drinks.

"What's happening in New York?" I asked.

"Legal stuff."

"To do with the book?"

"Not exactly." He took a sip of his drink. Then he set the glass down on the arm of the chair. "The fact is, I'm setting up my own production company."

I had been foraging in the bowl of almonds the waitress had brought along with our booze. I stopped what I was doing and looked up at him. "Production company? Like for movies and TV? *That* kind of production company?"

"Well . . ." He seemed faintly uncomfortable. "Yes."

"Wow," I said. I lifted my glass in a toasting gesture. "That's really something. Congratulations."

"Thanks." He scratched his chin. "The only reason I'm doing it is . . ." He shifted around in the chair, picking up his drink. He gazed at me very earnestly. "Liz, I really hated the mini-series that were done of my last two books. I can't tell you how much I hated them."

I was silent. I hadn't liked them much, either.

"I want a little more creative control. Hell, I want a *lot* more creative control."

I ate some nuts. "I don't blame you. I would, too."

"Hollywood, Jesus," Marcus said, sighing. "The stories I could tell you about the place."

"Oh, please do."

"They'll curl your hair."

"It needs it." I hitched my chair a little closer to the table. "Go ahead, curl my hair."

He then embarked on a long and ludicrously convoluted account of what had occurred when his first book had been optioned for the movies. He didn't curl my hair, but he did a real number on my eye makeup. I was laughing so hard listening to him that I wept it all away.

We had a third drink.

That night was a quiet one for Jack and me. I made no attempt to restage the sex carnival of Tuesday evening. Or of this morning. I prepared a simple dinner of chicken, rice, and salad. We ate it without a great deal of conversation.

All I could *think* about was all the things I couldn't *talk* about with Jack.

Like green ribbons.

A few times during the meal I caught him looking at me. There was a touch of puzzlement in his expression, and a concomitant curiosity. And something else, too. I couldn't quite figure out what.

Maybe I didn't want to.

SIXTEEN

Marcus had told me to do whatever I wanted while he was out of town, so I did. Thursday morning, as he was probably going into his first meeting with his lawyers in Manhattan, I was riding a bus from Boston to Manchester.

Sometimes it's really a pain in the ass not to have a car. Or the license to drive one. But I make do.

I was fed up with cross-indexing. I wanted to be out in the field, investigating. I wanted to root around some more in the garbage dump of Henry Kmiec's past.

I wanted . . . action.

I took a taxi from the bus station to the address where Kmiec had lived before his arrest. The cab driver looked a little dubious at leaving me on the trash-lined street, with its condemned and abandoned buildings. He asked if I wanted him to wait. I said no, thanked him, and paid and tipped him.

The taxi drove off and I walked to the end of the street, two blocks down from Kmiec's house. I had Marcus's camera with me. I took a few long-range shots of the house. Then I walked the entire length of the street—eight blocks—to get a sense of the rest of the neighborhood.

It was all lousy. It may in fact have been one of the worst streets in Manchester. One entire block on the side opposite me was burned-out hulks. The sidewalks were buckled, and in the summer weeds would grow up through the cracks.

Kmiec's house was actually one of the better ones. I mounted the disintegrating concrete stoop and rang the DeWitts' bell. A short, overweight woman in pale blue polyester slacks and a University of New Hampshire sweatshirt strained by her copious bosom answered the door. She looked me over uninterestedly and said, "Yeah?"

"Mrs. DeWitt?"

"Who are you?"

I smiled. "My name is Elizabeth Connors. I was here last week to speak with Mr. DeWitt. If he's free, I'd like to talk with him again for a few minutes."

She shrugged. "He's out back." She closed the door in my face.

What a charmer. I shook my head and descended the stoop.

A ten-foot-wide passage, lined with trash cans, ran between this house and the condemned one next door. I picked my way down it. If a rat had scuttled out from behind one of the trash cans, I wouldn't have been surprised. I wouldn't have been too thrilled, either.

The path, or alley, led into a small backyard bordered partially by rusted hurricane fencing and partially by pickets of varied heights and widths. In the far left corner stood a small shed. I was willing to bet it had once been an outhouse. DeWitt stood in front of it, stuffing a black lawn and leaf bag with broken-up pieces of lathing and plaster. When he glanced up, I waved to him. He stopped what he was doing and gave me that same incurious gaze as his wife, or whoever the chunky charmball at the door had been. The DeWitts sure were an animated duo.

As I walked across the yard to DeWitt, he resumed stuffing the trash bag.

"You mind answering a few more questions about Henry Kmiec?" I asked.

Like his wife, DeWitt shrugged. An all-purpose response I interpreted in this case as yes. He knotted the top of the trash bag and heaved it into the space between the shed and the hurricane fencing. I wondered how long it would stay there.

DeWitt sat down on an overturned tin bucket and reached into his windbreaker pocket. He took out a cigarette and lit it. There was nothing for me to use as a perch, so I remained standing. I wasn't going to hunker down on the frozen earth.

"What ya want to know?" DeWitt said.

I got out my notebook and consulted the record of the first conversation—if it could be called that—that Marcus and I had had with DeWitt.

"You said that Kmiec lived here for about a year and a half before he was arrested. That was in November of 1990. So"—I counted backward—"he became your tenant in, say, June or July of 1989. Does that sound right?"

DeWitt ruminated. The smoke from his cigarette spiraled around his head. "Think it was earlier than that," he said finally.

"May?"

He seemed to be putting intense mental effort into answering the question. "Naw." He rubbed his chin, which still had on it the same day's worth of stubble that had adorned it the last time I'd seen him. "Earlier."

"April?"

He frowned slightly. "End of March."

Between the end of March 1989 and the end of November 1990 was longer than a year and a half, but I wasn't going to quibble.

"Just about a week or so before the big fire."

I glanced automatically back at the house. "Not here, was it?"

DeWitt jerked his head to the left. I remembered the row of burned-out and boarded-up buildings I'd passed by earlier.

"Big fire," DeWitt repeated. "Started late in the afternoon. They didn't get it put out till near midnight."

"Was anyone hurt?"

DeWitt shook his head. "Wasn't nobody livin' in them places. 'Cept the rats."

There seemed no need to reply to that comment, so I didn't.

"Whole street was out there watchin' that fire," DeWitt continued. "Me and the wife. The neighbors. Kind of excitin'."

Why hadn't they just thrown a block party? I wondered.

DeWitt dropped the butt of his cigarette on the ground and crushed it with his boot. "Kmiec thought it was a real gas, watchin' them buildings burn."

He would. "He was there?"

"Oh, yeah. Fire musta started a little before he got home from work. First he was pissed off 'cause he couldn't find no place to park his truck, 'cause of the fire engines and all. Then he really got into it. Sat around on the front steps drinkin' beer and watchin' the flames. Colder'n a witch's tit that night, too. Kept sayin' he couldn't wait for them to start bringin' out the body bags. Dumb shit didn't know there wasn't nobody livin' in them buildings."

Except the rats, I added silently.

"Yeah, old Henry was havin' hisself a real fine time, lookin' at them houses goin' up like paper." DeWitt chuckled, a sound like leaves rustling in a dry well. Then he hawked and spat on the ground. I averted my eyes quickly.

" 'Course, when one o' the ambulances backed into his truck, he got kinda upset." DeWitt chuckled again. "Fucked up the front end. Smashed a headlight."

His last words hit me like a bucket of ice water. "What?"

DeWitt looked at me blankly.

"Mr. DeWitt, you say a headlight on Henry's truck got broken that night?"

"Uh-huh."

"Can you remember at all when that happened?"

DeWitt shrugged. "It was dark. Night."

"Like ..." I made a circular motion with my hand. "Early in the evening? Later on?"

DeWitt shrugged again.

"Had the fire been going on for a while, at that point?"

"Couple hours. Three, four."

"I see."

On the April night in 1989 that Lisa Goodenough had disappeared, a red truck with a broken right headlight had been spotted in the parking lot of the administration building of Merrimack College, where Lisa had taught.

Lisa had been murdered on the first of the month.

I inhaled deeply. "Mr. DeWitt, I'm going to ask you something important."

"Yeah?"

"What day was that fire, can you remember?"

"I tole you. 'Bout a week after Kmiec moved in."

"The first of April?"

"Somethin' like that."

"Okay. Now, another important thing. Was Henry here *all* night, from the time he got home, watching the fire?"

"Far as I know."

"Till midnight, when they put it out?"

"Far as I know."

"He didn't leave for a few hours? Like between, say, five o'clock and, oh, eight?"

"Naw," DeWitt emitted his soft crackle of a laugh. "He was havin' too good a time waitin' for them to bring out the body bags."

Sure, what guy who collected snuff movies wouldn't?

"Mr. DeWitt, you've been a big help. Thanks."

I left him sitting on the upturned bucket and raced down the street to where it intersected with a broader and more prosperous thoroughfare. There I darted up and down until I found a drugstore that had a pay phone and a directory. I got the number of the cab company whose driver had taken me from the bus station to Kmiec's address and called. Then I went outside to wait for the taxi, fairly dancing up and down on the sidewalk with impatience and excitement.

The cab appeared in about ten minutes in real time, although it seemed more like ten hours. I told the driver to take me to the public library.

There I went through the back files of the Manchester *Union-Leader* to the April 3, 1989, edition of the paper.

The fire on Kmiec's street was large enough to have made the front page. I read the story quickly. No mention of Kmiec's presence at the event, but I hadn't expected to find one. The story didn't give exact times and dates for the beginning and end of the fire. On an inside page of the paper was the fire log. I skimmed it. The fourth item down was a brief notice of the blaze on Kmiec's street, called in at 3:57 P.M. on April 1 and extinguished at 12:17 A.M. on April 2.

If Joseph DeWitt's memory could be trusted, Henry Kmiec had been guzzling beer and cheering on a holocaust while, forty miles away, Lisa Goodenough was being abducted and stabbed thirty-four times along a riverbank in another state.

SEVENTEEN

Friday I spent in Marcus's suite at the Charles, trying to cross-index. I didn't make much headway on the job. Mostly, I thought about the significance of what I'd discovered Thursday. And fumed at Marcus for being in New York and not here so I could tell him about it.

That night, Jack and I went to dinner and to a movie afterward. It was a pretty good film, I suppose. I couldn't concentrate much on it.

I tried to be a lively conversationalist over drinks and dinner. But the one big thing I really wanted to talk about, I couldn't discuss with Jack.

When we went back to my place we went to bed, where I didn't have to think of anything at all to say.

Marcus had left word he'd be back in Cambridge late Friday night, and that if I needed to speak to him, he expected to be in his hotel room Saturday morning till about eleven. After that, he was going out to do some interviews.

Saturday morning I woke up at seven, something so unprecedented for me that I inspected the clock on the bedside table to make sure it hadn't stopped running at seven the previous evening. It hadn't

Of course I knew very well what had wakened me. My consuming need to get to Marcus and tell him that there was an excellent chance Henry Kmiec hadn't been anywhere near Lisa Goodenough the night she died.

I glanced to my left. Jack lay stretched out beside me, still deeply asleep.

Under different circumstances, I'd simply have waited until a decent hour, like nine or ten, and called Marcus at the hotel and told him what I had to. But with Jack here, I couldn't do that. What could I say to him? "Hey, honey, would you mind vacating the apartment for fifteen minutes so I can make a private phone call to Griffin Marcus I don't want you overhearing?"

I couldn't run to the corner store to use the pay phone there, with the excuse that I was going to buy the papers, because I had the *Globe* and the *Herald* and the *Times* delivered.

I wasn't out of milk or coffee or orange juice or bread or any other breakfast item, either.

Maybe while I was in the shower I'd think of some legitimate-sounding urgent reason to absent myself from Jack and the apartment for an hour or so. I slid out of bed very carefully, trying not to make the mattress bounce, and cat-footed it to the bathroom, which was off the kitchen, so maybe the sound of running water wouldn't disturb him.

Getting clean didn't give me any great ideas. Neither did brushing my teeth or putting on makeup. I tiptoed back into the bedroom in the same state of nude noninspiration in which I'd left it.

I inched open dresser drawers and closet doors getting out underwear and turtleneck and jeans and dressed in them with the speed of a character in a silent movie. As I did, I kept flicking glances at Jack. Still totally given up to sleep, as far as I could see. I found my shoes and was about to leave the bedroom with them in hand, to put on in the living room, when he said, "What the *hell* are you doing?"

I was so startled I dropped the shoes. I looked back at the bed. He was lying on his back, staring at me.

"Good morning," I said stupidly.

"Morning?" He checked the bedside clock. "It's seven thirty-five. That's the middle of the night by your standards."

"Well"—I shrugged—"I guess I just couldn't sleep."

"So you decided to get dressed and go for a brisk walk along the Charles?"

For all the years he'd known me and we'd been occupying the same bed, my normal habit if I woke up unusually early was to stay supine and read whatever book I happened to have put down the night before.

And on Saturday and Sunday mornings, whoever regained consciousness first lay around waiting for the other to come to life so we could make love. Weekday mornings there was generally too little time for that.

What could I tell him now—that I had to go plow the lower forty?

"What's the deal?" Jack said, raising himself up on his elbows.

I'm a terrible liar, and I get more inept at it under pressure. "I—Jack—"

"Yes?"

So I told him the truth. Sort of.

"I really have to go see Marcus. Just for a little while. But I do. It's important."

Jack rubbed a hand over his face. Then he shook his

head as if to clear it. "Right," he said. "You desperately have to go see Marcus at . . . what?" He glanced again at the clock. "Seven-forty on a Saturday morning? Uh-huh. Would it be out of line for me to ask why?"

I felt myself flushing. I know he noticed.

"Well," I began. "It's just that he has some papers he wants me to check over. And it has to be done this weekend. And he's going to be out interviewing people most of today and all of tomorrow, so this is the only chance I'll get to, you know, pick up the stuff."

Jesus, was that speech feeble. Jack apparently thought so too, because he said, "Well, if Marcus is going out, why doesn't he drop the goddam papers off here on his way to wherever the hell he's going instead of making you go to his hotel at"—Jack glanced yet again at the clock—"seven forty-two in the morning?"

I gestured helplessly. "I said I'd come get them."

"So call him and tell him you've changed your mind."

"Oh, Jack . . ."

"Call him."

I brushed my bangs back from my forehead, a tic of mine when I'm nervous and agitated. Jack knew that, too.

"Look," I said. "I'll just go grab the stuff. I'll be back here in less than an hour." I smiled. "We'll have the whole weekend ahead of us then. With no interruptions."

"Sure," Jack said. "Unless Marcus decides he *has* to see you, like, say, tomorrow morning. Or tonight."

I was starting to get angry as well as nervous and agitated. I made an effort to control the anger. I couldn't do much about the nerves and the agitation.

"Jack," I said. "What's wrong? Why are you acting like this?"

As if I couldn't guess.

He looked at me for a moment. There was nothing yielding in his expression. "I was just about to ask you the same thing."

I swallowed. Then I bent over and picked up my shoes. "I'll see you in a little while," I said, and left the room.

I got a cup of coffee at the corner store. Then I walked to Harvard Square. I was trying to focus on the news about Henry Kmiec and imagine how Marcus would react to it. I didn't want to think about the scene that had just played itself out in my bedroom. Hard not to, though. I'd blank out one image in my mind and another would rear up to take its place, the way the right side of a pillow rises if you punch down the left.

I knew I wouldn't get back to my apartment within an hour, as I'd told Jack I would. It was going to take longer than that to go over the new development with Marcus.

So why had I made a promise I couldn't keep?

"I don't believe it," Marcus said.

We were having breakfast in one of the hotel restaurants. I put the triangle of toast I was eating down on my plate and stared at him incredulously. "You don't *believe* it? Do you think I made it up, then?"

"No, no." He scowled at me. "Of course not."

"Well, I didn't make it up. Here. I can give you the transcript of my entire conversation with Joseph

DeWitt." I rummaged in my handbag for my notebook, retrieved it from the depths, and attempted to pass it across the table to Marcus. He waved it away.

"I'll read it later," he said.

I resumed eating the toast. Marcus was silent, holding his coffee cup in both hands, not drinking from it but rather frowning at its contents. I knew exactly what he was thinking.

If Henry Kmiec hadn't killed Lisa Goodenough, why had he claimed he had?

And if he hadn't killed Lisa, had he in fact killed any of the other six women?

Or was his entire confession just a fantasy? Or a weird hoax perpetrated by a very disturbed and very evil mind? Things like that *did* happen.

Marcus put his cup down on the saucer with a click and said, "Liz, look, I talked with Joseph DeWitt, too."

"Yes. I was with you when you did."

"And this guy, you have to admit, is not a giant intellect."

"Can't argue with you there."

"He's not alert. He's not smart. He doesn't strike me as the world's most reliable observer. He was very probably mistaken about Kmiec being at that fire the whole night."

I sighed.

"Let's dissect his statement," Marcus continued. "Did DeWitt tell you Kmiec was never out of his sight once, for the entire—what?—eight hours that the fire burned?"

"No, he didn't tell me that."

"And hell, you yourself said that DeWitt could barely remember when Kmiec became his tenant. You had to prod him to get a straight answer on that point."

I finished the toast and wiped my fingers on my napkin. "Griffin, what about the headlight on Kmiec's truck? It got broken the night of the fire. When an ambulance backed into it."

"So DeWitt says."

"Why would he invent a detail like that?"

"I'm not saying he did, damnit. I'm saying he might have confused or telescoped the time it happened. Maybe the headlight got smashed, like, around four or four-thirty that afternoon, when Kmiec was trying to find a place to park the truck. Which would still have given him plenty of time to drive down to North Andover and snatch Lisa. Because the truck wasn't damaged badly enough so that Kmiec couldn't drive it, was it?"

"DeWitt didn't say so."

"Then there you are."

"Okay," I said. "Let's not fight about it."

Marcus's eyes widened. "But we're not. I'm sorry if I sounded as if I was. And I'm sure as hell not mad at *you*. I think you did a great job. I think this is worth checking out some more, too. I'll go talk to DeWitt again. But"—he smiled at me—"I think we'll both find he's a little screwed up in his recollections."

"Maybe."

"You're a good investigator," Marcus said. "And interviewer."

"Thanks." I poured myself another coffee. "Griffin?"

"Yes?"

"Remember the other day when you were telling me about your talks with Keisha Madison?"

"Uh-huh."

"Well, one of the things she said to you is kind of nagging at me."

"What's that?"

"When Kmiec went after her with the knife, what was it he told her? 'I'm going to do to you what I done to them other two whores'?"

"That's right."

I twisted the napkin in my lap. "Okay. Why didn't he say to her, 'I'm going to do to you what I done to them other *nine* broads'? Or other nine cunts, or whatever revolting locution a degenerate like that would use?"

Marcus raised his eyebrows. "Well, the first seven weren't whores, were they?"

"No, but . . ."

"So Kmiec has his own bizarre way of classifying his victims. Liz, this guy's mind operates on a level you can't begin to plumb. You haven't met him. You haven't talked to him. I have."

"Right."

We finished breakfast. Marcus signed the check. As we were leaving the restaurant, he said, "Look, I hope you're going to take the rest of this weekend off. Don't spend it thinking about Kmiec. Relax. Have some fun. You earned it."

"I'll try. Good luck with your interviewing."

When I got back to my apartment at a little after eleven, Jack wasn't there. Somehow that didn't surprise me. I puttered around the place for the next few hours, doing odds and ends of housework. He didn't come back and he didn't call, and somehow that didn't surprise me either.

EIGHTEEN

I went to the bank to deposit the second thousand-dollar check Marcus had given me over breakfast that morning. Then I went for a walk along the river. Not for exercise, but to sort out my thoughts. And to try and figure out a way to stave off the mess I could see my personal life would become if Jack and I didn't get back on our old track quickly.

He was entirely correct in thinking I'd been acting oddly recently. If I could explain to him why, everything between us would probably be fine again.

But I was behaving oddly precisely *because* I couldn't explain to him why I was behaving oddly.

Swell.

After an hour's pacing down the footpath that ran alongside the Charles, I was no nearer a solution to the dilemma.

I leaned on the railing by the Charlesgate Yacht Club and gazed across the water at Boston. The view was wonderful, but it didn't give me any answers either. Nor did any of the joggers or power walkers or bicyclists on the towpath behind me.

I went home.

I let Lucy out and then fed her. I looked in the refrigerator. On a plate sat the game hen I'd defrosted for dinner. Too big for one person to eat. Perfect for two, though. Of course, that had been the intention.

Maybe, I thought, this can be played by ear.

I called Jack. He answered on the third ring.

"Me," I said. "Look, I have a great idea. Why don't we just paint a giant blob of Wite-Out over this morning, huh? Pretend it didn't happen and start over again? Okay?"

He was silent for a few seconds. Then he said, "Yeah. All right."

"Good," I said. "Now, will you please get the hell over here and have dinner tonight and breakfast tomorrow morning like you were supposed to?"

"I suppose," he said. The words themselves weren't enthusiastic, but the tone in which they were spoken was a lot lighter than it had been. Not light, exactly. But not heavy, either.

"Whew," I said into the mouthpiece, and hung up the phone.

I cleaned the bird and stuck it in the oven. Then I fixed my hair and makeup. I looked . . . not bad, I figured. Not bad would have to do. Didn't the Total Woman advise that if you really wanted to win over your man, you meet him at the door naked with his drink in your hand?

If I met Jack at the door nude with a tumblerful of bourbon and ice, he'd laugh. Then he'd have me committed for observation.

I couldn't pull off a stunt like that, anyway. I'd feel like a horse's ass.

He showed up forty-five minutes later, which meant he hadn't exactly broken any land speed records getting here. I gave him a kiss. Then I gave him a drink. Fully clothed.

We sat down on the couch, close but not touching.

"Didn't get off to a fabulous start this morning, did we?" I asked.

"No."

"Well, I'm sorry I had to go out so early, but it really couldn't be helped."

"It wasn't so much that you left that bothered me. It was the way you left." He looked at me. "You were trying to sneak out."

I sighed. "I was trying not to disturb you, was what I was doing. I'd have left you a note telling you I'd be back as soon as I could." I took a sip of my drink.

"If it was just this morning, I could shrug it off."

I scowled at him. "What are you talking about?"

"You've been acting weird for the past two weeks."

"Oh, really? How so?"

"For one thing, you're too quiet."

"Oh, sorry. Let me go get my noisemaker."

He made an impatient gesture with his left hand. "And for another . . . what's with these sudden attacks of nymphomania?"

I took another sip of my drink. "Since when," I said, trying to make a joke of it, "do you object to a woman with a hearty sexual appetite?"

"Only when she's faking it."

Comedy time was over. "I wasn't," I said. "I wasn't faking anything."

"It sure seemed like it to me. Remember, Liz, I know you."

I nodded.

"You haven't been the same since you started working for Marcus."

I ran a finger around the rim of my glass. "Well . . . is that so surprising?"

He stared at me. "Yeah, as a matter of fact, it is."

"No, look," I said. "Try to understand. I've never been in a situation like this one. It's a different kind of pressure than I'm used to. And a different kind of responsibility than I'm used to. My whole working life is different from what it used to be. So if *I* seem different to you, maybe that's why."

He didn't react immediately to my words. I watched his face intently. His expression suggested he was weighing and analyzing each syllable I'd spoken. Finally he said, "Yes. Okay. I can see that."

I reached over and took his hand. "And keep in mind, too, sweetie, that this situation I'm in is not going to last very long."

He gave me a slight smile. "A temporary aberration."

I smiled back at him. "Leading to temporarily aberrant behavior."

He put his arm around me. I leaned toward him, and we kissed.

"Now," I said. "Just let me go and check on what the dinner is doing. How's your drink?"

He held up his glass. "Fine."

"Good." I got up from the couch.

As I walked to the kitchen, I could feel myself slumping internally. And I wasn't smiling anymore.

What I had just told Jack was 85 percent of the truth. And I hadn't lied about anything. Nothing important, at least.

So why did I feel as if I had?

* * *

Despite that, we had a very good evening. Anyway, I recall it as having been good. Could be that I'm just con-
trasting the memory with what happened later. Dinner
was fine and we talked—*really* talked—before, during,
and after the meal, which was better than good. What
we talked about was Jack's ongoing investigations and
what I could do to advance my career after the Marcus
interlude had ended.

The good feeling lasted through the evening and night
and into next morning and early afternoon.

Late Sunday it cracked and shattered.

Jack was in the living room watching football and I
was in the bedroom leafing my way through a stack of
magazines when the phone rang.

"You want me to get that?" Jack called.

"No," I yelled back to him. "I will. Thanks." I
pushed up off the bed and went to the living room. Jack
turned down the sound on the television and then disappeared into the kitchen.

The caller was Marcus. He did not sound cool, calm,
and collected. "Yeah, hi," he snapped. "Can you get
over here? Now?"

"What?" I said, blinking.

"The shit's hitting the fan."

"What's wrong?"

"Look, I'm sorry, I don't have the time to explain. I
have another call coming in. It's an emergency. Can you
just get over here?"

Jack was coming back down the hall toward me. I
glanced at him and ran my free hand back through my
hair.

"You know, you're calling at a bad time," I said to
Marcus.

"I said I was sorry, for Christ's sake, didn't I? I need

to see you as soon as possible. Shit, here's my next call. Goodbye."

I replaced the receiver in the cradle and stared for a moment at the phone. Then I took a deep breath and turned to look at Jack. I didn't like the expression on his face.

"Guess who that was," I said.

"And let me guess what he wanted," Jack said. "You. Now. Am I right?"

I nodded.

"Shit," Jack said. "I hope you told him to go take a flying fuck at a rolling doughnut."

"I didn't tell him anything. He didn't give me a chance. He had another call coming in and hung up."

"Uh-huh. So?"

"Jack, he said it was an emergency."

"Yeah? What kind?"

"He didn't say. He *did* sound upset."

"And what does he want you to do about it? Hold his hand?"

"He didn't say that, either."

"Uh-huh. Right. I see. So you're just going to take off now? Think you'll be back sometime this evening? Or tonight?"

I stared at him. "I cannot *believe* what I'm hearing from you."

He shrugged.

I closed my eyes for a few seconds. Don't blow up, I told myself. Aloud, I said, "Jack, this is ridiculous. How many times have you had to leap up while we were in the middle of dinner, or in the middle of the night, because somebody got murdered and you had to go to the scene? Have I ever been unreasonable when that's happened? No. I accept it. I may not like it especially, but I accept it. Stuff like that happens. It's the nature of your job. Okay, so I have a job that places unusual demands on me. I would expect you of all people to understand that." I shook my head. "Jesus, haven't we had this conversation before?"

"That's different," Jack said.

"What's different?"

"I'm a cop."

"Sure. And I'm a writer. So what? The principle's the same in either case."

"No it isn't."

"What?"

He inhaled. "My kind of emergencies are different from your kind of emergencies."

"How?"

"Mine are more . . ."

"More what?"

He let out the long breath he'd taken. "Liz, they're more important, that's all."

I had crossed my arms. I uncrossed them now and let them hang down by my sides. "Excuse me?"

He shook his head. "Well, they are. You can't just leave a body lying someplace till it's convenient for you to investigate who made it a corpse. Whatever this is with Marcus, I'm sure it can wait till tomorrow."

"How would you know?"

"Liz, how big a deal can it be?"

"I have no idea," I said. "But, buddy, you sure do make me want to find out."

"You're going, then?"

"You're damn right I'm going. Right now." I went into the bedroom for my bag and notebooks. When I came back to the living room, he had risen from the couch and was standing in front of it. I got my jacket from the closet. " 'Bye," I muttered. I was seething.

I had my hand on the front doorknob when he said, "Liz?"

"Yes?" I said, over my shoulder and through my teeth.

"Can I ask you a question?"

"What?"

"What the hell is going on between you and Marcus?"

I released the doorknob and turned slowly to look at him. "I beg your pardon?" I said. "I really hope, I really do hope, that I just heard you incorrectly."

"I don't think you did."

I stared at him for a moment. Then I said, "Whenever I get home this evening, you better not still be here. Because I have absolutely nothing further to say to you."

NINETEEN

I was so shaken, so disoriented, that I walked four blocks without even remembering to look before I crossed the street. Given the insanity of Cambridge drivers, that I didn't get creamed by a car or a truck may have been a small miracle.

I was as incredulous as I was enraged. In all the years I'd known Jack, I'd spent a lot of time listening to him talk and I'd never once heard him say anything remotely like the words he'd spoken to me this afternoon.

It was, of course, the implied accusation of infidelity that galled me the most. But I wasn't any too charmed by his suggestion that my life's work was insignificant in comparison with his.

My credo is very simple: If I don't work, I don't eat. Period. I love writing, but one of the reasons I do it is that I get *paid* to do it. I have to take the business seriously. Otherwise, no food, no clothing, no shelter.

I work for the same reason every man does.

I found myself breathing quickly and heavily, almost panting, and leaned against the side of a building to try and regain control. There was no point in bursting into

Marcus's suite half hysterical. What went on between Jack and me was none of his concern, anyway.

There's a gate in my mind that I try to keep clanged down between my private and professional lives. Right now, I was concentrating on making it fall. The hinges seemed to be rusty. In any case, it was descending a lot more slowly and creakily than usual.

But the gate did, finally, drop into place.

When I walked into Marcus's suite, he was fighting with someone on the phone. Fighting down and dirty. I peeled off my coat and tossed it onto a chair. Then I wandered over to the window and leaned my forehead against the glass. I looked out at the JFK School and tried not to overhear Marcus's end of the conversation. My ears had been assaulted enough already today.

Marcus ended the call by slamming the receiver onto the phone. I straightened up and said, "What's the problem?" I was suddenly aware of a huge, exasperated weariness with men and their problems. Whatever they might be.

"The fucking problem is," Marcus said, "Kmiec's decided he's going to talk to the reporters from the local press."

I sat down quickly on the wide windowsill. *"Oh."*

"Yeah, oh." Marcus paced across the living room. "Swell, huh? I guess the son of a bitch decided he couldn't wait for the book to come out."

That thought had occurred to me days ago. I hadn't seen any point in mentioning it to Marcus.

"When did you find this out?" I asked.

"About twenty minutes before I called you."

"I see. So what's your next step?"

He stopped pacing and raked a hand through his hair. "I can get a magazine piece out in six weeks. Two places will hold a space for me. But, goddamnit, it's just not the same."

"I know." And I did. I could feel for him, having the rug of exclusivity ripped out from underneath his feet. But that sort of thing happened. It had often happened to me.

"Look, Griffin," I continued. "You still have the book. And it will be *the* book on Kmiec, no matter what else gets written."

He lit a cigarette.

"And," I said, "if you move fast, you can get your own production company to lock up whatever additional TV or movie rights you need."

He gave me a quick, sharp glance to see if I was being sarcastic. I was, but only a little.

"We're working on it," he said.

I stuck out my legs and crossed them at the ankles. "Well, since I can't go down to Walpole and shove a gag in Kmiec's mouth, what would you like *me* to do?"

"We have to plan for this coming week."

"And?"

"Well, that's what we have to do."

I was quiet. *This* was Marcus's big emergency? Figuring out the direction we were going to take next week? This couldn't have been done tomorrow morning? Or in ten minutes over the phone?

It suddenly occurred to me to wonder if the real reason Marcus had declared his emergency was so that he'd have an audience (me) before which to vent his rage at Kmiec.

Someone to hold his hand. So to speak.

For this I'd gotten into a cataclysmic argument with Jack?

I had an intense desire to bang the two men's heads together.

"Sure," I said curtly. "Let's plan."

Marcus noticed my tone. "Is something wrong?"

"Not at all," I said. "Everything's hunky-dory."

He nodded. "Look, want to go downstairs and have a drink while we plan?"

"Why not?"

Might as well get *something* out of this fiasco.

Over the next few days, the Henry Kmiec story became the hottest one in town. He talked publicly on Monday. That night, he was the lead story on the six o'clock news on all three TV stations. The *Globe* and the *Herald* had him on Tuesday's front page. He was also the subject of a few radio call-in shows. The consensus of the callers seemed to be that Kmiec ought to be strung up on the nearest lamp post. Hard to argue with that sentiment.

Marcus had rented a VCR and had me tape some of the TV programs as well as clip the newspaper articles. He was off running around frenziedly trying to sew up as many exclusive interviews as he could with the principals in the case.

When I wasn't taping or scissoring, I was answering the phones in the suite and taking messages. Most of them were from Marcus's agents and lawyers. I felt like a receptionist. The highest paid one in the Boston area.

I was, in fact, too busy to think about Jack. Or I kept myself too busy to think about him. A good thing, too. The thoughts would have become increasingly painful.

When I'd gotten back to my place early that Sunday evening, Jack hadn't been there. I wondered how soon after I'd left that he had. Probably very.

But not so quickly that he hadn't taken the time to remove his personal effects from the place. I realized that when I went into the bathroom and discovered the toothbrush and razor he kept there were gone. So were the few articles of clothing he'd stored in my bedroom closet.

TWENTY

Of all the programs on Henry Kmiec I watched and taped, the one that interested me the most featured a brief interview with Daniel Tucker, the New Hampshire State Police detective coordinating the investigation into the Carolyn Bragg, Denise Michaud, and Cheryl Timmons murders. I also recalled Marcus telling me that Tucker was one of his more helpful law enforcement contacts. Watching Tucker parry the interviewer's questions, I could see why. He was clearly intelligent, which isn't unusual among cops. He was also articulate, which often is.

And he made a damn good case for Kmiec being the Merrimack Valley Killer.

In manner he was reserved yet sufficiently at ease not to appear stolid (a typical cop posture with the media). He was giving away no information about the case he didn't want to give. He evaded very neatly the interrogatory traps the interviewer laid for him.

He looked to be, as Marcus had remarked, in his late forties or early fifties. His hair was gray and crisply short, his eyes a pale northern blue. His build was lean and wiry, and I made a guess that he was around my height.

His presence was impressive. No wonder the New Hampshire A.G.'s office had made him one of its spokesmen.

When Marcus returned from his interviewing late Wednesday afternoon, I played the tape for him. We sat side by side on the couch to watch. Marcus leaned forward slightly and focused all his attention on the television screen.

When the tape ended, I said, "Tucker's good. You were lucky you were able to establish a friendly relation with him. He'll make a superb source for the book."

Marcus nodded and lit a cigarette.

"Tucker really seems positive that Kmiec's the murderer."

Marcus exhaled some smoke and leaned back against the couch cushions. "Well, Kmiec knows details of each killing that were known only to the police here and in New Hampshire."

"Oh, like the business about a green ribbon being tied around each victim's neck? You got that verified?"

"Uh-huh."

"By whom? Tucker?"

Marcus nodded again. "Yeah. Off the record, though, for the time being."

"What were the other details?"

"Well"—Marcus took a final drag on his cigarette and butted it out in the end table ashtray—"for one thing, Kmiec knew that each victim's hands and feet had been bound by duct tape. *Another* fact known only to the police."

"Go on."

"And he was able to say exactly what kind of knife

he'd use each time, which corresponded exactly with what the cops got from the autopsies on each victim. The kinds of weapons Kmiec said he used would make wounds of the depth and width of the ones found on the bodies."

"I see."

"Kmiec is it. No doubt in my mind."

I sighed. "The evidence *is* pretty strong."

Marcus stared at me. "What do you *mean*, pretty strong? It's damning, is what it is."

I was silent for a few seconds. Then I said, "What about Joseph DeWitt's story?"

"What about it?"

"Well, DeWitt did maintain that Henry Kmiec never left Manchester the night Lisa Goodenough was murdered."

Marcus shook his head and smiled at me. "Liz, DeWitt is a loose cannon. I went back to talk to him myself, you know, last Sunday morning."

"And?"

"He's not reliable. Sorry, but he isn't. I went over the story he told you, and it just doesn't stand up."

"Griffin, I don't think he was lying to me."

"No, of course he wasn't. But his memory has big gaps in it."

"What kind of questions did you ask him?"

"Same ones you did. Only more and harder. The guy in fact eventually had to admit that no, he couldn't account for Kmiec's every minute the night of the fire, and yes, Kmiec might well have gone off somewhere and come back again."

"Even for as long as a few hours?"

"Even for as long as a few hours."

"Maybe . . ." I paused. "Never mind. Forget it."

Marcus lit another cigarette. "No. Go on with whatever you were going to say."

"Griffin, it's possible you pushed DeWitt too hard. And he gave you the answers he thought you wanted to hear so you'd get off his back."

Marcus grimaced. "Liz, give me a little credit for some finesse, huh? What do you think I did—smack the poor dumb bastard around with a rubber hose?"

"No," I said. "Sorry."

"It's okay." He stood up and stretched. "Jesus, I'm enervated. How about a drink?"

"No." I smiled to soften the refusal. "Thank you. But I'm meeting a friend in Boston in about half an hour."

"Oh. All right. See you tomorrow, then."

The friend I was meeting was a woman named Christine Cameron. She worked for one of the big consulting firms that had its offices in the Stock Exchange building. Years ago she had been, like me, a college English teacher. She'd abandoned that profession for the same reasons I had. She was also quite frank about her feeling that her current line of work, communications consulting, was bullshit. But she was nonetheless very good at it, and, as she told me she constantly reminded herself, the pay was great, you got to travel a lot, and you didn't have to grade freshman compositions.

I met Christine where I always did, in the clubby upstairs bar at the Parker House. She had arrived there first and taken a table for two. She seemed to be fending off the advances of a guy who had *I am an investment banker* practically inscribed on his forehead. This happens to her often; Christine is a nice-looking woman with a good-humoredly sexy air about her.

As I approached the table, the guy backed away from it and returned to the bar.

"What did you tell him?" I asked. "He sure took off fast."

She grinned at me. "I just thanked him for his offer to buy me a drink and added that I was only interested in lifetime commitments."

"That will discourage them," I said judiciously. "I'll remember that line. Probably more effective than threatening to hit the guy with a chair. Which is what I once did in a similar situation. He was unusually persistent."

"I guess. Did the chair trick work?"

"Barely. He thought I was playing hard to get."

Christine laughed, and I sat down opposite her. The waitress appeared. We ordered martinis, vodka for me and gin for Chris.

"So," she said. "What's up? How's the new job going?"

"Busy. Time-consuming. Fine. Interesting."

"Good. How's Jack?"

"I don't know. I haven't seen him or talked to him since I told him to get out of my apartment last Sunday afternoon."

Christine said, *"What?"*

The waitress brought the drinks and a pewter bowl of mixed nuts.

"Begin at the beginning," Christine said, "and don't leave anything out."

I did and I didn't.

When I'd wound up the story, we were ready for another drink. Christine flagged the waitress.

"Okay," I said. "What's your take on the situation?"

"Jack's jealous of Marcus. Isn't that obvious?"

I sighed. "Yeah, it is. But, Chris, that's so out of character for him I can hardly believe it. I mean, I have men friends. I've worked with and for men before this. Jack knows all that. It's never bothered him until now."

"You've never worked for anyone like Marcus until now."

"What does that mean?"

"Oh, Liz, come on. You know exactly what it means. Marcus is *somebody*. He's famous. He's influential. He's powerful, in a way. He's rich. He's even *Hollywood*."

"So? None of those things would bowl me over."

Christine shrugged Perry Ellis–draped shoulders. "Maybe Jack thinks they would."

I gave her an outraged look.

"Oh, calm down," she said. "I'm not saying that's what he consciously believes. Look at it this way. Suppose some gorgeous celebrity actress came to Cambridge to make a movie and hired Jack to be her personal bodyguard. Wouldn't that make you a little nervous?"

"No. I'm too conceited."

"Oh, balls. Admit it—you'd be nervous."

I toyed with the bowl of nuts. Then I said grudgingly, "Maybe."

"There's another thing, too."

"What's that?"

"You're taking a grand a week from Marcus. You refused to take any money at all from Jack."

"Oh, Chris. Please. Marcus is paying me for work I do for him, not for being his girlfriend."

"And I'm sure Jack accepts that rationally. Emotionally may be another story."

"All right, all right," I said. "You win."

"What am I winning? This isn't a contest. You're telling me your problems and asking for my thoughts, right?"

"Yeah."

"Well, okay. I'm giving them to you."

"Fine."

"You know, Jack's not completely at fault here. Even if he did say some asshole things to you, you've been acting funny around him and you can't tell him why. So naturally he notices that, not being stupid. So equally naturally he suspects the worst. That you're getting—uh, involved with Marcus."

"But I'm not."

"But you *are* attracted to him."

"Jesus, you missed your calling. You'd have made an ideal prosecutor, Chris."

She patted her handbag. "Correct, and I have the bamboo shoots in here to stick under your fingernails if you don't answer my questions. How attracted *are* you to Marcus?"

"Such a tiny little bit that it makes no difference. I'm not—I don't *want* to do anything about it. I'm sure not going to let Marcus do anything about it."

"If he finds out you and Jack are—what? Estranged? If he finds that out, he might try again with you."

"If the problem arises, I'll handle it."

"Okay." She picked up her drink. "Fine. Glad to hear it."

"Chris?"

"Yes?"

"Okay. So we can take it as a given that it's not completely unreasonable that Jack should be bothered by the way I've been acting recently. Even though he jumped to the wrong conclusion about why. *But*—"

"But what?"

"Did that give him a good reason to also belittle my job?"

Christine swished her martini around in the glass. "No. I can't find an excuse for that."

"Coming from him, it really hurt. I didn't realize how much until ... Well, it's been growing on me over the past few days." To my horror, I felt my eyes stinging. No way was I going to cry in a bar. In public.

Christine gave me time to compose myself. Then she said, in a reflective voice, "It's the most enraging thing."

I cleared the huskiness from my throat. "What is?"

"Oh, with women and work. A woman has a social date with a man. She breaks it because there's a crisis or something at the job and she has to stay late and help solve it. And the guy she had the date with accuses her of being—what? Selfish? A neurotic workaholic?"

"Or that she's having an affair with her boss."

"That too. *But*— but, but, but. If a woman skimps on her work or cuts it short because she has to fulfill a social obligation to a man or help him through one of *his* job crises, what happens then?"

"She gets accused of being irresponsible. Not serious about her career."

"Damned if she does and damned if she doesn't."

"Or," I said, "as Virginia Woolf put it, you can't fucking win."

Christine had taken a mouthful of liquor. She spat it back into the glass. "Excuse me, but wasn't that Dorothy Parker?"

"No, she said you might as well live."

Christine smiled. "Doesn't the one presuppose the other?"

"I guess it does."

"So what are *you* going to do?"

"Well, I'll certainly live. And I'll certainly work."

"Beyond that?"

"I don't know."

TWENTY-ONE

The next day I met Henry Kmiec.

The meeting took place in a small, characterless room deep within the maximum-security prison at Walpole.

Marcus and I sat at a rectangular table waiting for Kmiec to be led into the room under guard. I was on edge. This would be the second time in my life I'd come face-to-face with a serial killer. I wasn't sure how I'd react.

Marcus noticed my tension and put a hand on my arm. "Relax," he said quietly.

I nodded. I tried to concentrate on the rhythm of my breathing. Sometimes that helped.

Marcus, who had always seemed to me as incapable of extended physical repose as a toddler, sat calm and still. What was his technique for assuming such stasis?

"I'm surprised you were able to get permission to bring me along with you today," I whispered.

"Thank Tucker." Marcus said. "The guy's well connected down here. In addition to being well thought of."

"Yes."

The door to the room opened and Henry Kmiec was brought in by a guard. The guard was armed. Kmiec was manacled and shackled. The chain that linked his ankles was just long enough to permit him to walk with short steps.

Kmiec sat down across from us. He looked at Marcus and said, "How you doin', man?"

"Fine," Marcus said. "How's it with you?"

"Same as usual, man. Nothin' too much different around here, one day to the next."

Marcus gestured at me. "This is Elizabeth Connors, Henry."

Kmiec studied me for a moment. It felt as if his eyes were crawling over my face with slimy little steps. My right cheek twitched in response. Kmiec grinned.

"She the old lady?" he said to Marcus.

"No." Marcus said. "My associate."

In person, Kmiec was nondescript, the way the incalculably evil very often are. No horns, no tail, no cloven hooves, no cloak of darkness visible. His hair was a stringy dirty-blond and hung to just below his earlobes. It had been shoulder-length at the time of his arrest. And the mustache he'd worn then was gone. His skin was pitted and large-pored, and his nose had obviously once been broken. His teeth were yellowed and crooked and chipped. The upper right incisor was missing. Put him in East Cambridge or East Somerville or Charlestown and he would have been indistinguishable from any of the resident dirtballs.

Except for his eyes.

They were grayish-blue and had a hard, bright shine to them, like twin reflector plates. They had no depth. None. Behind the irises was . . . nothing. Just a steady surface burn.

Marcus had described Kmiec's eyes as from "the bottom circle of hell." Not too much of an exaggeration there.

"Okay, Henry," Marcus said briskly. "Let's get started."

"Sure. Whaddaya wanna talk about today?"

"How about Linda Tessier?"

Kmiec nodded. "Broad up in Methuen, huh?"

"That's the one."

"So whaddaya wanna know about her?"

"Well, a few things. Like—why her? Why did you pick her?"

Kmicc grinned. "My type, man."

My stomach tightened.

"Your type," Marcus repeated. "In what way?"

"She was little. Just the way I like 'em."

Marcus nodded. "Mn-hmm. Why do you like them to be little?"

"That's the way a broad's supposed to be, man." Kmiec jerked his head at me. "Not like your old lady here."

"My associate, Henry."

"Yeah, whatever."

"Okay. Anything else about Linda?"

"Sure. She was Catlick. Just like the rest of 'em."

"Uh-huh. All right, now—how did you go about taking her?"

Kmiec looked nonplused. "Huh?"

"Did you just happen to spot her and decide to snatch her and kill her right then and there, or was it more planned than that?"

Kmiec's face creased back into that feral grin. "Saw her one day when I was down cruisin' that mall."

"The Methuen mall."

"Yeah."

"Right. Excuse me—why were you cruising the mall?"

"Lookin' for my next broad, man."

"Uh-huh. Go on."

"So I seen Linda, man."

My palms were damp. I blotted them unobtrusively on my corduroy skirt.

"She was gettin' into her car," Kmiec continued. "Followed her home. Saw where she lived. Near that Catlick school."

"And then what?"

Kmiec shrugged. "Let her go inside."

"And you? What did you do?"

"Went home."

"To do what?"

"Think about what I was gonna do to her, man."

"Anything else?"

"Well, shit, man, sure. I had a plan how I was gonna do it."

I pressed my hands against the tops of my thighs, beneath the table.

"How'd you feel while you were planning what you were going to do to Linda?"

"Same as always."

"What's *same as always?*"

Kmiec's grin widened. "Good, man. Real good."

"Why did that make you feel good?"

"*Always* makes me feel good. Killin' bitches always makes me feel good."

I dug my nails into the corduroy.

"All right," Marcus said. "Henry, how long was it between when you saw Linda and decided she was the one and when you—"

"Grabbed her and cut her?"

"Yes."

"Coupla days."

"Two? Three?"

"Somethin' like that."

"What were you doing for those *coupla* days?"

"Thinkin' about her."

"I see." Marcus folded his hands together and rested his chin on them. "Okay, Henry. What I'd like you to do now is describe to me, as closely as you can, just how you killed Linda Tessier. Start from the beginning. From where you . . . grabbed her."

"Right outta the parking lot, man. Easy."

"When did you do that?"

"When it was dark."

"You remember the date?"

"Sure, man. December seventh."

"What year?"

"1989."

"What time of night was it?"

Kmiec hesitated. Then he shrugged. " 'Round seven, seven-thirty."

"Hmm." Marcus frowned thoughtfully. "December seventh, seven or seven-thirty P.M. Henry, the mall must have been pretty crowded with people doing their Christmas shopping and all."

Kmiec bobbed his head. "Yeah, sure. Place was fuckin' mobbed."

"So wasn't that kind of tricky, then? Snatching a woman under those circumstances? When somebody could so easily have heard or seen you do it?"

"Nobody heard me or seen me, man."

"How'd you swing that?"

"Soon's she come up to her car, I grabbed her. She didn't have no time to say or do nothin'."

"Why didn't she say or do anything when you grabbed her?"

"I put my hand over her mout' and tole her I'd kill her if she squeaked."

"What'd you do then?"

"Put her in my truck, man."

"Did you have to carry her, or pull her, a long distance across the parking lot?"

"Oh, shit, no, man. I put my truck right nexta her car."

"That was clever."

"No big deal. Just waited till the space was empty."

"Okay. Where'd you put her in the truck?"

"Front seat wit' me."

"You weren't worried she might jump out?"

"Fuck, no, man. Broad was too scared to breathe."

"What happened next?"

"We went to the woods."

"And after that?"

Kmiec's face went flat. The hard surface burn of his eyes dimmed. When he spoke again, the pitch of his voice had dropped down to a monotone.

Marcus sat up a little straighter in his chair.

The room seemed more still and small to me than before. Perhaps it was only that my awareness had shrunk to this space.

"Come on, Henry," Marcus said. "Tell us."

"The moon was out," Kmiec said. His voice was as flat as his features. "It was a nice night. Real nice."

Marcus nodded slightly. "Go on."

"Not too cold."

"Uh-huh."

"Parked the truck off the road, so nobody was goin' by could see it."

"Yes."

Kmiec's voice had not only flattened but slowed.

"Then the broad says, 'What're you gonna do to me?' And I says, 'You'll see, honey. Won't be long now.' "

"Uh-huh."

"Then I taped her up."

"Where? How?"

Kmiec raised his manacled hands. "'Round her wrists." He shuffled his feet. "Her ankles. And I put some tape over her mout' so she couldn't scream or nothin'."

"Then?"

"Then I took her down to the river."

"And?"

"Put her down on the ground."

My head felt thick, and I clasped the sides of my chair. Marcus gave me a lightning glance out of the corner of his eyes.

"Then I got on top of her and I took out the knife and I shown it to her."

"How'd you get on top of Linda, Henry? Were you lying on her?"

"Naw. Sittin' on her stomach."

"I see."

"Then I took the knife and I stuck it in her tit."

"Which one?"

Kmiec was silent for a moment. Then he said, "Left." Marcus nodded.

"So I did that seven times. Then I did it to her other tit."

"How many times?"

"Same. Seven."

"Why seven?"

"Don't know, man. I just like the number, is all."

"Was Linda conscious?"

"Oh, yeah, man, sure."

He must have wanted them to be that way, Marcus's voice echoed in my mind, *for them all to be aware of what was happening to them up to the very last minute.*

"Go on, Henry," Marcus said.

"Then I put the knife in her neck."

"How many times did you do that?"

"Seventeen."

"And?"

"The broad croaked, man. Whaddaya think?"

"Did you do anything to her after she died?"

"Yeah."

"What?"

"Cut off a little piece of her hair."

"From where?"

Kmiec gestured upward with his cuffed hands and moved his head to the right. "There."

"What'd you do with the lock of hair?"

"Threw it in the river, man."

"Why?"

"It's what I always do."

"Okay. Anything else?"

"Sure."

"What?"

"Tied a bow around her neck."

"What kind?"

"Green ribbon, man."

Marcus nodded. "What kind of green ribbon?"

"Oh, man, I tole you already. Same kind I used on them other broads."

"Uh-huh. Why?"

"Why what?"

"Why'd you tie a green ribbon in a bow around their necks, Henry?"

Kmiec smiled. "It made 'em look pretty."

TWENTY-TWO

"Godalmighty," I said.

Marcus glanced at me. "Yeah, I know." He put the Explorer in gear and we drove out of the parking lot to the checkpoint. The guard retrieved our visitor's pass and waved us on our way.

"I read all the notes you took on your previous conversations with Kmiec," I said, "and all the gory detail was there—how he carved up the other women . . . Reading that was bad enough, but . . ." I lifted my right hand, made a small meaningless gesture with it, and then let it drop back into my lap.

Marcus nodded. "Yes. You have to be with Kmiec in person, listen to him, watch him, before what he did and what he is really hits you. Otherwise it's just words on paper."

"Mmm-hmm."

Neither of us spoke again for the rest of the ride.

At four-thirty we were sitting in the bar section of a restaurant in Norwood, not too far past the Walpole town line. Neither of us had ordered a drink yet, although we both wanted one. We were waiting for Daniel Tucker to join us. Marcus had arranged the day before for him to meet us here after we'd finished up with Kmiec.

"Tucker's not coming all the way from New Hampshire just to see us, is he?" I asked.

Marcus lit a cigarette. "No. He had to be in Framingham this afternoon anyway, so it was no problem."

I nodded. Framingham was where the Massachusetts State Police headquarters was located. It was also adjacent to Norwood.

At twenty to five, Tucker came into the bar. I recognized him even before he spotted us; he looked much as he had on television, only slightly less drawn.

Marcus introduced us. We shook hands.

"Good to meet you," Tucker said.

"You too."

He had a nice smile, subdued and a little weary-seeming, but genuine. His pale blue eyes were faintly shadowed. He sat down across from me.

The waitress came to take our order. Marcus and I had the usual. Tucker asked for a draft beer. Then he settled back into his chair, unzipping his heavy parka and shrugging out of it.

"What were you doing with the Mass. State Police today?" Marcus asked. "Comparing notes?"

Tucker smiled his tired, pleasant smile again. "Something like that. There's a lot to coordinating these investigations that go from one jurisdiction to another."

"Complicated," I said.

"You got that right."

The waitress brought the drinks.

When she'd gone, Tucker looked from me to Marcus. "How was Kmiec today?"

Marcus raised his eyebrows. "Liz? Why don't you answer that?"

I took a deep breath and let it out slowly. "He's . . ." I shook my head. "He's just pure evil, isn't he?"

Tucker gazed at me for a moment. Then he nodded. "That about sums it up."

"He told us all about how he chopped up Linda Tessier," Marcus said.

Tucker was reaching for his beer. He grimaced at Marcus's words.

"He really enjoyed doing it, too," Marcus continued. "More so today than ever before."

Tucker drank some of his beer. "Maybe he enjoyed having a female audience."

"That's what I thought."

I laughed briefly and with no amusement. "He kept referring to me as Griffin's 'old lady.' "

"That's civilized talk for Henry," Tucker said. "He could have called you much worse."

"I'm sure."

There was a bowl of pretzel nuggets in the middle of the table. Tucker pulled it toward him. "First food I've had since six o'clock this morning," he remarked.

"Jesus," Marcus said. "Why don't you have a sandwich or something?" He started to signal to the waitress.

Tucker stopped him. "It's okay," he said. "Thanks, but I'll have a regular dinner in a little while."

"You could have an appetizer now," I said.

He smiled at me. "No, I'm fine. I'm picking up my son at five-thirty. He and I are going to grab something to eat and then catch the Celtics game."

I returned Tucker's smile. "Your son lives down here?"

"In Randolph, with his mother."

"How old is he?"

"Fifteen." Tucker took a few more pretzels. "He's a hell of a kid, too. Made the all-state swim team last year. I wish I could see him more often."

"Tell me about it," Marcus said abruptly.

Tucker looked over at him and then nodded.

"You worry about him?" Marcus asked.

Tucker snorted. "When don't I?" He finished his beer. "He's a good kid. He's not into drugs or booze, and he keeps his grades up. He's never been in any trouble. Still . . ." Tucker set his glass on the table and stared at it a moment. "Still, Christ. The job I have, I see kids just like my son, good kids from nice homes, plus good kids from not-so-nice homes, all the time getting hurt or killed." He exhaled softly. "It's always in your mind."

"Always," Marcus said.

The bar was filling up with the post-work crowd. Someone activated the jukebox that till now had been standing silent in a corner. A party of five guys in their mid-twenties took the table next to us.

"I have to be moving," Tucker said. "Pleasure to meet you, Liz."

I held out my hand to him. "I hope I see you again soon."

"Me, too. Thanks for the drink, Griffin. Good to talk to you."

"You, too," Marcus said. "Oh, and, hey, Dan, thanks for greasing the wheels with Kmiec."

"Sure. Talk to you later." Tucker left the bar. I watched him go.

"He seems like a sweet guy," I said to Marcus. "A little worn out and troubled, though. But then I guess he has reason, with the pressure of this investigation and all. I mean, they *do* have to prove Kmiec killed those women. They just can't take his word for it."

Marcus was swirling the dregs of his martini around in the glass and didn't respond.

"Griffin?"

"Huh?" He seemed absorbed by the sound of my voice.

I snapped my fingers at him. "You in a trance or what?"

He swallowed the last of his martini. "No. Just thinking."

"About what?"

"Leah. My daughter."

"What about her?"

He looked at the chair Tucker had occupied as if Tucker were still sitting in it. "Dan's right. Anything can happen to them. And no matter what *you* do, you can't prevent it."

"Griffin . . ."

He made a sharp movement with his right hand as if to silence me. "No. You don't have kids. It's something you can't understand."

"I can try."

"There's no *rational* reason for me to be afraid . . . something will happen to Leah. But I am."

I didn't say anything.

"Especially," Marcus added, "after I've had a session with Kmiec."

I leaned back in my chair and folded my arms. It was all I could think of to do. Just sit and listen.

"One of Kmiec's victims was exactly Leah's age. If it could happen to that girl, it could happen to . . ."

His voice was very quiet but very intense. The bar noise around us seemed to recede.

The waitress approached our table.

"Just the check, please," I said quickly, before she could ask us if we wanted a second drink.

Marcus smiled wryly. "You know what I'll do when I get back to the hotel this afternoon?"

"What?"

"I'll call my daughter's school and demand to speak to her."

I checked the clock over the bar. "Griffin, it's two o'clock in Los Angeles. She'll probably be in class and unable to come to the phone."

"Sure. But I'll raise holy hell until they get her. I do that every time I come back from talking with Kmiec."

There was the explanation for at least some of the yelling he did on the phone, I supposed.

I shook my head. "The headmistress or whoever must love you, disrupting Leah's schedule that way. Not to speak of the school's office."

"Well, fuck the headmistress. And I don't care if I'm disrupting the headmistress's office. I don't care if I'm disrupting the headmistress in the middle of an orgasm."

"She'd *really* be steamed if you did *that.*"

"I just have to talk to Leah myself and know that she's all right."

"And what does Leah think, once you've gotten her on the phone and started interrogating her about her well-being?"

"She thinks I'm nuts."

"I bet she does."

"You should hear her. 'Daddy, what *is* this? Are you, like, totally insane? I'm *fine,* Daddy. Now will you stop this? You're just embarrassing me incredibly.' "

I laughed at Marcus's rendition of an exasperated female teenage voice. "The poor kid. Do you let her date?"

"Of course I let her date."

"Well, aren't you liberal."

He laughed then, fully. "You're right. So is Leah. I'm a hysterical asshole."

"She hasn't called you that, has she?"

"No. She's too polite. But it's what she thinks. I can tell."

"Do you have a picture of her?"

"Of Leah? Of course."

"Well, may I see it, please?"

"Sure." He reached for his wallet, riffled through the credit card (there were many) compartment, and then removed a two-by-three-inch rectangle of stiff white paper. He turned it over and handed it across the table to me. I took it by the edges.

"She's lovely," I said. And she was. Long wavy glossy black hair and large hazel eyes in a tan oval face. A little bit like the actress Olivia Hussey, I thought. "Gorgeous."

"Thank you. I think so, too."

I handed the photo back to Marcus. He studied it for a moment. Then he returned it carefully to the credit card compartment.

"In fact, she looks a lot like you," I added. "Except for the difference that *she's* pretty."

"Very funny," Marcus said. He put some money on the table to cover the check and tip. "Well—shall we hit the road?"

"Ten-four."

We took the turnpike. We were passing by Braintree when Marcus said, "Thanks."

"For what?"

"What you did back there."

"What did I do?"

He glanced at me. "Made me laugh. Kept me sane."

"Oh, Griffin—"

"Well, you did."

I sighed and smiled at him. "If you say so."

"I say so. Again, I'm very glad I hired you. You probably can't imagine how glad."

I felt a little flustered. "That's—I'm happy to be working for you, too."

"Not *for* me. *With* me."

"All right. With you."

It was a little after seven when we got back to my place. I deliberated for a second. Then I said, "Would you like to come up for another drink?"

He smiled. "Sure. Thanks."

We climbed down from the Explorer and went up to the apartment. As soon as I opened the door, Lucy lunged over the threshold to take her usual flying leap into my arms. Then she spotted Marcus behind me and gave a short, suspicious bark. She pressed her body protectively against my legs.

"It's all right," I said. "It's just Mr. Marcus. Be nice to him and maybe he'll let you call him Uncle Griffin." I grinned at Marcus. "She has a very large extended family of aunts and uncles."

Marcus bent down and extended his hand. The dog sniffed it and then lickcd. Her tail waved.

"Seal of approval," I said. "Do come in."

I took his coat and hung it and mine in the closet. "Please sit down."

"Thanks." He went to the couch, Lucy following him.

I checked my answering machine for messages. There were none.

"Feel free to use my phone to badger poor Leah," I said.

"No," he said. "I think I can contain myself till I get back to the hotel."

I laughed and went to the kitchen. When I returned to the living room, it was with two vodka martinis and a bowl of mixed nuts.

"You make wonderful drinks," Marcus said when he'd sampled his.

"Thank you. It's one of my pitiably few talents."

He lit a cigarette. "You have more than a few talents."

I wrinkled my nose and ducked my head.

"You're not very good at taking compliments, though. Neither am I."

We drank. Lucy lay down before the coffee table and yearned at the bowl of nuts.

"She looks like she'd kill to get into them," Marcus said. "Don't you ever feed her?"

"Constantly." I was sitting at the opposite end of the couch from him. I angled around to face in his direction. "What are we doing tomorrow?"

"I have to go to the city."

When he said "the city" in that tone, I knew he meant New York and not Boston or even L.A. People born in New York tend to refer to it that way forever. They could be on the outskirts of London and still make the same reference. If they were going to London, they'd say they were going to *London*. If they said they were going to the city, they meant they were hopping a plane at Heathrow and taking it back to JFK. I know. I'd had to break myself of the same habit.

"Have a good time," I said. "Plus a nice day. What do you want me to do up here in the sticks?"

Marcus stubbed out his cigarette in the coffee table ashtray. "Write up everything you saw and heard today in that room at the prison."

"Okay."

"I'll do the same. Then we can compare. I'm sure you picked up on stuff I didn't."

"Maybe. Be interesting to see."

"Yeah. So let's not talk about Kmiec now, huh?"

"Fine with me."

Marcus reached for the bowl of nuts. As he did, Lucy's head and ears sprang to full alert. He laughed and took a few of the nuts. "Can I give her one?"

"If you want to be pestered by her for the rest of the time you're here, you can."

He tossed a Brazil nut to the dog. She snapped at it, missed, and went scrambling across the rug after it. Marcus popped a cashew and a pecan half into his mouth. Lucy wolfed the Brazil nut and then trotted over to Marcus's side and put her head on his knee. He held up his empty hand to show her it was empty and said, "All gone. Sorry, love." She stepped back a few paces and gave him a look that was limpid with devotion.

"This is getting sickening," I said. "Would you like me to leave you two alone so you can get better acquainted?"

"No. She's a nice dog, but I'm not into bestiality."

"I can't tell you how relieved I am to hear it."

He grinned and finished his drink.

"Like another?"

"Need you ask?"

Lucy—so much for the steadfastness of canine attachments—got up and trailed me as soon as she saw me heading for Food Central. In the kitchen I opened a can of the revolting pinkish-gray chicken byproduct slop she adores and dumped it into her yellow plastic dish. She was gulping it down as I left the room with Marcus's second drink. I still had half of my first one.

When I'd settled back down on the couch, Marcus said, "So what's new with you? In your life?"

"Nothing much."

"How's Jack?"

I couldn't help it. The glass holding my hand jerked a little and some of the martini dripped down onto my skirt. Automatically I brushed at the spilled liquor with my free hand.

"I don't know," I said. I remembered giving the same answer to Christine Cameron when she'd asked me the same question.

Marcus looked at me. "You don't—" He paused. "Sorry. It's none of my business."

I shook my head mutely and drained my drink. Then I got up and made another.

We sat quietly for a while. Then Marcus said, "If you want to tell me what the problem is, and I gather there *is* a problem, I'll be happy to listen. If you want me to shut up and get lost, I'll be happy to do that, too."

I was holding my glass in both hands and staring at it. I couldn't exactly say, *The problem is you, Griffin.*

Then on the other hand, maybe I should.

"We had a big fight last Sunday. After you called."

"Oh?"

"He was angry that I left him to go to you. He—we said some hard things to each other. Finally I told him I didn't want him to be here when I got back that evening."

"Back from seeing me," Marcus said softly. "Jesus. Liz, I *am* sorry."

"Not your fault."

"Even so . . ."

"It's okay."

He stared at me. "Obviously it's not. Not okay."

I nodded.

"Was he angry at you leaving then? Was it just that?"

"No. It's been building up. And he was angry when I went to see you Saturday morning, too."

"Why?"

I shook my head.

"Liz . . ."

"It's . . . he doesn't like me working for you."

"Why the hell not?"

I shook my head again.

"Never mind. I can guess." Marcus lit another cigarette. "Son of a bitch."

"I don't want to talk about it anymore, Griffin."

"No, of course not. I understand."

"Thanks."

"God. Shit. I feel as if I've completely screwed up your life."

"Don't. You didn't."

"No?"

"No. It's his problem. My problem. Not yours."

Marcus nodded.

I took a sip of my drink.

"Liz?"

"Yes?"

"He'll get over it. Men are . . . they act like jerks sometimes. Take *me,* for Christ's sake."

I couldn't help smiling.

"He'll get over it," Marcus repeated. "Give him a little time. He will."

"Sure," I said.

What I didn't add was, *Will I?*

The phone rang. I jumped at the unexpected noise. This time, though, I didn't spill my drink. I was clutching it too tightly.

The phone rang a second time.

"You want to get it?" Marcus said. "Maybe it's Jack."

"That, I guarantee you, it's not," I said.

The phone rang a third time. I set my glass on the coffee table, rose, and answered it.

An unfamiliar woman's voice said, "Is Elizabeth Connors there?"

"This is she."

"Oh. Hello. This is Marian Sandoval."

The name meant nothing to me. "Yes?"

"I have a letter from you here."

She did? I scowled at the receiver. "You do? I'm sorry, but I can't—"

"It's not a letter to me. It's to my parents. You wrote them last week."

"Who . . . ?"

"My parents are Charles and Julia Timmons."

I inhaled sharply.

"I'm Cheryl Timmons's older sister."

"Yes?"

"My parents don't want to talk to you. Or Griffin Marcus. Or anybody else, anymore, about Cheryl. Ever."

"I see."

Her voice was sharp. "But I want to talk to you."

I tried to keep my voice calm, neutral. "Okay. Good."

"Just you. Not Marcus."

"But—"

She cut me off. "No. I've seen him on TV. I know who he is. He may be a swell guy and a terrific writer, but I don't want to talk to him."

"Why not?"

"Because he thinks Henry Kmiec killed my sister."

I pressed the receiver closer to my ear. "And you . . . don't?"

"I *know* he didn't."

I scraped my free hand back through my hair. "You *do?*"

"I know it for a fact. A plain, provable fact."

I let out my breath. "All right. I want very much to talk with you. When and where? Tomorrow?"

"Fine. Perfect."

"You know the Charles Hotel? In Cambridge? Off Harvard Square?"

"I can find it."

"I'll meet you in the lobby." I described myself quickly. "At noon."

"See you," she said.

TWENTY-THREE

Marcus listened closely while I repeated to him my conversation with Marian Sandoval.

"What do you think?" I said.

"I think you should definitely meet her tomorrow and find out what she has to say."

I sat down on the arm of the sofa. "I wonder why she's convinced that Kmiec didn't murder Cheryl."

Marcus shrugged. "I imagine she'll tell you."

I glanced at him. "You don't seem too excited by the prospect."

He raised his eyebrows. "At this stage of the game, it would take a hell of a lot to persuade me that Kmiec was innocent of *anything*, let alone killing Cheryl Timmons."

After being in that grotesque and horrific presence today, I could see his point. Vividly. "Yeah," I said.

"Still," Marcus continued. "It's great that someone close to Cheryl is willing to talk at all. I want a personal take on that girl. So far she's only a crime statistic to me." He shook his head briefly. "And I want her to be a whole lot more than that."

"For the book."

"For the book."

"Do my best for you, boss," I said.

"Oh, don't give me that boss crap." He pushed himself up from the couch. "I should hit the road. Thank you for the drinks—and everything else."

"Anytime. Have a good time in New York tomorrow."

"Oh, yeah. It'll be a real blast."

I got his coat for him.

"Talk to you when I get back," he said, and went out the door.

I was closing it behind him when he said, "Liz?"

I pulled back the door. "Yes?"

He stood in the hall with his hands in his pockets. "You know, about your, uh, problem with Jack."

"Uh-huh."

"I meant what I said. I'm sure he'll cool off once he's had a chance to think."

"Maybe," I said shortly.

He looked as if he was about to say something more. He didn't. He smiled, very faintly, and went down the stairs. I shut the door.

My second drink wasn't finished. I went back to the couch, curled up in the corner, and took the glass from the coffee table.

Eight years I had been with Jack. *Eight years.* We'd had some arguments in that time. None that had created a major rift, though.

Why was something that had seemed so solid and lasting apparently now falling apart so quickly?

A better question—why wasn't I in agony over the collapse?

I was lacerated inside, all right. Badly. But was it Jack's absence that was causing the pain?

No. Not entirely.

I knew what was stabbing at my guts. The knowledge that the man I'd spent eight years of my life with didn't trust me. Had tried to demean me.

And, to a certain extent, had succeeded.

I woke up at three the next morning. I'd been doing that a lot lately, waking at odd hours.

I lay quietly in bed, staring at the ceiling. I didn't put on the light. I knew it would take me at least an hour to return to sleep. If I did at all.

How much was I to blame for the breakdown with Jack?

Even if the blunders I'd made were innocent blunders or at least well-intentioned ones ... still, they'd been made, and couldn't be unmade.

It was ironic that the secret I'd withheld from Jack, the one that had opened the crevasse between us, was no longer a secret. It hadn't been since Kmiec had confessed to the world.

Had I reacted too sharply to the things Jack had said to me last Sunday?

And if I had—*why* had I?

No answer came to me out of the darkness.

Funny, that was the title of Marcus's book.

Toward five I drifted off to sleep. It wasn't a good and restful one. I don't know what I dreamed, but I woke up crying.

Marian Timmons Sandoval was about five-seven and thin. She was Cheryl's much older sister, perhaps in her early thirties. Cheryl had been blond and blue-eyed, with fair skin and a round-cheeked face. Marian's face was narrow and sharp-boned. Her skin was olive and her hair and eyes were dark brown.

Cheryl—judging by her picture, anyway—had had one of those twinkly ready-to-laugh expressions. Marian had the look of someone who saw little in the world to smile at.

I was slouched in a chair in the Charles lobby when she appeared. It took me a moment to realize that someone was standing beside me. When I did, I uncoiled from the chair like a spring.

"Marian Sandoval?" I said.

She nodded.

"Liz Connors." I held out my hand, and she touched it briefly.

Around us the lobby burst into sudden frenetic life. A blond woman came through the revolving glass doors, followed by perhaps six or eight people carrying luggage. The woman leading this procession looked awfully familiar. I squinted at her. Of course she looked familiar. She was Candice Bergen.

Actually, I shouldn't have been surprised. The Charles was the command post for about 70 percent of the TV and movie people who came to Massachusetts to film or do promotional work.

I'll be damned. Murphy Brown, lady journalist, up close and personal. Maybe I could offer to buy her a drink. Maybe she'd shed some light on my personal and career problems.

Marian Sandoval said, "Is that . . ."

"Uh-huh. Come on. Let's go upstairs. I've ordered a lunch from room service."

We took the elevator up to Marcus's suite. Marian Sandoval stood with her head down, hands in the pockets of her forest-green trenchcoat. I unlocked the door of the suite. Marian paused for a moment on the threshold, peering inside as if making an inspection of the sitting room. *Then* she set foot in it.

"May I take your coat?" I offered.

She shed it and handed it to me, still glancing around at the surroundings. Underneath the coat, she had on a cream silk blouse, a tan flannel blazer, and brown slacks. The blazer hung a little awkwardly over her right hip. As if she was wearing a holster beneath it.

I froze. Then I remembered a line from Marcus's book proposal.

. . . Cheryl, the younger sister of a police officer . . .

Marian Sandoval was a *cop*.

My God.

"Sit down," I said. "Anywhere that looks comfortable. Or that doesn't have a file folder on it."

The room service waiter appeared. They were pretty snappy with the amenities here at the Charles. I directed him where to put the cart and forged Marcus's signature on the bottom of the check, adding a tip.

I'd ordered a variety of salads, rolls, and coffee.

Marian Sandoval perched on the edge of an easy chair and focused her gaze on me. Despite the alertness of her posture, and her wary reticence, she didn't seem ill-at-ease.

She was a cop, all right. Nobody but a cop could go into a strange place with a stranger and look as if *she* was the person controlling the situation.

"Well," I said, gesturing at the cart. "Let's help ourselves. Then we can talk."

Marian Sandoval looked at each item on the cart very carefully. Then she served herself a small amount of pasta salad and green salad. I took bigger portions of everything.

"You're a police officer," I said. "Where?"

"Portsmouth."

"Do you live in New Hampshire, too?"

She nodded and ate a spinach leaf.

"How long have you been with the department?"

"Five years."

"Are you patrol or . . . what?"

"Patrol for the first three years."

"Days or nights?"

"Nights."

I smiled. "Where the action is."

She nodded again.

"You know," I said. "The Cambridge Police Department—at least the night captain of it—has a saying. 'There's day men and there's cops.' "

She looked up from her plate and, for the first time, gave me something resembling the glimmer of a smile.

"What about the past two years?" I said.

"Detective."

"Oh, really? What unit?"

"Sexual assault."

"Tough job."

"Yes."

We finished lunch and got coffee. Marian leaned back slightly in her chair. I told her something about myself. She listened quietly, not interrupting, taking it all in without question or comment or visible reaction. I could only hope she approved of what she heard.

Ultimately I suppose she must have, for when I finished speaking she set her empty cup on the end table and said, "Okay."

Meaning that was what she thought I was? I felt as if

I'd passed an initiation rite, one that qualified me for membership in the small and select club of people who met with Marian Sandoval's approval.

"Do you want to tell me why you think Henry Kmiec didn't kill your sister?" I asked.

"He couldn't have."

"Why?"

"He wasn't anywhere near Plaistow the night she died."

TWENTY-FOUR

"Before we go on," I said, "do you also want to tell me why you're coming to me with this information? I mean . . ." I made a small circular gesture with my right hand. "You're a cop. Shouldn't you be talking to your colleagues about this?"

"I have."

"And?"

Her face hardened. "If I'd gotten anywhere with them, I wouldn't be *here,* would I?"

It's nice to be wanted.

"I don't know," I said. "Would you? Am I your court of last resort?"

"Maybe."

I got myself more coffee and offered her some. She refused with a shake of the head. "What about Dan Tucker?" I asked. "The guy from the New Hampshire A.G.'s office. Have you spoken to him?"

"Yes."

"What'd he say?"

Her face went from hard to bitter. "Oh, he was polite. He listened. Then he told me he'd look into it and showed me the door."

"And did he? Look into it?"

"Oh, who knows?" Her voice was weary. "I doubt it. He and the others already had their minds made up. They didn't want to hear any information that might confuse the issue."

I nodded and drank some coffee. Some cops *did* have a tendency to do that, fixate on one suspect and ignore or disregard any evidence that might exculpate him. And inculpate another. Yet Tucker had seemed more . . . broadminded to me. I said so.

"Oh, he's like all the rest," Marian Sandoval said impatiently.

Maybe, I thought, she'd rubbed him the wrong way. I could see that happening. This was a prickly woman sitting before me.

I kind of liked her.

"Well, I'm open," I said. "If Henry Kmiec wasn't in Plaistow the night Cheryl was killed, where was he?"

"In Keene."

Keene was on the other side of the state from Plaistow. It was a fair drive between the two.

"Where in Keene was he?" I asked.

"At a bar, a pigpen, called Jimmy Mac's. Actually, it's right outside of Keene. He was there all night. From seven till closing time." Marian's voice had a flat finality to it as she added. "Drinking beer."

"You sound very sure."

"I am."

I looked at her for a moment. How had she gotten this information? Surely she hadn't gone to every bar and roadhouse in the state on the off chance that Kmiec had hit one of them the night of her sister's death.

I asked the question I was thinking.

"I interviewed a few people who knew Kmiec. One

of the things I found out was the places he liked to hang out. I made a list. There were nine or ten. A couple bars in and around Manchester. One in Laconia, one in West Lebanon."

"He liked to travel to do his boozing, didn't he?"

"Yeah. What it was is, I think he got bounced from so many local places he had to go further and further afield to find new ones. He even went up to North Conway sometimes."

"Goodness, he must have blended in beautifully with the chi-chi ski resort crowd."

Marian gave me another tiny smile. I felt rewarded. "Yeah, right. He also had a place in Portsmouth and one outside Concord. One up by Plymouth."

"All buckets of blood, I imagine."

She nodded. "Real dumps. What other kind of place would let him in the door?"

"Hard to think of many. So. You checked all these places? Did you have any prior indication that Kmiec might be at one of them the night your sister died?"

"Well, that landlord of his, that—" She fumbled for the name.

"Joseph DeWitt," I supplied.

"Yeah, him. He told me Kmiec had certain places he liked to go to certain nights of the week. Jimmy Mac's was one of his Monday-night places. The other was the place up in Laconia."

"Did he alternate Mondays?"

"Well, sort of. It wasn't Keene one week, Laconia the next, then back to Keene. He wasn't . . . didn't have *that* much of a routine. Sometimes he'd do Keene three in a row. Or Laconia two in a row."

"It was a Monday night Cheryl died."

"Yes. January 22, 1990."

"And Kmiec was in Jimmy Mac's all that night. Drinking beer. From seven P.M. onwards."

"And Cheryl was last seen alive at nine that night."

"In Plaistow."

"Who at Jimmy Mac's IDed Kmiec for you? The bartender?"

She nodded. "I showed him a couple different newspaper photos of Kmiec. Plus mug shots I got from the Manchester P.D."

"From when he tried to rip off the video store?"

"Yeah."

"And the bartender seemed to you a credible witness?"

"Well . . . yeah."

Her "yeah" was full of conviction, but I noticed the hesitation preceding it. I knew where it came from. In a place like Jimmy Mac's, which catered almost exclusively to scumbags, the bartender was probably a dirtball himself. Maybe not a paragon of reliability.

"I know what you're thinking," Marian said.

"I guess it has to be thought, doesn't it?"

Marian's face hardened again. "You sound like Tucker."

"Marian, I'm sorry, but . . ."

"Shit," she said. "You're just like all the others. I'm sorry I wasted my time. Thanks for the lunch." She rose.

"Wait a minute," I said. "Now wait just a goddam minute."

She stared at me.

"Now *you* listen to *me.*" I told her Joseph DeWitt's story about the night of the fire, and how, according to DeWitt, Kmiec had been so enraptured by the flames that he hadn't stirred from the scene all night long.

Halfway through the recitation, Marian sank back into her chair, still staring at me.

"He didn't kill Lisa Goodenough then, either," she said.

I sighed. "I don't know, Marian. I just don't know. Marcus talked again to DeWitt after I did. Marcus's take was that DeWitt was confused about the times Kmiec was actually there and watching the fire."

"Bullshit," Marian said. "Marcus wants to believe what he wants to believe. He doesn't want holes punched in this theory any more than the cops do." She pronounced the word *cops* as if she weren't one.

And what about you? I thought. Maybe you don't want holes punched in your theory, either.

"Look," I said. "I think there's a lot to what you say. I want to pursue this with you. But can you give me anything else?"

For answer she began rummaging in her large brown purse. From it she withdrew a bulky set of papers folded in thirds. It looked like a computer printout.

"What's that?" I asked.

"A list of all the late-model red Chevy pickups registered to owners in and residents of New Hampshire."

"The kind of truck Kmiec drove."

"He bought his, used, in 1985. It was a 1983 model."

"Uh-huh."

"So on this list I checked off the names of all the registered owners of 1983 red Chevy pickups that were on the road between 1986 and 1990."

"When the murders occurred."

"Right."

"How many names were there?"

"Twenty-seven, including Kmiec."

I nodded. "Go on."

"All right, twelve of them I was able to eliminate pretty much right off the bat, for a lot of reasons. You want me to go into them now?"

"No. Later you can, if it's necessary."

"So that left me with fifteen possibles. Some of the possibles look better to me than others. Like maybe five."

"I see."

"One of them, a guy named Robert Woodruff, lives right in Plaistow. Plus, he has a record."

"For what?"

"Aggravated assault."

"Against a woman?"

"His girlfriend. He went after her with an ax."

"God."

"Okay. And here's another one for you. Dell Washburn. No record, but a weirdo."

"In what way?"

"Oh, he's a spaced-out creep. And Dennis McCarry. Another peach. A convicted rapist. Served five years for that."

"Nice."

"Okay, and we got Richard LeFleur and Paul Herrick. LeFleur was picked up once in Concord on a porn-distribution charge. Herrick was a suspect in a child molestation case in Franklin."

"How much backtracking have you done on these guys?"

"Basically what I've told you. I'm still working on it."

"In your free time?"

She nodded.

"Can any of these guys account for his whereabouts the night Cheryl was murdered?"

"Nothing I've been able to verify. *Yet.*"

"Were they investigated by the . . . the other detectives?"

Her face went hard again. "In a half-assed way. The cops already knew who their man was."

"Kmiec."

"Kmiec."

"You're really convinced the investigation of the New Hampshire murders was . . . inadequate, aren't you? Not just your sister's, but the others'. Denise Michaud's and Carolyn Bragg's."

"That's what I think."

"Well, what about the Massachusetts murders?"

She shrugged.

"What about the two Boston women Kmiec initially confessed to killing? Maria Acosta and Carla Whitlow? And the one he attacked? Keisha Madison? There was a lot of physical evidence to connect him to those crimes."

"I think he *did* do *them.*"

"But not the seven murders before them."

"Well, he didn't kill Cheryl, that's for sure. And not Lisa Goodenough, either, from what you say."

"Then why did he say he did?"

Marian was silent, gazing at me. Then she said, "New Hampshire has no Son of Sam law."

I had been leaning forward in my chair. Now I sagged backward. "Of course. So theoretically Kmiec could literally profit from his crimes. Or what he *claimed* were his crimes."

"That's why he wants Marcus to do the book, isn't it?"

I grimaced. "He thinks it will make him a star. He even asked Marcus one day who Marcus thought should play him in the mini-series that'll get made of the book."

"Is Marcus paying him?"

"God, no."

"Is there anything to stop Kmiec from selling his story elsewhere?"

I bit my lip. "I'm not sure. I don't ... I can't say what deals could be worked out independent of the book Marcus is doing. I suppose something could."

"Well, maybe Kmiec thinks he can peddle his bullshit to the movies."

"He might think that."

"If he did, he could make a bundle, couldn't he?"

"Well ... maybe," I said. "It depends on what your idea of a bundle is. A movie or TV company might pay him two thousand dollars for an option. With a camera-roll fee to follow."

"A what?"

"*If* production actually began on a mini-series or a movie about him, they'd follow up the two grand with more money. Up to a hundred thousand, I suppose. That's a camera-roll fee."

"Jesus," Marian said. "What's Kmiec think he can do with that kind of bread in Walpole?"

I was tempted to say, *Spend it in Vegas while he's on a weekend furlough from prison,* but I didn't. this was no time for tacky jokes about the laxity of the Massachusetts correctional system.

My mind flashed back three weeks, to the scene inside Edith Kmiec's trailer. What was it, exactly, that she'd said about her son?

Henry's a good boy. He's away now. But he'll be back soon. He'll take care of me then. I know he will. He said. He said he'd take care of me.

"Maybe he wants the money to give to his mom for her old age," I said.

"It's happened before. Hard as it is to believe that a crud like Kmiec could have family feelings."

"Yes, I know." And I did. A lot of Boston cops believe that the real reason Albert DeSalvo confessed to being the Boston Strangler was for the money entailed by the rights to his story. Money he could pass on to his wife and kids for their support, since he was going to be in prison for the rest of his life anyway on a variety of non-Strangler-related sex-crimes charges.

There's no such thing as a bad boy.

"All right," I said to Marian Sandoval. "All right. Where do you want to go from here?"

TWENTY-FIVE

The afternoon was gray and chilly, and there was a smell of impending snow in the air. Nonetheless, Marian and I left the hotel and walked down JFK Street to the river. We crossed Storrow Drive by the Larz Anderson Bridge and skirted around the Weld Boathouse to the riverbank. The Charles looked dirty and cold, which it was. Across the way the buildings of the Harvard Business School massed together in red brick mutual congratulation.

"Tell me about Cheryl," I said. "All I know about her was that she was a lovely-looking girl."

"She was," Marian said. She kicked at a stone lying in her path and sent it skittering into the river. It hit the water with a dispirited plop. "She was the baby of the family."

"Are you the oldest?"

Marian nodded.

"How many between you and Cheryl?"

"Three boys. Well, two really. One of my brothers died when he was eighteen months old."

"I'm sorry."

She nodded. "He would have been, oh, twenty if he'd lived. Cheryl was sort of his replacement, I guess."

And they'd lost the replacement. I flinched inside my parka. Why did the burden of tragedy fall so heavily and so indiscriminately? Of course, Charles and Julia Timmons didn't want to talk about Cheryl, to me or to Marcus or to anyone else. What could they possibly have to say?

"Cheri was a good kid," Marian said. "Happy. Smart. Always did well in school."

"What were her plans?"

"Well, college, first. She was thinking about law school afterward." Marian smiled very briefly. "She wanted to be a federal prosecutor."

"No kidding. Did she do a lot of reading about the law and the criminal justice system in her spare time?"

"Tons."

"She must have been fascinated by your job."

"She was. She was always after me to take her to court with me when I had to testify."

"Did you?"

"Sometimes." Marian was quiet for a moment. "I wish now it had been more often."

I remembered something else from Marcus's book proposal. "You have a cousin who's an A.D.A. for Essex County, don't you?"

She nodded. "Joe Stearns. My mother's younger sister's son."

"Cheryl must have spent a lot of time with him."

"Whenever she could."

"Have you approached him with your doubts about Kmiec?"

Marian nodded again, somewhat stiffly.

"And?"

"He's bought into the whole Kmiec thing, too. Bastard. He and I don't talk much anymore."

"I see. Well, let's get back to Cheryl. Tell me more. You say she was happy. Did she have lots of friends?"

"Loads. She was real popular."

"Boyfriends?"

"A couple. They seemed like okay guys to me. I never really met them but once or twice. My parents thought they were all right. Though I guess my dad probably didn't think anyone was good enough for her."

I recalled Marcus fretting over Leah. "That seems to be pretty much a universal condition."

We passed the Weeks Bridge and continued downriver.

"Marian," I said. "This is a hard question I'm going to ask."

She looked at me.

"Could Cheryl have had a fight with her boyfriend, whoever she was going with at the time she died, and he—"

"Killed her?"

"Yes. You of all people would know how often that happens."

"Yes, I do."

"Well?"

"No. It wasn't Cheryl's boyfriend. He was away that night, out of the state, on a school trip somewhere."

"I see. What about a past boyfriend?"

She shook her head.

"You sure?"

"Yes."

"You investigated this?"

"Of course," she said, with a kind of tired exasperation.

"Okay."

We'd walked about a mile. The cloud cover had seemed to lower and darken, and the damp chill in the air had sharpened. Time to head back to a warmer environment.

We crossed Storrow Drive and started down the sidewalk that ran along in front of the Harvard houses, Dunster, Leverett, Winthrop, and Eliot.

"Tell me about yourself," I said.

"What do you want to know?"

"Are you married?"

"I was. We got divorced about three years ago."

"Was your husband a cop, too?"

"No. A salesman."

"It's none of my business and you can tell me to go jump in the river if you'd like, but—what happened?"

"He didn't like my job."

"The danger of it?"

She shrugged. "That was part of it, I guess. But not a real big part. Mostly he didn't like my hours."

I nodded. I knew all about that situation, from both sides, didn't I?

"What he really didn't like, though, was me being in a cruiser with another guy for eight hours."

"Right." Something else I knew about now. Jealousy. "Was it a bad divorce?"

"You ever hear of a good one?"

I laughed shortly. "Stupid question. I withdraw it."

By the time we got back to the hotel, we were both shivering. An early February day in Massachusetts not only gets under your skin, it gets into your bones.

It was four-thirty. Close enough to the cocktail hour.

"Would you like a drink?" I asked. "In order to defrost?"

"No. I have an hour-and-a-half-drive. Through rush-hour traffic."

"Sure. Well . . ." I held out my hand. "Good to meet you."

"You too."

We shook. And then we stood looking at each other for a moment.

"Are you with me on this?" Marian said.

I took a deep breath. "Yeah. I'm with you."

I had breakfast with Marcus in the suite the next morning. Over cantaloupe and crepes, I told him about Marian Sandoval. He listened attentively, which I assumed he would. Then he proceeded to pick apart all the evidence Marian had gathered, which I also assumed he would.

The first point he attacked was Joseph DeWitt's account of Kmiec's drinking habits. Then he went after the Jimmy Mac's bartender's assertion that Kmiec had been guzzling beer in his establishment the entire evening of January 22, 1990.

"How the hell could he remember that far back, to an exact day?" Marcus shook his head and ate some scrambled egg. "I'm not saying Sandoval isn't a good investigator—I'm sure she is—but she was probably feeding the bartender his lines. Maybe without even knowing she was doing it."

"She seemed pretty thorough and conscientious with me, Griffin."

"I'm not denying that. But, Liz—she is not exactly an objective party here. She obviously has a very heavy emotional investment in seeing Cheryl's killer caught.

And maybe feels that she as a cop ought to be the one to do the catching."

I sighed. "What about the five guys with red Chevy pickups and police records? Well, four of them have police records. The fifth, Dell Washburn, is just an unsavory character."

"They may be all degenerate scum. They sound like it. But that doesn't make them serial killers. Did Sandoval have anything else concrete on them?"

"No," I admitted.

Marcus raised his eyebrows. "Well, then?"

"Yeah."

"Still, I'd like you to maintain the contact with her."

"That's good, because I already promised her I would."

He grinned at me. "She'll be a great background source. And what a subplot, you know? Sister of murdered girl tries to catch killer. She sounds like a fascinating character, all moody and tetchy and vengeance-driven."

"Uh-huh. I don't think she thinks of herself as the heroine in a mini-series, Griffin."

"Oh, fuck, I didn't mean *that.*"

"Sure."

"She really opened up to you, huh?"

"Seemed like it."

"You're good at that. Getting people to open up."

"Must be because I'm such a nice girl."

He laughed. "Liz?"

"Yes?"

He drank some coffee. "You sound pretty impressed with Sandoval."

"I was."

"She convert you to her point of view?"

"Oh, for Christ's sake, Griffin. I think the issues she raised bear some closer examination, that's all."

"Okay, okay." He set down his cup. "Calm down."

I ate some cantaloupe. Then I said, "How was New York?"

"How would I know? I spent the entire day cooped up with two lawyers and three accountants."

"So the production company's really getting off the ground, then."

"Looks like it."

"Congratulations."

"Thanks."

"*Oh.*" I put down my fork. "Speaking of movie stuff—guess who's staying here in the hotel?"

"Cecil B. DeMille."

"He's dead. No. Candice Bergen."

Marcus's eyebrows went up again. "Candy's here?"

I looked at him. "*Candy?*"

He looked puzzled. "What's wrong?"

"Nothing. Is she a friend of yours?"

"Well, I know her."

"And you're having breakfast with *me?*"

"She already had a date."

I giggled. "I can live with being second choice. What are we doing today?"

"Don't we have to compare notes on the Kmiec interview?"

"That's right." I reached for my purse. "Got mine right here."

"Great. Well, let's trade and get to it."

The rest of the weekend passed quietly. It was the first one I'd spent without Jack in I couldn't recall how long. It felt odd and lonely having that time and space to myself. I invented errands and projects to keep me occupied so I wouldn't feel worse than just odd and lonely.

I wondered what he was doing.

Although I was only slightly less sure than Marcus that Henry Kmiec was the Merrimack Valley Killer, I was nevertheless nettled that Marcus had so easily dismissed Marian Sandoval's opposing conviction. Her doubts cast enough of a shadow to be taken seriously.

And hadn't I told her I'd help her? Didn't that mean giving her the benefit of the doubt?

Monday morning, while Marcus was off reinterviewing Kmiec's high school guidance counselor, I called a woman I know, Ellen Davis, who works at the Harvard Observatory.

Kmiec had said that the night he'd killed Linda Tessier had been "real nice," with a visible moon. It would be interesting, I thought, to see how closely his memory corresponded to reality.

A lab assistant put me on hold and went to locate Ellen. It took several minutes. When she came to the phone, I said, "It's Liz. Sorry to drag you away from your astrological chart or whatever."

She snorted and said, "What's up?"

"I have a question for you."

"What's that?"

"Can you tell me what the climate conditions were the night of December 7, 1989?"

"Where? In Sri Lanka?"

"Funny. No. Right here. In the Merrimack Valley. Specifically, the Methuen area."

"All right. Can I get back to you in about an hour?"

"Of course. Talk to you later." I gave her the number at the Charles Hotel.

It was more like an hour and a half before she called.

"Liz?"

"Uh-huh."

"Okay, the night of December 7, 1989, in the Merrimack Valley region, specifically the Methuen-Lawrence-Andover-North Andover area, we had dense cloud cover."

"No moon visible?" I cut in sharply.

"Maybe if you had X-ray eyes. Shall I go on?"

"Yes, yes."

"Low dense cloud cover with intermittent snow from about five P.M. to eight P.M. Around eight P.M., the snow became steady and heavier. It tapered off around midnight. Temperature was hovering around—oh, you don't understand Celsius, do you?"

"Who does?"

"It was around thirty degrees Fahrenheit."

"I see."

Didn't sound like a real nice night by most people's standards.

"Anything else?" Ellen asked.

"No," I said. "Thanks, though. Thanks a lot."

"Anytime. Is this for an article?"

"Sort of."

"Do I get a credit?"

"I'll ask my coauthor."

"Gee, thanks. 'Bye."

" 'Bye."

I hung up the phone. "Son of a bitch," I said.

I was waiting to lob this latest discrepancy at Marcus as soon as he walked in the suite. I didn't. The expression on his face—and the lack of color in it—silenced me. He stood just inside the door staring in my direction. Then he took off his coat and let it slide to the floor.

"Griffin?" I said. "Is something wrong?"

He rubbed his forehead, hard. "You could say that, yeah."

"What?"

"Kmiec is dead."

"What?"

"They found him hanging in his cell this afternoon."

TWENTY-SIX

It was seven that evening, and Marcus and I were sitting in the Quiet Bar with Daniel Tucker.

"So what the hell happened, Dan?" Marcus was saying.

Tucker shook his head. He looked exhausted. The lower lids of his pale blue eyes were pouched and dark. "I don't know," he said. "I just don't know."

"I thought the prison authorities were supposed to be keeping a special watch on Kmiec. To keep something like this from happening."

"Did he really commit suicide?" I said.

Both men looked at me sharply. I shrugged. "Logical question, isn't it?"

"The first one *I* asked." Tucker wiped a hand over his face.

"Well? *Could* he have been murdered by some of the other inmates?"

"Possible, I guess," Tucker said. "Although if those guys are going to cancel somebody's ticket, they usually aren't so neat about it."

"I suppose."

Serial killers and child molesters and the most vicious

multiple rapists were always getting murdered—or perhaps executed—by their co-felons. And the co-felons weren't merciful in carrying out the death sentence. About fifteen years before, a guy had been sent to Walpole after having been convicted of raping and murdering three five-year-old boys. Four guys in his cell block jumped him one night. First they poured Drāno down his throat. Then they went at him with a hedge clipper. They each took turns.

"Kmiec hung himself, then?"

"Pending the outcome of the investigation, I'd guess yeah, he did," Tucker said. "There was no sign anybody helped him."

"How'd he do it?"

"Tore his shirt into strips. Braided the pieces together into a rope. Made a noose. That's what it looks like, anyway."

"God."

"But *why?*" Marcus said. "Why, godamnit? Why'd he have a fit of—what? Remorse? Guilt? What? Why'd he have that *now?*"

"Who knows?" Tucker said. "All I can tell you is, we see it all the time. For a lot less reason than Kmiec had. A guy gets picked up for a moving violation and he takes the pipe."

"Shit," Marcus said feelingly. Tucker drank some beer.

"Now what?" I said.

Tucker gave me a curious glance.

"Does this mean that the investigation into the Merrimack Valley killing is over? Now that the chief suspect is dead?"

Tucker nursed his beer. Then he set the glass on the marble-topped table. "I can't speak for the Massachusetts end of things. Up my way, it's the attorney general's decision."

Translated, that probably meant, *Yes, we're closing the books on this one. Unofficially, anyway.*

I wondered what Marian Sandoval was thinking now. We hadn't spoken since the day we'd met. Maybe she was off pursuing her own lines of inquiry.

"Liz seems to think there's a little doubt about Kmiec's guilt," Marcus said.

Oh, thanks, pal.

Tucker looked at me with a glimmer of interest. "Really?"

"Griffin's pulling your leg," I said. "I—and someone else—just picked up on a few discrepancies in Kmiec's story, that's all."

"Yeah? Like what?"

I couldn't see any harm in telling him, now that Marcus had put me in the position of almost having to.

When I finished, Tucker said, "Interesting. Who's the other person you say noticed this stuff too?"

"Cheryl Timmons's sister," Marcus said. "A Portsmouth cop named Marian Sandoval."

"I know her," Tucker said. "I've met her, anyway. Good police officer, I think."

"But maybe on the wrong track here," Marcus said.

"I can understand her situation exactly," Tucker said. There was a very slight edge to his voice, as if he were subtly reproving Marcus for having been cavalier at Marian's expense.

I liked him for that.

Marcus had the sensitivity to catch the reproof. And the grace to look uncomfortable.

"You going to keep on hunting for your discrepancies?" Tucker asked.

"I think it's worthwhile," I said.

He nodded. "You never know what might turn up." He gave me a tired smile. "But, Liz, I got to say—"

"I know, I know. Chances are ninety-nine out of a hundred that Kmiec is the killer."

"Sure seems that way to me."

"I like to be thorough."

"Tell me about it." Tucker finished his beer. "You give Marian my best when you see her. I liked her. I respect what she's doing. She probably isn't too crazy about me, though. Day she came to see me, I kind of brushed her off. Not because I wanted to, but because I had an assistant A.G. breathing down the back of my neck."

"I'll tell her."

"Do that." He rose.

"Hey, I thought you were going to join us for dinner," Marcus protested.

Tucker shook his head. "I'll take a raincheck. I need to get back now."

Marcus shrugged. "If you have to . . ."

We both shook hands with Tucker, and he left. Marcus and I watched him walk out of the bar, a middle-aged man of medium height and wiry build and unassuming manner. Yet it all added up to an impressive presence.

"Nice guy," I said.

"Yeah." Marcus lit a cigarette. "I think he's relieved Kmiec is dead, though. In a way."

"Oh? Why?"

"Pressure of the investigation was getting to him. Maybe now he can move on to something else."

I nodded. "Well—do you still want to have dinner

out? Even though our guest has bowed out of the picture?"

"Sure."

"Where?"

"How about that trendy place you took me to?"

"The Harvest?"

"Yeah, that. It's close by."

"All right."

We glanced at each other. The same thought, or recollection actually, must have struck us simultaneously:
what had gone on in Marcus's suite after we'd had dinner at the Harvest.

There was a silence that on my end at least felt awkward.

Marcus broke it. "Don't worry," he said. "I'm too
goddamn tired to be horny. Your virtue's safe with me."

I laughed.

"Anyway," Marcus continued. "I think you're still
spoken for, aren't you?"

I stopped laughing.

"I don't know," I said.

He gave me an odd, probing look. "You are," he said.

The dinner was very good, although I caught a
glimpse of the check when it arrived and paying it
would have put a major crimp in my pleasure. The total
was $197.65. Marcus acted like it was $4.37 for a BK
Broiler, large fries, and medium Coke at the East Somerville Burger King in Union Square.

Marcus and I walked back to the hotel afterward. It
would have been a replay of that other night, except that
we went to the parking garage instead of his suite. He
drove me home.

Lucy met me at the door with a big grin and a thrashing tail. When I'd realized I was going to be out fairly late, I'd called my neighbor, Sue McCreary, and asked her to feed the dog and let her out for her 6:00 P.M. backyard patrol. I watered Sue's Brazilian rain forest of house plants and retrieved her mail and newspapers when she was off on a buying trip for the pottery-and-crafts business she owned. A good arrangement. She didn't have to feel guilty about abandoning her aspidistra, and I didn't have to feel guilty about neglecting my dog.

I had a few phone messages. None from Jack. It felt strange and sad not to hear his voice in mechanical playback. We had liked to do that—leave joking or sexy messages on each other's machines. We had in fact a complicated running routine involving him being Stud-in-Chief of something called Dial-a-Hunk Phone Phantasies.

My mail was mostly bills. Whoop-de-do.

I switched on the television to catch the eleven o'clock news. The lead story was about the death of Henry Kmiec. I didn't hear anything I didn't already know. Then there was something about a fight in the Boston City Council. (So what else was new?) National and world news followed. The Serbs and the Croats were shooting at each other yet again.

The anchorwoman said, "And on the New England Newsline, a grim discovery was made late this afternoon by a woman out walking her dog in Newburyport. For details, we go to Sheila McAndrew at the scene."

The image of the anchor at her desk flickered into the ether and was replaced by that of a blond woman, microphone in hand, standing in what looked like a field. Behind her was a body of water.

"Tricia," she began. "I'm talking to you from the scene, where, at five this afternoon, the body of twenty-eight-year-old Joanne Parisi, a Newburyport resident, was found. Police are releasing few details, but Newscenter Five has learned that Parisi was stabbed multiple times in the neck and chest area. The body was discovered by one of Parisi's neighbors, who is refusing to speak with anyone from the media. We have no knowledge yet whether Parisi was brought here and killed or killed elsewhere and transported here later. We *do* know that the body was located approximately ten yards from the north bank of the Merrimack River. . . ."

TWENTY-SEVEN

Marian Sandoval called me at seven-thirty the following morning. I was awake. I hadn't been able to sleep much. I'm sure she hadn't, either.

"You heard?" she said.

"Yes." I'd already read the accounts of the murder in the *Globe* and the *Herald*.

"Marian," I said. "I know. This is really raw. But let's try to stay calm. It *is* possible this has nothing to do with the murder of Cheryl and the other six women."

"Jesus! Do you—"

"Marian! Listen to me! You have got to calm down. Look, do you know anyone in the Newburyport Police Department?"

"No."

"Shit." I drummed my fingers on the telephone table. "What we need are verifying details. Was Parisi tied up in duct tape? Did she have a green ribbon in a bow around her neck? Can you find that out through your other cop contacts?"

"I don't know," she replied. "I'm not exactly on friendly terms with a lot of them anymore. They think I'm a pain in the ass."

"Shit," I repeated. "Damn. Marian, let me do a little more checking on my end."

"With who? Marcus? He'll tell you it was somebody imitating Kmiec."

"Marian, will you stop yelling at me? Please?"

"Sorry."

"Okay. Look. I *am* taking this very seriously. Would you please believe that? Now—I'll find out what I can. You do the same. I'll call you this afternoon. Will you be in?"

"If I'm not, leave a message and I'll get right back to you. But call my home number *only.*"

"Okay. Talk to you later."

I hung up the phone. Then I took off for the Charles Hotel.

Marcus wasn't in the suite. Nor was he in the hotel restaurant. I was so annoyed and frustrated I almost punched a hole in the blond wood paneling of the lobby.

Instead I reread the *Globe* and *Herald* articles about the murder of Joanne Parisi. The details were sketchy.

I refolded the papers and put them in my bag. The guy who'd written the *Herald* story I knew pretty well. He also owed me a favor. I could call him and ask if he had any additional information. Or speculation. Or rumor. *Anything.*

He wasn't at his desk. I left a message that I'd call back later. Then I called the Newburyport Police Department. After about five minutes I got put through to a detective named Roberts. I identified myself and explained what I was doing and what I wanted. He said he had no additional comment to make about the Parisi killing beyond what had appeared in the papers. Exactly what I thought he'd say. But had to make the effort. I requested he send me a copy of the initial police report, something I could legitimately do since it was part of the public record. Roberts said he would. I decided not to hold my breath until he did.

Then I went for a walk. There wasn't much else I could do at the moment.

When I checked Marcus's suite again at ten o'clock, he was there, drinking coffee and eating a muffin.

"Hi," he said. He gestured at the room service cart. "Get you something?"

I stared at him. "Did you catch the news?"

"Sure."

"Well?"

He put down the muffin and wiped his hands on a napkin. "It was awful."

"It might be somewhat more than that, Griffin. That woman was stabbed, and I quote, 'multiple times in the chest and throat and left by a bank of the Merrimack River.' Sound familiar?"

"Boy, you're in fine fettle this A.M. Sit down and have some coffee."

"Griffin!"

He looked at me very steadily. "You think I haven't been out inquiring about this since the crack of dawn? I bet I've been up longer than you have working on it."

I took a deep breath. "Okay. Sorry." I went to the room service cart and poured myself some coffee. I moved some file folders off an easy chair and sat down in it. "What have you found out?"

"Joanne Parisi had no green ribbon around her neck."

"I see."

"And she wasn't tied up in duct tape."

"Uh-huh. Where'd you get this information?"

"Tucker."

"Really?"

"Really. You think he's not in on something like this from the word go?"

"They brought him in as a consultant?"

"Well, of course. You don't think they noticed the similarities you did?"

"Do they have any idea who killed her?"

Marcus shrugged. "It may have been an imitative thing. God knows there's been enough about Kmiec in the papers and on TV to inspire some degenerate dipshit to go out and . . . you know."

"Do you think that's what it was?"

"No."

"What, then?"

Marcus sighed. "I think she was killed by a drug dealer."

I set my cup in its saucer. "She welched on some payments?"

"No. She had testified against this guy about five years ago. After he was convicted, he swore up and down he'd get her when he got out of the joint. He was paroled two weeks ago. And—guess what?"

"What?"

"When the cops went looking for him yesterday, they couldn't find him."

"I see."

"This guy—his name is Dominguez—has a reputation for being incredibly violent. And now he seems to have jumped parole."

"How many times was Joanne stabbed?"

"About fifteen."

I shook my head.

"Fewer cuts than Kmiec liked to make," Marcus said.

I looked at him. "But sufficient to do the job."

"Oh, yes."

Marian very grudgingly accepted the possibility that Joanne Parisi's murder might not have had anything to do with her sister's. She gave me a lot of argument about it, though. I was beginning to feel like a dual personality, acting as her devil's advocate to Marcus and his to her.

"Maybe," Marian said, "Parisi didn't have any green ribbon around her neck because the killer was disturbed by something, a noise that startled him, say, or a car going by, and he had to hurry so he wouldn't be caught."

"Could be," I said noncommittally. "Why do you think he didn't tape her up, though?"

"Same reason, more or less. No time."

It was that afternoon. Marian had picked me up at my place an hour and a half after I'd phoned her. We were on Route 93, heading to Manchester. I had a few questions I wanted to ask Joseph DeWitt. Marian wasn't happy with that plan, but I insisted loudly enough to overrule her objections.

If DeWitt was surprised to see the two of us together, he didn't show it. But then, he didn't show much to anything. I was beginning to think, however, that he was a lot shrewder and a lot more observant than Marcus had given him credit for.

When we arrived, he was coming down the sidewalk carrying a paper bag of what was probably groceries. We caught up with him as he was letting himself into the house. He allowed us to follow him down the hall to the kitchen. At least, he didn't tell us we couldn't. We sat at the table while he moved around the kitchen put-

ting away cans of soup and beans and tuna and pack-
ages of dry cereal and instant mashed potatoes.

On the ride up, I had wondered aloud why DeWitt
was always at home when one of us came to see him.
Marian had run a brief background check on him and
learned that he'd been injured on the job in a Manchester mill ten years ago and been collecting Social Security ever since.

DeWitt folded the empty paper bag very neatly and
put it in a cabinet next to the stove. Then he joined us
at the table.

I also wondered why he was apparently so willing to
put up with these repeat interrogations about Henry
Kmiec. Then it occurred to me that in his remote way,
he might find them entertaining. Better than daytime
television, anyhow.

I took him through the story he'd told Marian about
Kmiec's drinking habits. I couldn't shake him on any
points. In his laconic way, he was very definite.

Marian sat with her arms folded across her chest,
looking bored and a little impatient. I ignored her.

"So," I said. "Jimmy Mac's in Keene was one of
Henry's regular Monday-night places, is that correct?"

"Yup."

"He told you that?"

DeWitt gave his soft crackle of a laugh. "Tried to get
me to go with him one night."

"Did you?"

DeWitt just looked at me. I supposed that meant no.

I put away my notebook and glanced at Marian. "I
guess that wraps it up."

She rolled her eyes and started to get up from the table. When we were back in the car, I knew she'd ha-
rangue me for wasting her time. What she really was

was insulted that I'd cross-checked the story she'd gotten from DeWitt. Just as I'd been miffed when Marcus had cross-checked the fire story *I'd* gotten from DeWitt.

The thought of Marcus reminded me of something that had been bothering me ever since my first extended conversation with Marian.

"Mr. DeWitt?"

"Yuh?"

"Why didn't you tell Griffin Marcus and me these things about Henry the first time we came to see you? You in fact told us you *didn't* know where Henry spent his evenings."

He shrugged.

"Mr. DeWitt."

He stared at me with no particular expression on his face. Then he said, "Didn't like that Marcus."

"Really? Why not?"

"He's a pushy bastard."

For the first time that afternoon, Marian smiled.

TWENTY-EIGHT

The pushy bastard and I had a quick breakfast together the following morning. Then he went off to interview the parents and ex-husband of Denise Michaud, the second of the Merrimack Valley Killer's victims. Marcus gave me his blessing to join Marian in tracking down Richard LeFleur, one of *her* prime suspects for the murder of Cheryl and the other six women. "Fantastic subplot for the book," he kept maintaining.

LeFleur was the thirty-one-year-old sleazeball from Concord who not only drove a 1983 red Chevy pickup but who had been arrested a few years earlier in the bust-up of a pornography ring. The porn wasn't the usual tacky trash like *Big-Boobed Blondes* or *Hung Like a Horse*. No. Three quarters of it was child pornography, with titles like *Six Men and a Baby*. The other quarter consisted of snuff films with adult female victims. It was, one of the FBI agents involved in the case later told a reporter, the worst filth he'd ever seen: "I couldn't eat or sleep for a week afterward."

LeFleur hadn't been one of the kingpins in the operation—more of a gofer, really. He had, however, turned state's evidence and the charges against him had been dropped in 1988. The producers and distributors were convicted and sent to prison.

It was about an hour-and-fifteen-minute drive from Cambridge to Concord. I used the time to read through the file of material Marian had accumulated on LeFleur.

His arrest on the pornography charge hadn't been his first. In 1980, he'd been picked up for car theft; in 1982, for the illegal sale of fireworks; in 1984, for breaking and entering; in 1985, for assault and battery with a dangerous weapon. He'd served a one-year prison term for that. A busy boy.

His employment record was sporadic, to say the least. When he worked, it was on a loading dock somewhere. He got fired a lot. He lived with—and probably off of—a string of women. Along the way, he'd fathered two children. Except for that, his personal history was a lot like Henry Kmiec's. Scum will be scum.

"Marian?"

"Yes?"

"Does LeFleur have any record of violence against women? I mean, apart from the fact that he was on the fringes of an operation that made movies about killing them?"

"He sent his last girlfriend to the hospital with a broken jaw and two cracked ribs."

"God. Did she press charges against him?"

"No."

I sighed.

"She's the one we're going to see today," Marian said. "LeFleur was living with her when Cheryl died. That's the address I have for him, anyway."

"What's her name?"

"Grace Hapgood."

"What's her story?"

"Pathetic. You'll see."

"Why is she willing to talk to a cop and a writer about LeFleur?"

Marian made a face. "Probably wants to tell us what a swell guy he is, despite the fact that she spent three weeks in the hospital because of him."

"One of those, huh?"

"Yes."

A few years ago I'd done an article on battered wives and girlfriends. One of the women I'd interviewed had her arm in a sling and a turbanlike bandage around her head. Her upper lip was held together with a crisscross of dark thread. The flesh above it was swollen and purplish-yellow.

"Why'd you let him do this to you?" I'd asked.

She'd looked at me with dull incomprehension. Then she'd replied, "He's my husband. He has the right."

What appalled me was the number of other women I'd spoken to who'd said much the same thing, in mostly the same words.

Grace Hapgood's apartment was in a gray frame three-decker in one of Concord's less select neighborhoods. The street was part residential, part industrial, part boarded-up, and completely rundown. Concord, like Manchester, was originally a mill town. When the shoe and textile businesses had moved south, many of the old factory buildings had been left abandoned. In recent years they'd been turned into condos or office parks or malls with crafts boutiques and hanging-plant restaurants. Not on this street, though.

Marian found a place to park in front of a low red-brick structure that had once been a tannery.

"Have you ever noticed," I said, "that your business and mine don't often take us to the garden spots?"

"Plenty of times," she said.

Shabby as Grace Hapgood's building was, at least it had a working buzzer and intercom system. Not that either mattered for security purposes; the front door was unlatched and slightly ajar. In the foyer, a rusted bicycle frame rested against one wall. The lighting fixture in the ceiling had been removed, exposing a tangle of wires. The floor looked as if it had last been swept during the Carter administration.

"She's on the third," Marian said.

We groped our way up a dim and creaky flight of stairs.

"Apartment seven," Marian said.

I could hear a baby wailing. The air was stale.

Marian knocked on the apartment door. The volume of the child's cries increased.

"How many kids does she have?" I asked.

"Three."

"Is LeFleur the father of any of them?"

"The youngest, I think."

The apartment door opened, and a thin woman in jeans and a pink T-shirt peered out at us. Her hair was a lank light brown scraped back from a center parting into a ponytail. The bridge of her nose had a slight indentation, as if it had once been broken. The skin beneath her eyes was puffed and grayish. Elsewhere it was sallow.

Marian introduced herself and me.

"Oh hi," the woman said. "Yeah. You wanna come in?" She opened the door wider.

We walked into a boxy living room that looked as if it had been furnished by things left out on the street for trash collection. A cot with a maroon chenille spread and two green-and-white-print throw pillows did service as a couch. Half of it was taken up by a pile of folded laundry and a large opened bag of disposable diapers. The floor was a yellowish speckled linoleum. On it sat a skinny boy, perhaps four or five, gazing raptly at the small color television on a card table in the corner. On the TV screen some cartoon character cavorted.

The baby's fretful wail rose to a screech.

"Fuck it," Grace Hapgood muttered, and left the room.

"Hi," I said to the kid on the floor. He didn't respond. His feet were bare and, I noticed, cold-looking.

The screeching in the other room subsided.

Marian stood with her hands in her pockets, surveying the place. She was wearing her cop face: expressionless.

Grace Hapgood returned with an infant cradled in her left arm. The baby wore a graying yellow blanket sleeper and sucked on a pacifier. Grace sat down on the empty part of the cot/sofa and jiggled the kid absently.

"Can we ask you some questions about Richard LeFleur?" I asked.

"Whaddaya wanna know?"

"Is he living here now?"

Grace shook her head.

"Has he been here recently?"

Grace looked at us both warily. "Has Richie done somethin'?"

"Not that I know of," Marian said pleasantly.

"I ain't seen him in a month."

"Do you know where he is?"

She shrugged. "At his mom's, maybe. He stays with her a lot."

"Where does his mother live?"

"Derry."

Marian sat down on the edge of a straight-backed wooden chair and opened her purse. She removed a small notebook and flipped back the cover. She checked something written on one page.

"Richie's recorded as living here between November of 1989 and March of 1991," she said. "Is that correct?"

Grace was quiet for a moment. The wariness was back on her face. She jiggled the baby with more energy.

"Richie's in trouble again, ain't he?" she asked flatly.

"Not with us," I said.

"Grace," Marian said patiently. "All we want to know for now is if Richie was living here between November of 1989 and March of 1991."

"He don't like me talking about him with no one," she mumbled.

Yet she'd agreed to do so before. Maybe she'd had a chance to think over the implications and gotten scared. LeFleur was the kind of guy who liked to use his fists on those who displeased him.

"He won't find out from us that you answered a few questions about him," I said. "That I promise."

Marian nodded.

The suspicion on the woman's face dissolved and reformed as stubbornness. "Why you wanna know about him?"

Marian glanced at me. On the drive up, she and I had prepared a scam in case one was necessary. Apparently it was.

"We think Richie may have been a witness to an auto accident in Manchester," I said.

"Yeah? So?"

"The insurance company I work for as an investigator has a big interest in finding out exactly what happened in this accident. Our party was badly injured." I paused. "We'd be willing to pay a thousand dollars for any information that might lead to a favorable settlement for our client."

When I'd finished speaking, I looked down at my nose to see how long it had grown. Not more than a centimeter.

"When was the accident?" Grace said.

"January 22, 1990," Marian said.

"Lemme think."

"Take your time."

Grace bent her head, her face puckered with concentration. I glanced at Marian. She was watching Grace very closely.

Grace Hapgood was obviously not smart. I hoped she wasn't stupid enough to lie to us. Would she try to scam the scammers in order to get the thousand dollars for LeFleur? I'd seen the flicker in her eyes when I'd mentioned the money.

Maybe she thought he'd give some of it to her. Illusion was all she had.

She raised her head. Then she shook it, dumbly.

"Grace?"

She hesitated, then sighed. "Richie wasn't livin' here then."

"Are you sure?" Marian said. "Not that January?"

Grace nodded, a gesture of resignation more than assent.

"Was he living with his mother in Derry?"

"No."

"Do you know where he was?"

"He tole me he was gonna go look for work."

"When was that?"

Grace scowled in thought. "Right after Christmas."

"Where'd he go?"

"He said he was goin' to California."

"Did he?"

Grace shrugged again, joggling the baby. "I guess."

"When did you see him again?"

"Oh, I dunno. I think it was like the enda February or somethin'."

"Was he in California that whole time?"

A strand of hair had come loose from her ponytail. She pushed it back behind her ear. "I guess. He sent me a postcard."

"What kind of work was he looking for in California, Grace?" Marian asked.

The woman gave a little snort of laughter. "Richie's like a dreamer, you know? He was gonna try and get somethin' with the movies."

I could imagine what kind of movies. "Did it work out for him?"

"Naw." Grace looked at me with sudden eagerness. "Richie, he's had some really rough times, see? He's really a mellow dude, you know? But people keep hasslin' him. He never gets the breaks."

It seemed to me that LeFleur had gotten a giant break when the pornography-distribution charges against him had been dropped. I didn't say so. I looked at the kid on the floor and the baby in Grace's arms. They were the same age as some of the victims in the movies LeFleur had helped put in circulation.

Grace had three children. So far I'd seen only two of them.

"Where's your other kid?" I asked abruptly.

Grace gave me a blank look. "Huh?"

"Where's your other child?"

"Oh. She's with my ma today."

Marian cut into the dialogue. "Grace, you're sure you didn't see Richie anytime in January 1990?"

"Yeah."

"Is there any possibility he could have been in New Hampshire or even New England then? Even if he wasn't here or in Derry?"

"I dunno."

"Please," Marian said urgently. *"Think.* It's important."

I frowned at her. The frown said, *Don't get so excited. Don't push.*

She and Marcus had more in common than she thought.

Then I had an idea.

"Grace," I said. "Did Richie drive to California?"

"What?"

"Did he take his truck to California? The red Chevy pickup?"

"Oh. No."

"How'd he get out there?"

"Took a plane. Borrowed the money from his ma."

"What'd he do with the truck?"

"Left it here. With me."

"I see. Did you drive it?"

"Yeah. Sometimes."

"Did anyone else?"

"Naw. Richie woulda killed me if he'da found out even I drove it."

"I see. Did you use the truck much?"

She laughed raspily. "How was I suppose to? It broke down right after he left. I hadda have it towed. Cost me an arm and a leg."

Marian leaned forward quickly. "Did you have it repaired?"

Grace gave her a look of weary scorn. "Where was I suppose to get the money?"

"What happened to the truck? Where'd they tow it?"

"Oh, Jesus. They left it here." She jerked her head in the direction of the street.

"How long was it out there?"

"Till Richie come home."

"And it was never moved in that time?"

"It couldn't go nowhere."

"So it just sat outside this house all January and February?"

"Yeah. I guess. What the hell difference does it make?"

A big one, if whoever had killed Cheryl Timmons had been driving a red 1983 pickup the night of the murder.

I looked at Marian. "Anything else?"

"No," she said. To Grace, she added, "Thanks for your help."

The television cartoon show ended. The boy got up from the floor, walked over to his mother, and leaned against her thigh. "I'm hungry."

"Yeah, yeah, in a minute, Jimmy," she said impatiently. The baby spat out the pacifier. Then it gave a choky little cry that sounded like the windup to a scream. Grace read the sign the way I did. "Oh, shit," she said under her breath.

I reached into my handbag for my wallet. I opened it and took out a twenty-dollar bill and put the money on the TV set.

"My company wants to repay you for your time," I said.

Marian stared at me.

I looked down at the boy's feet. "Maybe you can get him some shoes and socks."

"Oh, yeah," Grace said. "Yeah. I guess he needs 'em, huh? Thanks."

"Sure."

We were ready to go out the door when Marian stopped. She looked back at the woman on the cot. "Grace?"

"Huh?"

"When Richie came back from California and he found out the truck was broken, what did he do?"

Grace turned her head away from us. "Nothin'."

"Really? He wasn't mad?"

"No."

"You sure?"

"Well ..."

"Grace."

"Yeah." She fussed with the zipper on the baby's sleeper. "Yeah, I guess he was pissed at me."

"What'd he do?"

Grace shifted the baby to her right arm. "Well ... I guess he ... you know ... he slapped me around a little."

"He broke your jaw and ribs, didn't he?"

"Well ... I guess so." She raised her head. "But ... I mean ... you know ... he was like really pissed. I don't blame him. It was like my fault the truck got all fucked up, you know. I shouldna drove it after he tole me not to."

Marian inhaled raggedly. "Come on," she said to me. "Let's get the hell out of here."

* * *

Marcus was on the phone when I let myself into the suite. He gave me a brief distracted wave as I closed the door. "Yeah, I know, baby," he said. "Just be careful, that's all."

If there'd been someone to bet with, I'd have wagered a hundred dollars Marcus was talking to his daughter. I slipped out of my coat and draped it over the back of a chair.

"Okay," Marcus said. "Bye-bye, sweetie." He hung up the phone.

"So how's Leah?" I said.

Marcus looked half amused, half embarrassed. "Fine."

"Good. Tell me—do you make these persistent annoying phone calls to your son as well?"

"Andy's older. By almost five years."

"Oh? Yes?"

"And . . ."

"And what?"

"Well, he's . . ."

"A boy," I finished. "Correct?"

"Well . . ."

"You sexist."

Marcus gave me a sharp glance. I grinned at him and said, "Gotcha."

He laughed.

I sat down on the couch. Marcus joined me. He put his feet up on the coffee table and lit a cigarette. "How'd it go today?"

"Depressing," I said, and told him.

"Sounds like a swell time. Sorry I missed it."

"Well, I suppose it was useful, in the sense that Marian and I learned that LeFleur probably didn't kill Cheryl."

"How did Marian take that?"

"She accepted it. Anyhow, she has four other suspects she wants to check."

"I can eliminate two of them for her."

I frowned. "What?"

"Sure. Dennis McCarry and Paul Herrick. The rapist and the child molester."

I sat up straight and stared at Marcus. "Griffin, how—"

He interrupted me. "On the night of January 22, 1990, McCarry was in a jail cell in Vermont. He got picked up in White River Junction for drunk driving. At five P.M. He was in police custody until the next morning."

I was silent.

"Paul Herrick was in the Dartmouth-Hitchcock Medical Center in Dartmouth, New Hampshire, on January 22, 1990. He was admitted there on January twelfth and released on the thirtieth."

"Why was he in the hospital?"

"Got in a fight with a guy who pulled a knife on him."

"I see."

Marcus stubbed out his cigarette.

"You're sure of this," I said.

"Positive."

"Where'd you get the information?"

He smiled at me. "Oh, from a reliable source."

"Don't give me that reliable source bullshit," I said. I was suddenly quite angry. I could feel my face tighten and my mouth compress.

Marcus noticed. "What's wrong?" he said.

"I could have gotten that information myself," I said.

"Or Marian could have. Was it absolutely necessary for you to preempt us?"

"I saved you some time and effort."

"Yeah. Thanks."

"You're welcome," he said coolly.

"I'm sure Marian will want to do her own checking on Herrick and McCarry anyway."

Marcus put his hands behind his head. "You know something, Liz? I don't really give a good goddamn *what* Marian wants. In fact, the sooner you stop following her around on this wild-goose chase, the happier I'll be."

I gaped at him. "Excuse me? Excuse me? Griffin, I recall distinctly you telling me only this morning what a swell idea you thought this so-called wild-goose chase was."

He shrugged without moving his hands from behind his head. "What a difference a day makes."

I shook my head in disbelief.

Marcus took a deep breath. "Okay. All right. I'm sorry. Let's both calm down."

I didn't say anything.

Marcus lit another cigarette. "Look, Liz, all I meant was, I don't want you getting overinvested in a losing proposition, that's all. Marian's obsessed. I don't want you getting sucked into the obsession with her."

"So what do you suggest I do? Phone her up tonight and say, 'Sorry, pal. Marcus thinks you're a head case, so I'm bailing out'?"

He made an exasperated noise. "No, you know damn well that's not what I want you to do. I just want you to . . . pull back a little."

"Oh, humor her?"

Marcus closed his eyes briefly. "No. And you also

know damn well that's not what I mean, either. So knock it off."

I slumped back against the couch cushions. "Well, what *do* you mean?"

"Just what I said. Follow through with Marian on the last two guys on her list. What are their names, now?"

"Dell Washburn and Robert Woodruff."

"Yeah, right. Okay, you and she check their stories. Then, if she wants to continue after that, with whatever other list of suspects she may come up with, let her. But you should start to disengage. Stay in touch with her, but . . ."

"Yes?"

"As I said before, don't get overinvested."

I shrugged. "Don't worry about it."

"Okay. I won't."

My anger had diffused into a kind of weary irritation. And a feeling of futility. How could I argue with him further? He, after all, paid the piper. Didn't that entitle him to call the tune?

God, I was getting tired of being jerked back and forth between people. First between Marcus and Jack, then between Marian and Marcus. Where was I in all this?

It all turned out to be irrelevant in the end, because the next morning Marian Sandoval was dead. They found her lying in the entrance hall of her house in Portsmouth, two gunshot wounds in the heart.

TWENTY-NINE

"Okay," I raged to Marcus. "You explained away Joanne Parisi. Now explain away Marian."

"Jesus," Marcus said. He grabbed my forearms, pushed me back a few steps and down into a chair. "I'm not doing anything until you get hold of yourself."

"Griffin, Marian was murdered because she was too close to finding out who the real Merrimack Valley Killer was."

"Liz, she was murdered because she interrupted a burglary in her own home."

"Gee, what a neat coincidence, her getting killed that way."

Marcus drew a long breath. "The house was ransacked. Her jewelry was taken. So was the money in her purse, and some silver. And the CD player and the VCR."

"So? That could be a cover-up."

"Yes, it could. For anything. But in the absence of any information that points that way, I'm going to take it for what it looks like. A burglary gone wrong."

"There are no suspects."

"So what?" Marcus lit a cigarette. "Anyhow, we

don't *know* that there aren't. Maybe the Portsmouth cops and the New Hampshire State Police *do* have a suspect and they're not saying. My God, Liz. You know cops. They never tell everything they know or think."

"That's true."

He sat down in the chair across from me. He reached out and touched my knee with the hand that wasn't holding the cigarette. "Look, I know how you feel. Exactly. Remember that book I did on the murders in Rochester?"

"Yeah."

"Well, I had a source for that I got very close to." He paused, and then added, "Let's leave it that she died. Horribly."

I bit my lower lip. "I'm sorry."

"Yeah, so was I. Actually I was devastated."

I nodded.

"Is this the first time something like this has ever happened to you?"

"No." I looked away from him at the window. "It's the third or fourth."

His hand was still a warm pressure on my knee. "Doesn't get easier with repetition, does it?"

"No." I got up quickly. His hand fell away from my leg.

"What are you doing?" he asked.

"Going to go for a walk, by myself, for about half an hour," I said. "Pull myself together."

He looked up at me. "Okay. That's probably a good idea."

I shrugged into my jacket. He stubbed out his cigarette and rose. "I have some phone calls to make."

I zipped up the jacket. "When I get back, I'll be ready to work again."

He smiled at me. "I never doubted it for a minute."

Despite the gray chill of the day, Harvard Square was active. I walked on automatic pilot along the curve of Eliot Square and turned right onto John F. Kennedy. Down to the river. The last time I'd taken this route had been with Marian, the day I'd met her.

The weather had been the same, too. Sometimes things ended just as they'd begun.

I sat on a bench on the riverbank and looked at the sluggish gray water. Of course I wasn't really seeing it. I was watching mind movies of Marian and me and the things we'd done together in the brief time I'd known her.

The film didn't have a happy resolution. But I left the theater knowing what I had to do. And Marcus, by God, was going to help me.

I walked back up Kennedy Street, past Leverett House, the Boathouse Bar, the French café, the Spanish restaurant, the Thai restaurant, and the Mexican restaurant. Before I went back to Marcus, I wanted to stop at Out of Town News and buy the New Hampshire papers. I'd read the brief *Globe* and *Herald* accounts of Marian's death. Maybe the *Union-Leader* and the Portsmouth and Concord papers would have more details. Not that I needed them: I knew what I knew.

Out of Town News was mobbed, as it always was, with barely enough room to move in the aisles. I could

hardly open the door against the press of bodies. Jack
was in there, buying some magazines.

Seeing him for the first time since that Sunday afternoon in my apartment was like getting hit very hard in
the stomach. I stopped alongside a revolving rack of regional monthlies. What I wanted to do was hide. Or
walk away fast. But I couldn't move. I felt a little thick-
headed and dislocated.

He handed the kid at the cash register a ten-dollar
bill. While he was waiting for the change, he glanced
idly around the interior of the stand. His gaze swept
over me without pause. Then it halted by a display of
souvenir T-shirts and came back to me, focusing.

I was shaking. Someone jostled me from behind, hard
enough to push me one volitionless step forward.

The kid gave Jack his change and he pocketed it. We
were poised about five feet apart. He looked at me with
nothing particular in his face and said, "Hi."

"Hi." I was vaguely astonished I could speak.

"How's it going?" he said.

"All right. How about you?"

"Fine."

"Good."

He nodded. "Nice to see you." He gave me a faint
meaningless smile, the kind you give someone you've
met very briefly at a party and then bump into on the
subway a week later.

"Same here," I said.

He tucked the magazines under his arm. "Well, take
care."

"Sure. You too."

He left, and I stayed fixed where I was. I moved only
when I got elbowed—roughly—for the third time by a
guy trying to get to the skin-magazine rack. God forbid

I should delay his acquisition of this month's *Hooker*. I retrieved the New Hampshire papers and paid for them.

If I'd been a different kind of person, maybe I'd have run after Jack. Grabbed him by the arm, swung around in front of him, and yelled something at him.

As in . . . what?

You son of a bitch, don't treat me *like a stranger.*

Then again, maybe that was precisely what we had become to each other.

Being the person I was, I walked back to the hotel.

Marcus had ordered some coffee and sandwiches from room service.

"Good timing," he said to me as I entered the suite.

His tone was light, carefully so. He was looking at me in the same tentative way and trying to be unobtrusive about it. Checking to see if I'd pulled myself back together. I smiled to reassure him I had.

"Want some coffee?" he asked.

"Great."

He poured me a cup and set it on an end table. The solicitousness of the gesture amused me a little. I sat down in the chair by the end table and dropped the New Hampshire papers on the floor beside it.

"You never told me how your interview with Denise Michaud's parents and ex-husband went," I said. "Did you get good material?"

He was making himself some coffee and selecting a sandwich from the tray on the room service cart. If he was taken aback—or relieved—that I'd so quickly and apparently completely resumed my professional demeanor, he didn't show it. Then again, why should he be taken aback or relieved? He himself had said earlier that he had no doubt of my professionalism.

"Yeah," he said. "The interview went very well. At least Denise is more of a person to me now than a crime statistic."

I stirred my coffee.

"The parents were a little resistant at first," he continued. "But they ended up being very cooperative. The ex-husband was sort of hostile."

"Why?"

Marcus shrugged. "Not sure, really. My best guess is that he was afraid I'd portray *him* unfavorably."

"And will you?"

He grinned. "It's a temptation. He *is* kind of an oaf. And stupid. I'm not surprised Denise left him. I'm kind of surprised she took up with him to begin with, though."

"Why?"

"Well"—coffee cup in one hand, sandwich plate in the other, he sat down on the end of the couch nearest to me—"she was clearly a lot brighter than he is. And nicer."

Marcus's sandwich looked good. I felt a small gnaw of hunger in the base of my stomach. I got up and went to the room service cart. A split chunk of sourdough loaf stuffed with very thinly sliced meats and cheeses caught my eye.

"Why do women do that?" Marcus asked.

I transferred the sourdough concoction to a small plate. "Do what?"

"Oh—marry men a lot dumber and jerkier than they are. You see it all the time."

I smiled at him over my shoulder. "Well, Griffin, hav-

ing never been married, to a jerk or otherwise, I don't
know if I'm qualified to answer that question."

"Oh, come on. You know what I mean."

I returned to my chair with the sandwich. "Okay," I
said. "Why do high-rent women marry low-rent men?
Hmmm. Let me think."

"Go ahead." A tiny blob of mustard dropped from his
sandwich and spattered on his tie. "Shit," he said without any heat, and dabbed at the spot with a napkin.
"Well. So. Tell me."

"All right." I took a bite of the sourdough and cold
cuts, chewed, and swallowed. "If you want the real
blunt truth, as far as I see it, it's that those women don't,
if they want to marry, have that wide a choice of potential husbands."

"What?"

This was going to take a tedious amount of explanation. "Griffin, Denise probably married—what's his
name?"

"Warren."

"Yeah. Well, she probably took up with Warren, to
use your phrase, because he was the best option available at the time. And she couldn't foresee a chance to
meet somebody better."

Marcus scowled at me. "But he's an oaf. A boob."

"I'm not disagreeing with you."

"Then what the hell *are* you doing?"

I decided to cut to the chase and make the conversation simpler. "Denise was a bright woman, right?"

"I already told you that. And ambitious, and hardworking."

"Okay, so she probably would have liked to—or
we're assuming she would have liked to—marry someone more on her level."

"That's what I've been saying. So why didn't she?"

I smiled at him again. "Griffin, it's a sad but true fact of life that most smart men don't like smart women. At least, not to marry."

"That's not true."

I looked at the ceiling and sighed.

"I like smart women," he said defensively. "Do you think my wife is an idiot?"

"No I don't. And I didn't say *all* smart men, Griffin. I said *most* smart men."

He was silent.

"Well?" I said.

"You may have a point," he said finally, grudgingly.

I took another bite of my sandwich.

"Does that bother you?" he asked.

"What?"

"You know. About smart men and smart women. *You're* smart."

I put my sandwich on the plate. "It bothers me the way the fact that the sun comes up in the east bothers me. It's a reality of life—maybe even a natural law—I can't change. So I don't worry about it."

"But . . ."

"But what?"

"Doesn't that—the situation—affect *you?*" He made a circular gesture with his hand. "Cut down on your, uh, opportunities?"

"To what? Meet men? Have relationships with them?"

"Well, yes."

"I'm not suffering from emotional or sexual deprivation, if that's what you mean."

"You sure don't seem to be."

"In the case of Denise," I said, "I can only guess at

her motives. Perhaps she wanted, at a certain point in her life, to be married more than she cared about who she was married *to*. A lot of women are like that. Despite feminism. Or maybe because of it. Who the hell knows? Anyway, do you follow me?"

"I follow." He rose and went to the cart. He picked up the coffeepot and held it out to me. I shook my head. He poured himself more coffee and returned to the couch.

"There's another thing, too," I said.

"What's that?"

"Doesn't the traditional Freudian psychological line hold that women put up with crap—or at least unacceptable behavior—from men because they're masochists?"

"I've heard that."

"Actually," I said, "I think the reverse is true. Women are optimists. They try as hard as they can to make the best of a bad situation. Or a bad man. Maybe Denise did that with Warren—for as long as she reasonably could. Maybe she looked at the guy and said to herself, 'Well, he's kind of dumb and sort of a slob, but hey, he's got other good qualities, so I'll concentrate on those and disregard the rest.' "

Marcus drank some coffee. "Possibly. Okay. I can buy that." He put his cup on the end table. "What about battered women?"

"What about them?"

"Does some version of your theory apply to them?"

I took a deep breath, thinking of Grace Hapgood. "A very distorted and exaggerated and unhealthy one, maybe."

Richie, he's had some really rough times, see? He's really a mellow dude, you know? But people keep hasslin' him. He never gets the breaks.

Was that the voice of an optimist? A masochist? Or someone too beaten down by life to be either, surviving as best she could?

Marcus and I were quiet for a while after that, finishing our lunch. Perhaps we'd exhausted the topic. And who did I think I was, pontificating on the relations between men and women? Since when was I an expert on the human heart? I didn't even know what the hell was going on in my own.

I had more coffee. Marcus went to the bedroom to make another phone call. I read the New Hampshire papers.

When Marcus came back from the bedroom, I said, "What do you have planned for tomorrow?"

"Not sure," he said. "Things are up in the air at the moment."

"Let me bring them down to earth for you," I said.

He raised his eyebrows. "What do you have in mind?"

"You and I together are going to do something for Marian."

"What's that?"

"Track down her last two suspects."

"Oh, Liz—"

"*Griffin. Listen* to me. We are going to do this. Damnit, we owe her that much. Her memory."

He grimaced.

"Griffin," I said. "We do this, you and me, or I walk. And I'm not kidding."

He stared at me.

"I'm dead serious about that."

"I'll say."

"Well?"

He let out a long breath. "It's a goddam waste of time."

"I don't care."

We stared at each other.

"Christ," Marcus said. "There's no way I can talk you out of this, is there?"

"None at all."

He exhaled louder. "Shit." He lit a cigarette. "Christ," he repeated. "All right. What are the names of these two assholes again?"

"Dell—Delbert—Washburn and Robert Woodruff."

"And where are they from?"

"Woodruff lives in Plaistow. Washburn, just outside of North Conway."

Marcus shut his lighter with a noisy click. "North Conway?"

"Yes."

"Isn't there a bar up there Kmiec used to hang out in?"

"Yes."

Marcus threw the lighter on the coffee table. "All right," he said. "It's Washburn, then. We'll go to goddam North Conway and track the fucker down. And maybe while we're up there you'll allow me five minutes to visit the bar Kmiec liked so that I can do a quick bit of useless research on *him*, huh?"

"Fine with me."

He gave me a nasty smile. "You're too kind."

THIRTY

"Now," I said. "Do you want to take Route 93 to Route 128 to Route 1 to the Spalding Turnpike to Route 16, or do you want to take Route 93 all the way up to the Kankamagus Highway?"

"I don't care," Marcus said wearily. "What's your preference?"

"Route 16 is shorter by a bit," I said. "But the Kankamagus is a lot more scenic."

Marcus deliberated a moment. "Ninety-three straight up," he said finally. "It sounds a lot less complicated. Anyway, I know the road." He put the car in gear.

It was nine the next morning. I had arranged with Sue McCreary to keep Lucy for the next few days. The dog didn't seem unduly disturbed to see me go. She was probably looking forward to a change of venue herself.

"You know, I very likely could have spent today interviewing Peggy Letourneau's husband," Marcus said.

"He'll keep."

Marcus grunted.

"Oh, lighten up. This will be a very productive trip. You'll see. Trust me."

"I hate people who say, 'Trust me.' It reminds me of Hollywood."

"Oh, my God," I said. "Bite my tongue."

Thirty minutes after we'd left Cambridge, we were crossing the broad blue band of the Merrimack River. A hydroplane swept down over the bridge nor more than fifty feet above us. I craned my neck to watch it land.

"What a shame," I said.

"What is?"

"It's really such a beautiful river. Why did it have to be used as a . . . as a . . ."

"Killing ground?"

"Something like that."

"People like Kmiec are despoilers," Marcus said. "They take pleasure in it. It's maybe more gratifying to them than anything else."

I nodded.

"Murder, of course, being the ultimate act of despoliation."

"Yes."

Once we got beyond Concord, we lost about three quarters of the traffic. Marcus was an excellent driver—maybe it was all that California freeway experience—and I felt comfortable riding with him. Usually, I'm a nervous passenger. I spend a lot of energy stomping my right foot on an imaginary brake.

We stopped in Lincoln for coffee, just before the entrance to the Kankamagus.

"Have you ever been in the White Mountains?" I asked.

"No."

"Do you ski?"

"Uh-huh."

"Oh, you'd love it up here. It's wonderful. A little

overrun with tourists, but wonderful. Where do you usually ski? Aspen? St. Moritz?"

"No. Lubbock, Texas."

I laughed.

The Kankamagus Highway is about thirty miles long
and is a national park. Along it are campgrounds and
lookouts, where you can park and goggle at some of the
most breathtaking views in New England. Perhaps anywhere. During foliage season the highway is bumper to
bumper.

We were about two thirds of the way along the road
when I said, "Can we take time out for fifteen minutes?"

Marcus looked at me in surprise. "I suppose," he
said. "Why?"

"I want to show you something."

"What?"

"It's called Rocky Gorge. You'll see the entrance up
on the left in a bit."

"All right."

We passed a sign that informed us the danger of a
forest fire was low today.

"I can't tell you how relieved I am," Marcus said.

I poked him in the upper arm with my index finger.
"Oh, shut up."

We turned onto the Rocky Gorge access road. The
parking area was deserted.

"Oh, goody," I said.

Marcus stopped the car. "I'm a city boy," he said.
"You're not dragging me in here to introduce me to
Bambi or Alvin the Chipmunk or anything, are you?"

"Don't worry." I hopped down from the Explorer.
Then I put my head back in the car, grinned at him, and
said, "Trust me."

"You're making me nauseous." Nevertheless, he got out of the car and followed me through a stand of trees down to the river.

"Is this a tributary of the Merrimack?" he asked.

"No. It's the Swift River. It runs east to the Atlantic. The Merrimack starts out as the Pemigewasset, west of here."

"Yes," Marcus said. "I've looked at the map, too."

I ignored him. "Isn't this gorgeous?"

Rocky Gorge is a long terrace of glacial rocks, pools descending into rapids. On either side, the mountains rise in slopes gentle only to the eye.

"Yeah," Marcus aid. "It's nice." He leaned against the trunk of a birch and watched me.

I jumped off the bank onto a large slab of flat granite. From there I made a five-foot leap onto another squat lump of stone. Six feet away sat another boulder with a shelf at its base. The water boiled around it. I launched myself at the shelf.

"Jesus," Marcus said. "Be careful."

I stood on the outcropping, my hands on my hips, smiling at him. "You should have seen me at Stonehenge. And on the Scottish moors."

"I bet. What the hell did you do, turn into a Druid?"

"It's in the blood," I yelled back at him, over the rush of the water. "Come out here."

"No, thanks. I'll get my thrills other ways."

I shook my head. Then I made the three serial leaps back to the riverbank. My foot skidded on some mud and decayed leaves, and I started to slip. Marcus bent down, grabbed my hand, and yanked me upright.

"Whoops," I said. "Thanks."

"You're welcome. Now can we get the hell out of here?"

"Sure."

We trudged up the bank.

"But, Griffin, don't you think this is spectacular?"

"It's okay."

"What an endorsement," I said. "The park service will want to quote you in its brochures."

We got back in the car and back on the highway.

Route 16 through Conway and North Conway was clogged with traffic, half of it from out of state. This was a major resort area. For those who didn't ski, there were factory outlets to shop in. I personally had trouble figuring out why anyone would drive two or three hundred miles to buy the same stuff you could buy at the Filene's Basement or T. J. Maxx at home. But then, I'm not a shopper.

"Where are we staying tonight?" I asked.

"The Burton Farm Inn."

"Oh." I had heard of the Burton Farm Inn. I had also heard that a room there cost around three hundred dollars a night.

"Did you make a reservation?" I asked.

He nodded absently; he was concentrating on the traffic.

It took us twenty-five minutes to travel two miles.

The Burton Farm Inn was an enormous two-story white frame structure with a veranda. It sat in wide lawns at the base of a hill. You approached it via a long and winding oak-tree-lined drive. The parking lot was discreetly tucked away behind a stand of pines. Most of the cars in the lot were Saabs or Mercedeses or BMWs. And there was one pristine white Rolls Royce.

"Gee," I said. "Maybe we should leave this heap next to the Dumpster."

Marcus laughed and backed the Explorer into the empty space next to the Rolls.

We got our overnight bags from the backseat and walked up the path to the inn.

The lobby had wainscoting, wide-planked floors, and Oriental rugs. To the right was a mahogany registration desk. To the left, a lounge area with camelback sofas and Queen Anne chairs. In a long low fieldstone fireplace some logs burned with a muted glow. I sniffed. Applewood. On either side of the fireplace were floor-to-ceiling bookcases, filled. Beyond the registration desk, a staircase rose to the second floor.

Marcus got us checked in quickly. He strolled back to where I was standing and handed me a key. A bellboy materialized, snatched up our bags, and conducted us up the staircase.

My room was about twenty by twenty feet. The bed was large and four-postered. There were also a highboy, a lowboy, two wing chairs covered in rose chintz, and an armoire. A door in the right wall led to a bathroom. The door in the left wall led to a sitting room somewhat bigger than my bedroom. It had a fireplace with a marble mantel. The bellboy was kneeling to light the fire.

I crossed the sitting room to the door in the opposite wall and tapped on it.

"Yes?" Marcus said.

"Me."

"Come in."

I pushed open the door. His bedroom was a replica of mine.

"Really, Griffin," I said. "You didn't have to rent the presidential suite, you know."

"Oh yes I did." He paused in the act of unzipping his bag. "If I'm going to go on a fool's errand, at least I'm going to go in comfort and style. Besides, this was all they had left."

I made a face at him.

"I'll meet you downstairs in ten minutes," he said.

"Okay."

At his insistence, we had lunch in the inn's dining room amidst a welter of white napery, crystal, and silver. The food and service were superb. It was well after 2:00 P.M. before we started off in search of Dell Washburn.

"All right," Marcus said. "Where does this clown live?"

I looked at the notes Marian had given me. "West End Road."

"Does he work?"

"Yeah, he's an attendant at a ski place called, uh"—I checked my notes again—"Indian Ridge."

"So where's that?"

"About a mile north of here, on Route 16."

We were in the middle of another traffic jam when Marcus said, "Have you given any thought to how you're going to approach this guy?"

"I'm not, at first. I'm just going to check him out."

"Can you recognize him by sight?"

"He'd be hard to miss, if the description I have of him is accurate. For one thing, he's six and a half feet tall. For another, he has a big lantern jaw."

"Where'd you get that information?"

"Marian."

"Where'd she get it?"

I looked at him sharply. "She never had a chance to tell me, Griffin. I imagine she had her sources."

He was silent.

We didn't get to Indian Ridge till a little after three.

And it took an additional ten minutes to find a place to park. Indian Ridge was one of the bigger—and busier—of the region's ski areas. The main trail looked like Fifth Avenue at five o'clock on Christmas Eve. The line of people waiting to board the lift snaked down almost to the parking lot.

At the head of the lot was an oversized log cabin, where you could buy ski passes, hot drinks, and snacks and avail yourself of a men's or ladies' room. Marcus stayed out on the porch, while I went into the cabin. The place was crowded. The sandy-haired guy selling lift passes was short and moon-faced, which meant he wasn't Dell Washburn. Maybe Washburn was a waiter. I peered into the snack bar. It, too, was heavily populated, mostly with raucous college-age kids. All the snacks and drinks were dispensed by vending machine, which meant no waiters or waitresses. There was a guy sweeping the floor, but he was around my height, with a thin jaw. I went into the ladies' room. It was basic—four stalls, four sinks, a hand dryer, and an overflowing wastebin. I was willing to bet that the men's room was pretty much the same, which indicated that Dell wasn't a washroom attendant.

I joined Marcus on the porch. He looked at me. I shook my head.

We walked toward the lift, skirting the line. At the gate a guard checked passes. The guard was blond and female.

We turned around and headed back toward the cabin.

"Maybe he runs the snow-making equipment," Marcus said.

"Jesus," I breathed, and grabbed Marcus's arm.

"What?"

"There he is. That's him."

"Where?"

"He just came out of the control booth. Griffin, he must operate the lift."

Marian's description had been accurate but limited. Yes, Washburn was very tall. And yes, he had a lantern jaw. So probably did a lot of men. But you would not have mistaken any of them for Dell Washburn.

He was massive, almost antediluvian in his bulk. From shoulder to shoulder he must have measured thirty inches. His upper arms looked like transplanted thighs.

"Christ," Marcus said softly. "I feel like a midget."

Washburn wore jeans, duck boots, a plaid flannel shirt, and a down vest. He moved with an oddly arhythmic gait, like someone trying to walk on a badly sprained ankle without the aid of a crutch or cane.

His hair was thick and dark and fell down over a high and very slightly concave forehead. His cheekbones were prominent and the hollows beneath them deeply shadowed. His lower lip was full and slightly pendulous, the upper lip a thin curved bow.

I released Marcus's arm.

"What are you doing?"he said.

"I want to get a closer look at him."

Washburn went into the cabin by a rear door. I darted up the steps to the front porch and in the main entrance. The sandy-haired man was alone behind the pass counter. I walked into the snack bar.

Washburn was standing in line at the coffee, tea, and hot chocolate machine, jingling change in a hand that looked the size of a baseball glove.

Next to the hot drinks machine was one that sold packets of potato chips and crackers. I got two quarters from my purse, wandered over to the vendor, and pretended to inspect the selection. Then I dropped the money in the slot, punched a button, and got a bag of cheese puffs in return.

I turned away from the machine in such a way that enabled me to look directly into Washburn's face.

He glanced at me briefly and with no interest.

His eyes were as profoundly dark as his hair. And they were far more beautiful than they were dark, with a soft and liquid glow that seemed untarnished by age or human experience.

THIRTY-ONE

It was after five when Marcus and I returned to the inn. The cocktail hour was in full swing, the lobby lounge filled with people in *aprèsski* couture swigging gin and single malt.

"Suppose we meet down here in an hour?" Marcus said.

"Fine."

We went to our rooms. Marcus was probably going to work the phone. I had no similar plan.

I sat on the bed and looked at Marian's notes. The material she had on Washburn was sketchy. He was born in Laconia, forty-one years ago. Orphaned at an early age, he'd been adopted by a couple named Fraser. No college or military service recorded. No arrests, either.

Yet Marian had described him as a "creep."

Rumor? Gossip?

If so, where had she picked it up? Washburn's neighbors? Co-workers?

I thought of his eyes.

Angel eyes.

I put away the notes.

I changed from jeans and fisherman's knit sweater to a straight black wool skirt and a teal blue crushed satin blouse with a low neck and billowing sleeves that would have made Errol Flynn weep with envy. The impulse that had made me pack such an outfit this morning was still obscure to me. But I was glad I had given in to it.

I went downstairs to the lounge. Marcus, being Marcus, had managed to commandeer a piecrust table and two wing chairs near the fireplace. He rose as I crossed the room.

There were two martini glasses on the table and a crystal bowl full of nuts. We settled down across from each other. Marcus smiled at me.

"Nice blouse," he said.

"Thanks. It's my Jolly Roger shirt."

"Looks better on you than on Roger."

I laughed and took a sip of my drink.

Marcus leaned back in his chair and crossed his legs. "You know, I keep thinking about that conversation we had yesterday."

"Which one was that?"

"Where you were telling me why someone like Denise would have married someone like Warren."

"Well, don't take my words as gospel. I could be wrong."

"You sounded right."

I smiled and held out my hands, palms raised. "Who knows?"

"I'd like to talk about that in the book," Marcus continued. "Maybe tie it in somehow to the larger theme, men who serially kill women."

I ate some nuts. "It's a good tie-in," I said. "Smart, ambitious, hardworking women tend not to be passive and obedient. And what's a serial killer doing but imposing the ultimate form of obedience and passivity on the women he kills?"

"Right, right."

"All the Merrimack Valley Killer's victims were smart and hardworking."

"And only two were married," Marcus said. "Lisa Goodenough and Peggy Letourneau."

"Well, Griffin, Cheryl Timmons was only seventeen."

He made an impatient gesture. "You know what I mean."

"Sure."

He sank back even further into his chair. He was frowning. Thinking.

"Griffin?"

"Hmmm?"

"How long have *you* been married?"

He looked at me as if startled I'd asked the question. I was startled I'd asked it, too. It had just come out of my mouth without any conscious impetus behind it.

"Twenty-five years this May," he said. "If it lasts. I don't think it's going to."

"No?"

"It's been running on empty for about the past ten years. This separation isn't the first. It *is* the longest."

I finished my drink. "You told me the first time I met you, that you thought maybe you and your wife could work things out."

He shook his head. "That doesn't seem like a realistic hope any longer."

"I'm sorry."

He shrugged. "That's the way life goes." Then he peered at me. "Why are you asking?"

"I don't know," I said. "I shouldn't have. It's none of my business."

He smiled slightly. "I don't mind. Would you like another drink?"

"Yes, please."

He signaled the waitress. While she was taking our order, I glanced around the lounge. At a table about ten feet from us was another couple, perhaps in their late twenties. They were holding hands, not talking. Looking at each other. Oblivious to everyone else in the room, oblivious to everything outside their own magic circle.

The waitress brought our drinks and replenished the nut bowl.

"I know why I asked you about your marriage," I said.

"Why?"

"All of a sudden I'm intensely interested in the reasons why long-term relationships collapse."

"You and Jack?"

I nodded.

"Well, my marriage didn't fall apart overnight. The process was a lot more gradual."

"What happened?"

He frowned again. "It's—I can't put my finger on any one thing. I think we just sort of started diverging. The common ground got less and less and less and . . ."

"Yes?"

"Then finally there wasn't any at all. Except Leah and Andy. And they're grown and gone. At least Andy is. And Leah will be soon. Maybe . . ."

"What?"

"Maybe that's why I try so hard to hang on to *her*."

I smiled. "Probably."

"So what about you and Jack?"

"What about us?"

"Can that be repaired?"

I took a deep breath. "*Our* common ground seems to have turned into a trench."

I looked at the fire. After a moment Marcus said, "Let's talk about something else."

"Let's."

He lit a cigarette. "So what *would* you like to talk about?" He smiled. "Since we already seem to have covered love and death."

"There's always war and famine and pestilence, if you want to stay in a cosmic vein."

"Oh, please. Maybe some other time."

"All right. Tell me some more funny stories about the movie and TV biz."

"How about over dinner?" He glanced at the dining room door. "Let's eat here, okay? The food seems acceptable."

"Sounds good to me."

"Okay." He grinned. "Now finish your drink like a good girl."

"How about I just throw it in your face, little fella?"

He laughed loudly enough to attract the attention of the people at the table nearest us. "I thought you were the kind of feminist who could take a joke."

"I am," I said. "But I always have to top it with a better one."

We got up from the table together. As I edged around it, the waitress hurried past me with a loaded tray of drinks. I pulled back so we wouldn't collide. As I did, my shoulder bumped Marcus's upper arm. He put a hand on my back to steady me.

"Drunk again," he said.

"That'll be the day."

He kept his hand on my back, very lightly, as we threaded our way through the crowded lounge to the restaurant.

Somebody must have told the maître d' that Marcus was the person occupying the most expensive accommodations in the inn. He escorted us to the primo table, the one in the bay window alcove. It was private, but visible to the other restaurant patrons. It was also on a platform raised six inches above the floor where the hoi polloi dined. Some hoi polloi. Among them I recognized the junior senator from Massachusetts and an anchorwoman from the NBC affiliate in Boston. Like a lot of television people, she looked smaller, softer, and prettier in person. The junior senator looked as if he'd spent a little too long in the cocktail lounge. Or maybe he'd just had a rough time on the slopes. You could get a red face from windburn.

The maître d' made a big production of lighting the candle in the center of the table. Then he did a fast fade and was replaced almost instantly by the sommelier.

"I don't want another martini," Marcus said. "But I wouldn't mind some wine. What about you?"

"Wine would be nice."

"What would you like?"

"You pick. I think I'm going to have some kind of fish for dinner, if that's any help."

"White," Marcus said. He glanced at the wine list and said something to the sommelier. The sommelier was almost orgasmic in his endorsement of Marcus's choice. He bowed, smiled, and left us. "I'm sorry I didn't ask for cherry Kool-Aid," I said. "Or diet Dr Pepper."

Marcus laughed. "He is a little oleaginous, isn't he? Oh, well—look at it this way. With him around, we won't need butter for the rolls."

At that moment, a waiter deposited a wicker basket of bread on the table. I couldn't keep my face straight, so I covered the lower half of it with my hand.

"A little giddy, aren't we?" Marcus said.

"Just a little. Don't worry. It'll pass."

"I hope not. I'm enjoying it."

I opened the menu. The sommelier reappeared with the wine. He and Marcus went through the whole ritual: label exhibition and verification, tactile, olfactory, and visual examination of the cork, and swirl and taste. This completed to everyone's satisfaction, the sommelier poured us each a glass, put the bottle in a pewter bucket, and disappeared.

The wine was wonderful. So was the food that followed.

We finished dinner at nine, with coffee. Neither of us wanted dessert. As we left the dining room, our shoulders bumped again.

"Would you like a liqueur or a brandy or something?" Marcus asked.

"That would be nice," I said. "With some more coffee."

We wandered out to the lounge. It was packed. The junior senator from Massachusetts was holding court by the fireplace. Marcus looked at the crowd with faint distaste.

"We could probably get a table," he said. "But . . ."

"I don't care for mob scenes myself."

We looked at each other.

"We have a private living room of our own," he said. "Why don't we use it?"

"Good idea."

We went up to the suite.

Someone had kindled another fire in the fireplace while we were at dinner. The applewood logs on the grate burned with a low flame and a steady pleasant hiss punctuated occasionally by a soft pop.

I sat in one of the wing chairs flanking the fireplace while Marcus phoned room service. Five minutes later, a waiter appeared with a cart full of coffee, cups, sugar, cream, glasses, and a bottle of Rémy Martin.

"That okay with you?" Marcus asked.

"It looks divine."

He signed the check and the waiter left.

Marcus poured some cognac into a balloon and handed it to me.

"Thank you." I smiled up at him. I felt very warm and loose and relaxed. I kicked off my shoes and stretched my feet toward the fire.

Marcus said, "I feel like I'm posing for a magazine ad for the good life."

"You are. A Dewar's Profile. Tell me, what was the last book *you* read?"

"Valley of the Dolls," he said. "I really enjoyed its subtle examination of the female psyche."

I laughed. He sat down in the other wing chair.

"Liz?"

"What?"

"You ever think of writing a book of your own?"

I hesitated. Then I said, "Sometimes."

"Why don't you?"

"Oh, I don't know."

"You should. You're good enough."

"Thank you."

"I mean that."

"Well, maybe I will."

"I could introduce you to a very good agent."

"Thank you."

"Will you think about it?"

"Yes."

"Good. Let me know when you're ready."

I got up to get myself some coffee. "Would you like some?" I asked Marcus.

"Not yet."

I returned to the chair with the cup. I liked alternating sips of cognac and coffee. The sensation in the mouth was so heavy and rich.

"Can I ask you another question?" Marcus said.

"Of course."

"Well"—he took a sip of his drink—"it's going to sound as if it's coming from left field. But what the hell. Remember the first day we drove up to Manchester? To see Joseph DeWitt and Roger Freeling and Edith Kmiec?"

"Uh-huh."

"And you told me that you didn't drive?"

"Uh-huh."

"And you told me you'd tell me *why* you didn't drive some other time, that it was too boring to go into then?"

"Yes."

"Well, can you tell me now?"

"Why do you want to know?"

"I'm just ... curious, that's all."

I sighed. "When I was seven years old, I had a friend named Monica. She lived diagonally across the street from us, oh, maybe two houses down. I went to play with her one afternoon. She was on the sidewalk trying out her new two-wheeler. When she saw me, she jumped off it and let it fall on the sidewalk. Then she ran out in the street, waving to me and yelling something. I don't know what. Maybe she was excited about having a real grown-up bike. Anyway ..." I stopped speaking.

"What?" Marcus prompted softly.

I set my glass on the rug beside the chair and folded my hands in my lap. "A car turned onto the street. It wasn't speeding or anything. Anyway, Monica ran right in front of it."

"Jesus," Marcus said.

"She bounced off the front end of the car and made a sort of pinwheel and landed in the gutter."

"Did—"

I nodded. "She died. Probably before she hit the gutter. Then her mother came out of the house, and she started screaming, and she screamed and she screamed and she screamed."

"Okay," Marcus said sharply. "Don't go on. Unless you want to."

"No. I don't."

We were quiet for several moments. Then Marcus said, "Have you ever told anyone else about Monica?"

"Just Jack. Now you."

He nodded.

We each had a little more brandy.

"As long as I'm in a confessional mood," I said, "I should tell you something else about me."

"What's that, sweetheart?"

His use of the endearment registered with me only much later. "I killed somebody once," I said.

He stared at me. Then he said, *"What?"*

I looked at the fire. "It was a few years ago. It was a man who was a very big real estate developer in Boston. Also a very big crook and, as it turned out, also a murderer. I went after him because of—well, he did something terrible to Jack. Had him framed for a rape and a murder because he, the developer, was the target of an investigation Jack was doing. Jack even spent some time in jail." I lifted my glass and swallowed some brandy. "Anyway, I went after this guy like a fury, with a lot of help from some cops and reporters who were friends. And . . ."

"Yes?"

"Finally it came down to a confrontation between this guy and me. He attacked me physically. I fought back. He said he was going to kill me. The upshot of it was, he was the one who died."

"What did you do?"

"I pushed him away from me. He fell. The fall killed him."

"Did you intend to kill him?"

"I . . . I don't know."

"Sweet Jesus," Marcus murmured.

The silence in the room was broken only by the soft hiss of the fire. Marcus got up and poured us another drink.

"Liz?"

"Yes?"

"Do you feel guilty about what you did?"

"I don't know that, either. All I know is that I think about it every day. I probably always will."

"I hope you don't feel guilty."

"Why?"

"Because you didn't do anything wrong."

He was standing over me, the bottle in his hand. I looked up at him. "Yes, that's what the authorities said."

"They were right."

"Griffin?"

"What?"

"Let's talk about something else."

He smiled faintly. "We've done that before this evening, haven't we?"

"What? Changed the subject?"

"Yes."

"There are things that are hard to talk about. And maybe a point beyond where talking about them doesn't do much good."

"Maybe not. Still ..."

"What?"

"I'm glad you told me the things you did."

"Why?"

"I know more about you now."

"I hope I didn't puncture any cherished illusions."

"No, you didn't. And don't be so goddam flip."

"Sorry. It's a reflex."

"Yeah. I know that, too."

I shivered.

"Are you cold?"

"No," I said. "It's just nerves. Or something."

I got up to get more coffee. Or I tried. I couldn't hold the cup to pour anything into it; my hands were shaking too badly. I set the coffeepot back down on the cart. And the cup and saucer, before I dropped them. I returned to the wing chair and folded my hands in my lap, tightly. Although I had my head averted from him, I could feel Marcus watching me.

"Why are you nervous?" he said.

"I don't know."

He gave a little dry cough. "Probably for the same reason I am."

I couldn't look at him.

"Liz?"

"Yes?"

"Look at me, will you?"

With an effort, I turned my head toward him. He was holding out his right hand to me. I extended my left hand to him, slowly. The silence between us was dense, as if it had a specific gravity much greater than that of air.

When I spoke, my voice didn't sound like my own. "What do you want to do?"

"I know what I *want* to do."

I took a deep breath. "Then why don't you just do it?"

THIRTY-TWO

At three o'clock the next morning, I went back to my own room. I was careful not to wake him as I left. I picked up my scattered clothing—what I could find of it in the dark—and took it away with me.

It wasn't that I thought I'd sleep better in a bed of my own. I probably wouldn't sleep at all. What I wanted to do was think, which I always did more clearly when I was alone. And by instinct I retreated into myself when I was overwhelmed. As I had been tonight.

I ended up not thinking, not really. My mind kept replaying a video of the previous hours. And I could still feel, on my skin and inside me, the quivering memory of the experience, a sexual vibration that lingered on well after the culmination of the act.

I *did* go to sleep. I'm not sure at what point. When I woke up, it was twenty past ten.

I showered and dressed slowly, a little reluctant to face Marcus for the first time since last night. How would I behave? How would he behave? Maybe I'd take my cue from him.

A little after eleven, I opened the door to the sitting room.

Last night's cognac and coffee had been cleared away and replaced by a breakfast service. Marcus was eating toast. As I came into the room, he looked up at me and smiled.

"I missed you this morning," he said.

"Well, you didn't miss much. I look terrible when I get up."

He laughed. "I bet you don't. Want some coffee? A muffin?"

"Sure."

I sat down across from him and took a cup.

"Oh," he said. He leaned sideways, fished around beneath his chair, and straightened up with a piece of white cloth crumpled in his hand. "This is yours, I believe, madam."

It was my bra.

"Thank you." I shoved it in my pocket. "I was wondering where that had got to. Where'd you find it?"

"Under the coffee table."

"Ah."

We looked at each other for a few seconds. Then we started to laugh. We leaned forward over the room service cart until our foreheads touched.

"Have a good time last night?" Marcus asked.

"Fair."

"Oh, *really?* Fair? Just fair?"

"Oh, all right. Good. I had a good time. I suppose."

"It sounded to me as if you had several good times."

"Hmmmm. Well. I could say the same of you."

He drew back and grinned at me. "Got any plans for what's left of this morning?"

"None in particular. Why? You have something in mind?"

"Uh-huh."

"Well, I guess Dell Washburn can wait."

Marcus loosened his tie. "He's going to damn well have to."

"Okay," Marcus said. "Now what?"

It was 2:00 P.M. and we were sitting in the Explorer in the inn's parking lot.

"I want to check out Washburn's house."

"All right. After that, I want to pay a visit to that bar Kmiec hung out in."

I smiled at him. "Fine with me."

We had resumed our professional demeanor toward each other. Rather studiedly so.

Marcus backed the car out of the parking space. "So where does Washburn live, again?"

"West End Road. It's not far from here. I'll show you."

"How come you know where it is?"

"I've been up here before on vacations."

The last two times had been with Jack. I put that thought out of my mind fast.

West End Road was very country, with truck and horse farms. The farther you got from North Conway center, the greater the spaces between the houses stretched. I kind of liked the rural isolation. It probably gave Marcus the willies.

Washburn's house was tiny—no more, I estimated, than four or five rooms. And those would be very small. It was a one-story structure and set far back from the road on the verge of a woods. A long gravel drive led up to it.

We continued on up West End until Marcus found a place on the side of the road where he could leave the car. Then we walked back to Washburn's place.

Across from it was an open field. The last house we'd passed before coming to it had been about half a mile back.

"This really is the sticks," Marcus said.

"God's country," I replied.

He made a face, and I laughed.

We picked our way diagonally across the wide expanse of lawn, or whatever, in front of Washburn's house. Some patches of snow lay on the sere earth. We avoided them. No need to leave ostentatious footprints.

The little house seemed well kept. The trim appeared to have been recently painted. The windows were clean, as were the plain white curtains in them.

I knocked at the front door.

"What makes you think he's home and receiving guests?" Marcus asked.

"I don't. I'm just observing the proper form." I knocked once more.

Of course no one answered. Marcus and I circled the house. All the windows were curtained. All the curtains were drawn.

"Damn," I said. "I was hoping to get a peek inside."

Marcus shrugged. "We'll come back when we're pretty sure he's home. Maybe he'll invite us in." He gave me a slight, malicious grin. "I'd *love* to hear you interview him."

"Oh, bug off," I said.

The house had a back door. I put my hand on the knob and gave it a perfunctory twist. It turned and clicked. The door opened inward about five inches. I was so startled I snatched back my hand.

"My God," I said. "It's not locked."

Marcus shrugged again. "Why would it be? Who the hell would come all the way out here to the ass end of nowhere to commit a burglary?"

I stared at him. He raised his eyebrows at me.

"I wonder," I said, "what the penalty is in this state for illegal entry in the daytime."

"I haven't a clue."

"Maybe," I said, "just maybe I'll risk it. You mind standing guard?"

"Oh, Christ," Marcus said. "No, I don't mind. Go ahead. Just be quick, huh?"

"Sure." I pushed the door open all the way with the tips of my gloved fingers and stepped into Dell Washburn's kitchen.

It was small and clean, with an old gas stove and one of those round-shouldered refrigerators last manufactured in the 1950s. I poked around in a few of the cabinets over the sink. Washburn's crockery was dime-store milk glass. He also seemed to like dry cereal and canned soups and stews.

A short, dimly lit hall led from the kitchen to the front of the house. The room on the left was a sort of parlor, tidy like the kitchen. There was an oval braided rug on the floor, a settee, and two ladderback chairs. No television. Nothing else interesting, either.

The room on the right was where Washburn slept. It had a single bed—how did someone Washburn's height scrunch into that?—and a plain maple dresser. A small closet held a few pairs of jeans and some flannel shirts. I went back down the hall, past a tiny bathroom with a primitive-looking stall shower, like an upright metal coffin.

The door to the back room was shut and locked, as I found when I tried the knob.

"Damn," I muttered.

I rattled the knob. It was loose. Then I pushed on the door. It was not a tight fit in the frame.

I went back to the kitchen and rummaged in a drawer by the stove till I found a table knife. I stuck the blade in the space between the door and the lock and wiggled it around until I felt and heard the latch retract. The door swung open and into the room.

"Hey," I heard Marcus yell. "You going to be finished soon?"

"In a minute," I yelled back at him, and crossed the threshold.

At first I thought I was in a workroom. There was only one piece of furniture in it, a long wooden table across the back wall. On it were various tools, neatly arrayed: screwdrivers (regular and Phillips); a tack hammer; a clear plastic box with compartments containing different-sized nails; a wrench; a roll of duct tape; a sledgehammer; and some knives. One of them was a hunting knife in a leather sheath.

The light in the room was inadequate and my eyes were slow adjusting to it. I didn't see a lamp anywhere and there wasn't an overhead fixture.

"Will you move it, please?" Marcus yelled.

"Yes, in a minute."

There were things taped to the right-hand wall, very carefully and in precise geometric arrangements. I squinted. Newspaper clippings. Photographs.

"Liz! Move it!"

I went closer to the wall.

"Liz!"

Before me was the newspaper article from the Manchester *Union-Leader* about the discovery of the body of Denise Michaud. Next to it was a color photograph, a Polaroid.

It showed the body of a woman sprawled on her back on a pile of fallen leaves. Her mouth was taped shut, her eyes open and glazed. Her arms were hidden beneath her. Her throat had been torn side to side in a gaping half-moon.

Her blouse and coat had been ripped open and shoved down her shoulders. Her breasts and thorax were dotted with wounds like red insatiable maws. The leaves around the body were sloppy with blood.

I swayed and closed my eyes and clamped my hands over my mouth.

Tied just above the cut in the woman's throat was a green ribbon, in a jaunty butterfly bow.

THIRTY-THREE

Because my legs wouldn't hold me upright, I folded down onto the floor. Marcus yelled again. The sound filtered through the buzzing in my ears, distant and inconsequential. I shook my head, at what I don't know, and gagged into the palms of my hands.

There were footsteps in the kitchen, then in the hall.

"Liz? Where are . . . ?"

In the posture I was, I didn't see him enter the room.

"Liz . . . God! What's the matter?"

He was kneeling beside me. I lifted my head.

"Look at the wall over there," I said.

"What?"

"Just *look* at it, will you?"

He got up and crossed the room.

"Holy Jesus," I heard him say. "Sweet Jesus Christ."

"I can't believe it," Marcus said. "I can't believe it."

"Believe it," I said. "It's true."

He was more shaken than I.

It was five o'clock, and we were in our private sitting room at the inn. I had no real recollection of the drive back there. I didn't even recall getting up from the floor of Washburn's workroom and leaving his house.

"I need a drink," Marcus said. "You?"

I nodded.

"There's still some of the cognac from last night. That okay?"

"Fine."

He got two water glasses from his bathroom, splashed them each half full with cognac, and handed me one.

"I can't believe it," he repeated.

"Griffin, it's true. Washburn is the Merrimack Valley Killer. He has to be. Where—how do you think he got those photos? He took them himself, while those women were dying. Or right after they died. All of them, Griffin. Carolyn. Denise. Lisa. Peggy. Cheryl. Diane. Linda. Oh, yes. And Joanne Parisi, too. They were all there, hanging on the wall."

"All right, all right." He shook his head furiously. "But . . ."

"But what?"

"How the hell did Kmiec get all the details of the killings right? If *he* didn't do them?"

I sighed. "Somebody fed him the details, Griffin."

"But who? Why?"

"Somebody who was covering for Washburn."

"Why would anybody cover for Washburn?"

"I don't know, Griffin. But—it could happen, for reasons we're not aware of yet. Things like that *have* happened. Probably whoever it was, was also the person who shot Marian."

"How do you figure that?"

"Well, if you're covering for someone, you want that cover to stay intact. So you get rid of whomever might be on the verge of breaking it. Marian was on that verge. No, she was beyond it. She was the only person to finger Washburn."

"By that logic, maybe she was killed by Washburn himself."

I shook my head. "He'd have stabbed her. That's his m.o."

Marcus pointed his right index finger at me. "Serial killers can break their patterns. Didn't your forensic shrink friend, Brenda, tell you that?"

I nodded wearily. "You know she did."

"So?"

"Marian's murder wasn't a serial killing where the murderer used a different weapon to commit the same crime. It was a setup deal meant to look like a botched burglary. We were supposed to think the burglar panicked and shot her on impulse."

"You've said that before."

"Yes, and I still think it's true. After what we saw this afternoon, more than ever."

Marcus was silent, holding his glass to his mouth but not drinking from it, brooding.

"Griffin?"

"Hmmm?"

"We're going to have to do something. Fast."

"I know."

"What? Washburn can't be allowed to stay on the loose. My God! He may be planning another killing. Stalking someone while we're sitting here talking."

"Yeah, I know." Marcus took a swallow of his drink.

"Well?"

He gazed at the fireplace. "Jesus," he said softly. "What a story this is. What a book it's going to make."

I looked at him. "I agree. It's an incredible story. The scoop of the century. But, Griffin, Washburn has to be taken out of circulation. Now. Immediately. Before he kills another woman."

Marcus nodded abstractly.

"Now, Griffin."

"Yes, yes, right."

"So?"

Marcus turned to face me. "I want to follow him for a few days. Talk to him. Maybe force his hand."

"And then?"

"We'll see."

"Griffin!"

"Liz, I promise you, Washburn is done killing. One way or another, I will see to that."

I slammed my fist down on the top of the piecrust table. "How can you promise that?"

"I can. Believe me."

I took a deep breath. "Three days, Griffin. You can have three days. Then I'm going to the cops."

"Liz, don't threaten me."

"I'm not. I'm just telling you what I'm going to do." I drank some of my cognac.

Marcus inhaled very audibly. "Jesus Christ," he said. He put his elbow on the mantel and his hand to his forehead. He massaged his temples with thumb and index finger.

"Since we only have three days," I said, "are we going to start tonight?"

He raised his head and stared at me. *"We?"*

"Of course, we. I'm going with you, Griffin. What did you think—that I was going to sit here in the inn waiting for you and twiddling my thumbs?"

"Liz, it's—"

"What?"

"This guy kills women. *Women.* You're a woman. You're in the age group he goes for."

"I'm too tall, though. He likes them petite, remember?"

"Oh, don't be such a goddam wise-ass. I'm telling you—this is dangerous."

"You know something. Griffin?"

"What?"

"I don't give a shit." I finished my drink. "Anyhow—this is *my* story too, now, isn't it?"

A half hour later we were five hundred feet from Washburn's house. There were no lights in the windows to indicate he was home. Nor was his red Chevy pickup parked in the driveway.

"All right," Marcus said. "It's your turn to stand guard."

"I'll take the side of the house. That way I can see if he drives up, or if anyone else does, and I can run around to the back and warn you."

He nodded, and we climbed down from the Explorer. There was no further conversation between us as we walked to Washburn's house. Marcus was still angry with me.

I didn't care.

Marcus had the Nikon with him. He was going to take shots of the picture gallery in Washburn's workroom.

The back door was still unlocked. Marcus vanished into the kitchen.

I stood by the downspout, my hands in my pockets. I glanced up at the sky. It was black satin with a few scudding puffs of clouds. Living as I did in the city, I tended to forget just how many stars there were up there.

The air was cold and very still. I sniffed and caught a faint wet smell beneath the chill. I wondered if there would be snow.

I wondered what would happen tonight when Marcus and I got back to the inn. I wondered if we would end up in bed together again.

Thinking about the possibility, and the promise it held, I felt a kind of liquid rippling in the base of my stomach.

Twin lights flashed at the foot of the driveway.

I dashed around to the back door, yanked it open, and said, "Griffin! Quick. He's here."

Marcus appeared before the echo of the last syllable I'd spoken had faded. He shoved the camera in his pocket.

"I got ten shots," he said. "Beauties. I hope. The worktable, the wall, the knife, the duct tape. Everything."

Tires crunched on gravel. As Marcus and I came around the side of the house, we were dazzled by the headlights.

I put my hand on my shoulder bag. It felt heavy, more so than usual. It should; my gun was in there, tucked in a special pocket sewn into the lining like an internal holster.

I hoped the gun would stay put tonight.

The truck stopped.

"Remember how we agreed to run this," Marcus whispered sharply.

"Sure."

The driver's side door of the truck opened, and Dell Washburn stepped down from the cab.

He had left the headlights on. I felt like a deer. Marcus raised a hand to his face to shield his eyes from the glare.

Washburn continued to stand by the truck, an enormous black silhouette against a darker backdrop. He was silent and unmoving.

"Mr. Washburn," Marcus said.

The silhouette remained quiet and motionless.

"Mr. Washburn," Marcus repeated.

After a few seconds, a voice came out of the darkness, very low, with a rumble to it. "Who are you?"

Marcus introduced himself and me. He gave our real names. We had briefly thought of using aliases but rejected the idea as pointless.

Washburn shut the door of the truck. "Anything I can do for you?"

His voice had an odd drag to it, almost like the drag of his gait. Not a slur or any kind of speech impediment. More as if he had to pause and think for a millisecond before he enunciated each word.

"Could we talk with you for a moment?" Marcus asked. "If it's no trouble."

Washburn moved a few steps toward us. "What about?"

"Well, could we go inside?" Marcus asked pleasantly. "It might be more comfortable in there. It's cold tonight, isn't it?"

Washburn glanced up at the sky. "Gonna snow," he said.

"Exactly," Marcus said. "So . . ."

"I don't know who you are."

"That's true, you don't. But we'll explain."

Washburn shuffled a little closer to us, as if to inspect us at a near range. I tried to smile at him. Put him at ease. Throw him off guard. My insides were quivering. His dark and luminous eyes focused on me.

Angel eyes.

He opened his mouth as if to speak.

Maybe he would have invited us into his house. Maybe he would have ordered us off his property. I don't know. He never had the chance. From behind me a voice said, "Shut up, Dell. Don't say one more word."

I gasped and jumped. Then I swung around in a half circle.

Five feet away, just outside the apron of light cast by the truck's low beams, stood a man. He was holding a shotgun. He held it in my direction. He was Daniel Tucker.

THIRTY-FOUR

"Dan?" Marcus said.

Tucker moved the shotgun to the left so that it was pointing straight at Marcus's chest. "You shut up, too."

"Danny," Washburn said in pleased tones. "What you doing up here, man?"

"For Christ's sake, Dell. I told you to put a lid on it, didn't I? You don't want to talk to these people. You don't want to open your mouth in front of them, okay?"

Washburn seemed to retreat slightly. "Well, yeah. All right, Danny. You say so."

"I say so. So shut up now, huh?"

Tucker held the shotgun very steadily.

"Dan," Marcus said, quite calmly. "What—"

"Shut your goddamn face till I ask you a question I want you to answer," Tucker said flatly.

He looked at me. "Give your pocketbook to Dell."

I grabbed the strap of my bag reflexively.

He moved about a foot closer to me. I looked at the double barrel of the shotgun. I recognized its make. I had once seen a crime-scene photo of someone who'd been shot in the head by one of those things at close proximity. The person had had no head left. None.

"Do it." Tucker said.

I unhitched the bag from my shoulder and held it away from me straight-armed. Washburn fumbled it away from me.

"Keep that with you," Tucker said to Washburn, not taking his eyes from me.

"Yeah, sure, Danny." Washburn let the bag dangle loosely from his hand for a moment, as if puzzled what to do with it. Then he slung it on his left shoulder. It looked absurd hanging there.

"All right," Tucker said. "Marcus, where'd you leave your car?"

Marcus was silent.

"Marcus, that's one of the questions I want an answer to."

Marcus didn't say anything.

"Oh, just tell me," Tucker said, with a kind of weary exasperation. He pointed the shotgun back at me.

"It's up the road about two hundred yards," Marcus said.

"All right. Give Dell the keys."

Marcus dug in his pocket, fished out the car keys, and tossed them to the side without looking where they went. They hit the gravel with a small jingle.

"Okay," Tucker said. "Let's go." He stepped into the light. The lines in his face were very deep and the flesh beneath his eyes sagged.

"Dell," he said. "You walk ahead of us with this girl. Keep your hand on her so she doesn't trip or anything, okay?"

"Sure, Danny." Washburn took hold of my upper right arm.

"Marcus, you walk along back here with me, huh? You see where I'm pointing this gun, right?"

"Yeah," Marcus said. "I can see that fine."

"Good," Tucker said. "Dell? You ready?"

"Yeah."

"Let's go."

Washburn didn't pull or tug on my arm; nevertheless, I felt as if I were being dragged across the lawn. He walked fast, despite whatever his disability was, and it was difficult to match my step with his. The handbag bumped against him on his other side.

Nobody spoke till we reached the car.

"Okay, Dell," Tucker said. "Unlock the car. Then you get in the front seat. I want you to drive." He looked at me. "You stand over here." He gestured with the shotgun at the right front fender of the Explorer.

I did what he told me to do. He kept the gun on me as I moved into place. I glanced at Marcus. His eyes were closed. I wondered what he was feeling or thinking. I wasn't feeling or thinking anything. What was inside me was stopped and frozen.

Washburn got the doors unlocked.

"In the back," Tucker said to me. "Behind Dell."

I climbed into the Explorer.

"Now you," Tucker said to Marcus. "Up front, next to Dell."

Tucker got into the backseat beside me.

"Start the car, Dell," he said.

"Where we going, Danny?"

"That place by the river. The one you like."

"By Plymouth?"

"That's right, Dell. That's the one."

"What we gonna do there?"

"You'll see. Just drive. You know the best way. Not through town."

Washburn started the car and pulled it out onto the road.

Tucker said, "You know, Marcus, what I'll do if either you or the girl make any kind of move. The girl does something, she goes first. You do something, she still goes first. Okay? You understand?"

"Perfectly," Marcus said.

"Good. Glad we have that straight."

Tucker's voice was as worn as his face.

There was little traffic on West End. Washburn drove well. But then he knew these back roads and their convolutions. Just the way he knew the banks of the Merrimack.

Tucker held the shotgun across his lap, his finger curled around the trigger guard. He slumped a little. But I sensed that he would know if even the pattern of my breathing changed minutely.

We had ridden for about half an hour in perfect silence when Marcus broke it.

"Dan," he said.

Tucker's finger moved very slightly on the trigger guard. "Yeah?"

"What's Washburn to you?"

"He's my brother."

Perhaps forty-five minutes passed before somebody spoke again. This time it was Washburn.

"Hey, Danny, we're almost there," he said.

"I know, Dell. You want to find someplace where you can park this car way off the road, all right?"

"Sure."

"You know a place like that?"

"There's plenty."

"Okay. Well, just find the best."

"Sure, don't worry."

"I'm not, Dell."

I was still swaddled in my coccoon of numbness, still divorced from all sensation. Although I'd absorbed their meaning, I hadn't reacted to Tucker's last words to Marcus. I knew I should be terrified. But terror seemed almost beside the point now. Irrelevant. Where the fear should have been was just a white blank.

"This, where we're going, is where the Merrimack becomes the Merrimack," Tucker said.

I nodded.

"Liz?"

I looked at him.

"I'm sorry it had to be this way."

"Uh-huh," I said. "You killed Marian, didn't you?"

"Yeah."

"Because she was getting too close to finding out about Dell. And—your relationship with him."

"That's right. I didn't want to do it. I didn't have a choice. I tried to discourage her. It didn't work."

"Why didn't you shoot me, too? I was helping Marian. Following her lead."

He sighed. "I thought without her you . . . wouldn't be any real threat. And I figured Marcus could control you."

"*Control* me?"

He smiled faintly. "Bad choice of words. Excuse me. What I meant was, Marcus was convinced that Kmiec was the killer. And you worked for Marcus, so . . . you'd go along with what he was . . . with him. At least I thought that. Guess I was wrong."

"I pretty much did go along until this afternoon," I

said. "I only really decided to go after Dell as a gesture to Marian's memory. Then I saw his picture gallery."

Tucker nodded. "I wish you hadn't. I really do."

I realized, as I watched the play of his expression, that I believed in his regret. It was written on his face. I also believed in his pain. That had been incised on his face long before the regret.

"Dan?"

"Yeah?"

"Why the hell didn't you make Dell get rid of his collection?"

Tucker's eyes squeezed shut for a bare second. "I couldn't."

"Why not?"

He shook his head. "Not now, Liz."

I looked at the back of Washburn's head. There was no way he couldn't have overheard the dialogue between Tucker and me. But had any of it registered with him? He gave no sign.

He was a forty-one-year-old man and apparently the shrewd plotter and author of a string of bloody killings. Yet in manner and speech he was ingenuous. Almost childlike. Was he retarded? No. He had a driver's license and was clearly qualified to hold one. He lived independently and self-sufficiently. His job called for some mechanical skill and responsibility. Yet . . .

The car turned off the asphalt road and bumped onto rougher terrain. All around us were high woods. Washburn slowed the Explorer to about twenty miles per hour.

"Dan?"

"Yes?"

"You were the one who gave Kmiec all the details of the murders, weren't you?"

"Yeah."

"How'd you get him to confess to a series of killings he didn't commit?"

Tucker gave a short laugh. "He was going to stay in prison for the rest of his life. What did he have to lose?"

I remembered arguing the same point with Marian. "Maybe the question is, What did he have to gain?"

Tucker shifted around in his seat. "It made him feel like a big man. Powerful. Scary. Macho. And of course Marcus here was going to make old Henry a living legend, wasn't he? The baddest dude of all. You don't think Henry ate that up?"

"Oh, Jesus," Marcus said.

"You got scammed and suckered on that one but good, buddy," Tucker said.

"Kmiec's suicide," I said. "It wasn't a suicide, was it?"

"No."

"You?"

"Yes."

"Why?"

Tucker was quiet for a moment. Then he said, "I was afraid he might crack or slip, sooner or later. He wasn't the brightest bulb in the world, you remember. Besides, he served his purpose." Tucker looked at me with sudden energy. "Why? You feel sorry for Kmiec? You feel bad he's dead? Shit like that doesn't deserve to live."

"No."

Washburn brought the car to a sudden stop.

"We're way far off the road, Danny," he said. "This okay?"

"It seems fine, Dell." Tucker raised the shotgun and aimed it at me. "Marcus? Turn around."

Marcus turned.

"See how I'm holding this gun?"

"Yeah."

"All right. You get out now and stand in front of the car. You too, Dell."

Marcus slammed the door behind him. The car vibrated. Washburn frowned at him and said, "Hey, lighten up, man."

Tucker and I climbed down from the Explorer. I could feel the psychic pressure of the shotgun barrels between my shoulders.

"Okay," Tucker said. "We'll walk down to the river like we walked to the car. Dell, you and the girl go first. This guy and I'll be right behind you."

Again Washburn took hold of my upper arm. "You want to watch your step," he said. "This path isn't too good. Lotta holes in it. You can fall and hurt yourself bad."

I looked up at him. There was nothing in his face but a kind of amiable concern that I not stumble over a tree root and sprain my ankle.

His eyes were soft with that anxiety.

Angel eyes.

The path was as narrow and uneven as Washburn had said. It corkscrewed down a gentle slope through a press of pine and leafless trees. Nobody talked.

Marcus and I were on our way to die. Funny, I'd had other plans for this evening. Well, pretty soon none of my plans would matter. Nor Marcus's. Whatever his had been. Nice to have known you, Griffin. Fun while it lasted.

Jack.

What was the last thing he'd said to me?

Take care.

I did the best I could, babe. At least, I tried. I never meant . . .

The path opened onto a clearing about twenty feet wide by twenty feet deep. It very much resembled the clearings where Washburn had committed his murders.

This is a hell of an ending for the book, Griffin. Too bad you won't be around to write it.

My fault.

We stopped in the center of the clearing. The river ran broad and clear before us, reflecting the pale glimmer of the moon.

"You two," Tucker said. "Stand there. Side by side." He motioned at a decaying birch log fallen across the clearing floor.

Marcus and I shuffled together. He took my hand.

"Griffin," I whispered. "I'm so sorry."

He squeezed my hand and shook his head fractionally.

Standing off to one side, Washburn gazed at us with mild curiosity.

Tucker lifted the shotgun and pointed it at me.

"Dell," he said. "Look over there."

"What?" Washburn said.

"Over there. That oak tree. The big one."

"Which?"

"Over *there,* Dell."

Washburn twisted around, craning his neck.

Tucker fired the shotgun into the back of Washburn's head.

THIRTY-FIVE

A piece of skull blew sideways and hit Marcus on the cheekbone. He jerked his head. My legs got very soft. Marcus released my hand and grabbed me by the waist.

Tucker stood rigidly upright, his eyes closed, the shotgun still in firing position.

Marcus pressed his chin against the top of my head and tightened his arm.

Tucker opened his eyes and took a long, shuddering breath. He swiped at his mouth with the back of a hand.

"Okay," he said. "You two have to do something now." He looked for a long moment at where Washburn's body lay. "Marcus?"

"Yes?"

"That juniper over there." He pointed with the shotgun. "Get what's behind it and bring the stuff out here."

Marcus stared at him.

"Now." He raised the shotgun toward me.

"Sit," Marcus said. He pressed me gently down onto the birch log. I settled there awkwardly, my rubber-snake legs sliding out before me. Marcus walked over to the juniper. I heard some thrashing noises and the dry rustle of dead leaves.

"This?" Marcus said.

"That's right," Tucker said.

In either hand Marcus held a spade.

"Good," Tucker said. "All right, now, both of you are going to dig. Right here." He motioned with the gun at a spot about four feet from where I sat."

Marcus glanced at me and then at Tucker. "I'll do it," he said.

"No. You both will."

I pushed myself upright. "I'm fine, Griffin." I got to my feet. I only wobbled a little. I held out my hand to Marcus. "Give me one of those."

"You owe this to Dell," Tucker said. "Both of you."

"Oh, Christ, Tucker, what's the point?" Marcus said.

Tucker took a step toward him. "The point is this: You and she can dig the hole and give Dell a decent burial in a place he would have wanted it, or you, Marcus, can dig two holes. One for Dell and one for her. Your choice. You pick. What'll it be?"

Marcus gave me one of the spades.

"Get started," Tucker said. "When it's deep enough I'll let you know."

Marcus jammed his spade into the ground and brought his foot down on the upper edge of the blade a lot more heavily than necessary.

The earth wasn't completely frozen, but it was packed hard. After five minutes I was sweating inside my heavy jacket. And I'd thought the night cold before. I straightened up and looked at Tucker. He was leaning against the trunk of a pine, watching us very closely as we worked.

"You mind if I stop and take off my jacket?" I said.

"No. Go ahead."

I laid the coat on a pile of leaves and picked up the spade.

Marcus dug with an unflagging robotic intensity. His face and hair were soaked.

"Make it longer," Tucker said. "Seven feet. I don't want him all cramped up in there."

Marcus's spade hit a root. He hacked at it violently. "Tucker?"

"Yeah?"

"How long have you been planning this? These fucking shovels didn't grow up out of the ground like mushrooms overnight."

"No," Tucker agreed. "I put them there the other day."

"You knew this was going to happen?"

"I knew at some point I'd have to do what I did."

"And you thought you'd have some help?"

"Never mind that. Keep digging."

Marcus held the spade like an ax and swung it down on the root. The pulpy wood splintered into white bits.

My arms ached. The rocky soil seemed to weigh twice as much as it actually did. A nightbird cried somewhere in the woods behind me.

Despite the gathering cloud cover, the moon was still riding high, illuminating the clearing with a pale silver glow. The mountain of earth Marcus and I were creating was up to my waist.

"Stop," Tucker said.

Marcus leaned on his spade with both hands. I could hear him breathing.

Tucker walked to the far end of the trench we had excavated.

"All right," he said. "That looks good."

I let my spade drop to the ground beside me.

"Now," Tucker said. "Marcus, you and Liz pick up Dell and put him in there and cover him up."

Marcus flexed his shoulders. His hands clenched on the spade. For one excruciating second I thought he might try to chop at Tucker with it.

Oh, no, Griffin, please, no. I don't want to see you with half a head.

"You're out of your mind, Tucker," he said.

"Maybe," Tucker said. "So what? Do it." He turned the shotgun at me. *"Do* it. Both of you."

Marcus closed his eyes and inhaled harshly. "Liz?"

"Yes?"

He threw the spade to the ground. "Take its—take the feet."

We walked toward Washburn's body. I kept my face averted so I wouldn't have to look at what was left of his skull. The body was prone. We rolled it over. I put my hands beneath the ankles. Marcus grabbed the shoulders under the arms.

The body felt as if it weighed five hundred pounds. We hoisted it about a foot off the ground. I lost my grip on the left ankle. The body sagged and spilled sideways.

"Be careful, for Christ's sake," Tucker said.

I grabbed the leg I'd dropped, clutching at the denim that clothed it.

We hauled the body to the pit and lowered it into the trench. There was a mess of blood on Marcus's hands and arms.

"Cover him up now," Tucker said.

It was easier filling in the hole than digging it.

"Tamp the earth down nice and hard," Tucker said.

We walked back and forth over the grave, like forced partners in some *danse macabre,* stamping our feet up and down until the ground beneath it firmed. When we were finished there was a slight mound.

I felt nothing but a huge relief that the chore was completed.

The nightbird cried once more.

I was again aware that it was very cold.

"Can I get my coat?" I asked.

"Yeah, sure," Tucker said. "Then you and Marcus can sit down right on that log, where I can see you. I have a few things to say."

"I'd prefer to stand and listen," Marcus said.

Tucker gazed at him. "Suit yourself. Just remember who gets the next load of shot if you do anything."

"I'll remember that," Marcus said tonelessly.

I zipped myself back into my coat and stuffed my hands in my pockets. I didn't sit down on the log. I, too, preferred to stand. Tucker didn't say anything further about it.

He leaned against the pine trunk, cradling the shotgun in his arms. The shadows on his face deepened the lines and creases in his forehead and cheeks. When he spoke, it was in a voice as affectless as Marcus's.

"Dell isn't my blood brother," he said. "He was my cousin. My mother's sister's kid. My uncle was killed in Korea. My aunt died in a car crash a few years later. Dell came to live with us when he was about five."

Something stirred in my mind, a recollection of something I'd read in Marian's notes. I cleared my throat. "Dan?"

"Yeah?"

"I thought Dell was raised by a couple named Fraser. Theodore and Emma Fraser."

He nodded. "My mother and stepfather. My real old

man died in a logging accident when I was a kid. My old lady got married to Fraser a couple years later."

"I see."

"I kept my old man's name. Tucker. Dell kept his old man's name. Washburn."

I nodded.

"I know you think Dell was some kind of a moron," Tucker continued. "Because of the way he walked and talked. Slow and funny."

I was quiet.

"He wasn't, though. He had a high I.Q. They tested it a few times in school. He had that strange walk because he has a . . . like a clubfoot, I guess.

"Anyway, I was about sixteen when my aunt died and my mother and Ted took him in." Tucker shook his head slightly, as if in reminiscence. "Christ, I thought he was a weird little kid then. Well, he wasn't so little, even at that age. He was always real tall, much taller than the other kids in the neighborhood. Plus he wasn't coordinated because of that fucking foot. He got picked on a lot for . . . looking different. You know what shits kids can be about things like that. The bullies were always on his case."

I nodded a second time. Marcus stood a few feet away from me, unmoving. I could almost hear him absorbing Tucker's words.

"At first," Tucker went on, "Dell was nothing but a goddam pest to me. Especially since my mother expected me to act like his older brother. And baby-sit him. You know? Jesus, I was sixteen. Taking care of some nerdy kid wasn't where my head was at in those days."

"Did you end up becoming his protector?"

Tucker looked at me with a little surprise. Then his

mouth quirked in the briefest of smiles. "Well, yeah. I mean the little jerk was so lost and alone. He had no friends. Not one. *Somebody* had to . . ."

"Yes."

"I spent what time I could with him. The rest of the time he . . . made his own fun. He read a lot. Science and nature books. We lived in Concord then. He'd spend a lot of time down by the river. He'd collect all this crap, you know, rocks and fungus and leaves. Bring it all home. Used to drive my mother crazy. Once he brought home a dead fish and put it under his bed. Jesus, the smell."

"The Merrimack River," I said.

"Yeah. That river saved him when he was a kid. Gave him a . . . what? Refuge? Then, when he was about twelve, it almost killed him."

The moon went behind a cloud and for a moment Tucker was only one dark shape among many.

"It was a late spring afternoon, I remember. Dell was down at the river, messing around in one of the open places on the bank. A lot like this clearing, I guess, and he was there looking for some kind of goddam special moss."

"Yes."

The moon emerged from behind the clouds and Tucker's form resolved itself out of the shadows.

"Anyway, a group of about four boys came along, a little older than Dell, maybe thirteen, fourteen. Mean kids, all of them. Dell knew them; I guess they'd given him trouble before. He saw them and he tried to run. They went after him and caught him. They dragged him back to the clearing. Then they beat the shit out of him. No particular reason, you know, just because it was fun. Then they stole his clothing and threw him in the river. He could have drowned." Tucker paused. "Christ, maybe he should have."

I couldn't speak.

"I was twenty-three when this happened," Tucker said. "I was in the service by then. They had me stationed in Germany. There wasn't much I could do for Dell at that point. Then I got out of the army and joined the cops. I got married. My wife and I bought a place in Laconia. Dell was in high school by then."

"Did you see him?"

"When I could. But Annette—that was my wife—couldn't stand him. Didn't want him around. Thought he was weird. I didn't fight her on it. Maybe I should have. Oh, well, I guess it didn't matter in the long run. Annette and I broke up about ten years ago. And Dell . . . maybe there was never any hope for him. Even if I'd been there for him."

Marcus said, "You do what you can."

"Yeah," Tucker said. "Tell me about it."

"Dan," I said. "How long have you known Dell was the Merrimack Valley Killer?"

Tucker breathed in audibly. "Since right after the girl died in Plaistow. Marian's little sister."

"Cheryl Timmons."

"Yes. Her."

"Did you suspect before you found out for sure?"

"I didn't want to."

"How did you learn that Dell was the killer?"

Tucker squeezed his eyes shut. "He told me."

"Christ Jesus," Marcus muttered. "He *told* you?"

"I can't . . . describe what it was like. He just announced it to me one night, like it was the most casual thing in the world. The way you'd talk about going fishing and how you hooked a couple big ones. No, that's not exactly right. He didn't brag, like you would if you caught a twenty-pound salmon. He was just very matter-of-fact about the whole thing. God."

"Why did he tell you?"

"I don't know. He knew I was working on that case. On the New Hampshire murders, anyway. It wasn't like he was confessing."

"Trying to help you, maybe?"

"No. It wasn't that. He . . . I don't know."

"What did you do, after that?"

"The wrong thing, God help me. I made him go away. Leave the state." Tucker looked at the mound of earth in the center of the clearing. "I should have done then what I did tonight."

"When did he come back here?"

"About four months ago."

"And rented a house in North Conway and got a job at a ski lift and killed Joanne Parisi," Marcus said very softly. "Did you think sending him away would cure him? That when he came back he'd be normal? Not a killer anymore?"

"Griffin," I said sharply. "For God's sake."

"No," Tucker said. "I didn't think he'd come back . . . normal. I did it to give me time to think about what to do."

"And then Henry Kmiec murdered two Boston hookers and tried to kill a third. Because he'd read in the papers about the Merrimack Valley killings and thought, Hey, what a neat idea. I think I'll butcher me a few women and dump their corpses by the river."

"Griffin," I said. "Shut *up.*"

"No," Marcus said. "No, I won't. Tucker, Kmiec was the perfect solution to the problem, wasn't he? Tailor-made. Christ, the guy even wrote 'I will do this again' on one of the newspaper clips about Cheryl's murder."

"Yeah," Tucker said. "That's right. Kmiec was the solution. Till I could come up with something better."

"Dan," I said. "Why didn't you just turn him in?"

"I couldn't."

"Why not?"

Tucker's face clenched like a fist. "I couldn't, goddamnit. I couldn't. He was my *brother.* My *brother.* And I was the one who was supposed to watch out for him. Just before my mother died, she . . . she made me promise her that I'd look after him. 'He's so alone, Danny,' she said to me. 'He has no one. Only you.' And it was true. Everybody else treated him like shit his whole fucking miserable life. Like a freak. If he'd been arrested, do you know what they would have done to him?"

"Could it have been any worse than what *he* did?"

Tucker said, "You don't think I live with that every day?"

I took a deep breath. "Dan, if you wanted to protect Dell, why did you let him keep that collection of photos? The pictures he took of the women after they died. My God."

"I tried to get them away from him. He . . . he got violent."

"With you?"

"Not exactly. He said if I made him burn the pictures, he'd replace them with more. Of other women."

"And maybe you let him keep them because they were so incriminating," Marcus said. "Maybe you were hoping somebody would see them. And that would push you into doing what you did tonight?"

Tucker looked at him. "Maybe," he said. "Maybe."

"Dan?"

He transferred his gaze to me. "Yeah?"

"There was a big lapse of time between when Dell killed Diane Lamonica and when he killed Peggy Letourneau. Why was that?"

"He was working in Maine then. At a ski place there."

"And he didn't . . . ?"

"No. Nobody died in Maine. At least not because of him. I know that."

"How?"

"There's no Merrimack River in Maine."

"A woman named Sheila Gavin died in Andover, Mass., then. Are you *sure* Dell didn't travel down from Maine and . . ."

"I'm sure."

"How can you be?"

Tucker looked at me oddly. "If he had, you would have seen her picture on his wall, Liz."

I nodded.

Tucker sighed. "I think you know everything now."

"No," Marcus said. "Not really."

"What have I left out?"

"If Dell got beaten and nearly drowned by four boys when he was twelve and that set the thing off in his brain that made him a killer, what . . . why did he grow up to kill women? And not teenage boys? If he was going to get revenge for what had been done to him?"

Tucker was silent for a moment. Then he said, "I guess I did leave something out."

"What?"

He rubbed a hand over his face. "After the boys left, Dell was able to pull himself out of the river. I told you, they'd taken his clothes. He was a mess. Two black eyes, a broken nose. Blood and bruises all over him. He probably was concussed. He sure as hell was in shock. But he managed to drag himself out of the clearing and up the bank to the road. I guess he thought he could get help."

"Did he?"

"Eventually, yeah. He had to wait for a car to come by. Actually it was the police who picked him up and took him to the hospital. But before that, I guess ... well, the story I got from my mother later was that a group of girls came along. Maybe seven or eight of them. Walking home from school. They saw this naked, bloody kid. A big hulk with a clubfoot. A couple screamed. A couple laughed. They all ran. Not one even asked him if he needed help. Not one."

"So *they* became the villains in his mind?"

"I guess they must have. Well, I know they did." Tucker glanced at me. "You ever wonder why Dell always tied a green ribbon around the necks of the women he killed?"

"Plenty of times."

"Those girls who ran away from him that day were from the St. Ignatius School. The Catholic school. They all wore green uniforms. With green bow ties."

"Carolyn Bragg *taught* at the St. Ignatius School," I said. "She was the first victim."

"Uh-huh."

"Your *brother* must have found the connection very gratifying," Marcus said. He said the word *brother* as if it were an obscenity.

"Griffin!"

Tucker ignored us both.

"All the women Dell killed were small, too," he continued. "I guess in some way that made him able to see them as . . . those girls."

"He didn't put a green ribbon around Joanne Parisi's neck," I said.

"No."

"Do you know why?"

Tucker rested his head against the pine trunk. "He didn't have any. I found a spool of it in the glove compartment of his truck. I took it and got rid of it . . . without telling him."

"When was that?"

Tucker's jaw went rigid. "The night before he killed her."

"Did you think that would stop him?" Marcus said. "Taking away his green ribbon?"

"No."

"Did you *try* to stop him?"

"I followed him that night."

"And?"

"I lost him."

"Bullshit," Marcus said. "You're a cop. You could tail a flea if you wanted. You didn't want to find him."

"Griffin," I said wearily. "What's the point of this? It's done. We can't undo it."

"Liz, the point is that this son of a bitch let his fucking psycho *brother* get away with eight murders."

"Yes, and scammed us, too. Don't forget that."

Marcus took a step toward Tucker.

Tucker brought the shotgun into firing position. The barrel pointed at me.

"Now it's time," he said.

He moved the gun a few inches to the left to aim at
Marcus.

The nightbird cried a third time.

Tucker turned the shotgun, raised it to his mouth, and
fired.

THIRTY-SIX

"I could almost feel sorry for him," Brenda Adams said. *"Almost."*

"Yeah, me, too. But it's the child I pity. Not the man Washburn became."

"No."

We were sitting in her office in the clinic in the Middlesex County Courthouse. It was a month after that night in the woods by the river.

"And yet," Brenda mused, "maybe he never became a man. Maybe he was stuck at being a twelve-year-old forever."

"Time stopped for him that day. Or he got frozen in that one moment, like a fly in amber."

"Aren't we metaphysical," Brenda said. "Or whatever the hell term you writers use."

"Close enough."

"And Tucker," Brenda said. "My God. He must have spent the last few years living in hell."

"I know. I can't think of him as a bad person even now. What he did was awful, but . . ."

"Whatever he did would have killed him. If he'd turned his brother in, he'd have broken one trust."

"The promise he made to his mother."

"So he broke the public trust instead."

"No way out," I said.

"None at all." Brenda prodded her lower lip with the pencil she held in her right hand. "Liz?"

"What?"

"Why do you suppose Tucker had you and Marcus bury Washburn? He must have known the cops would only dig the body up."

"Oh, sure," I said. "But that was beside the point for him. He wouldn't be around to witness the exhumation."

"Yes, but . . ."

"I think he must have felt it was the last thing he could do for Washburn. Put him in ground he loved with some dignity. However temporarily. It makes sense to me. Tucker's family loyalty was . . . intense."

"I suppose we'll never know for sure, though."

We sat quietly for a few moments. The clock on the wall ticked softly. In the outer office a phone rang.

I opened the notebook in my lap. "Brenda?"

"Yes?"

"Washburn didn't start killing till he was in his, oh, mid-thirties. Why—"

"Did he wait so long to start?" she finished for me.

"Well, yes. It was over twenty years before the bomb went off in his head."

"I can't say. I *can* tell you that delays like that aren't at all infrequent. In fact, they may be the norm, if you want to use that word. Maybe something happened to him when he was—what? Thirty-five? And that triggered things."

"Or maybe it took that long for the rage to build up to the flashpoint?"

"Possibly. Another thing we'll never know for sure."

I shut the notebook and slipped it back into my purse. "Well, thanks for your help."

Brenda wrinkled her nose. "Such as it was."

I rose to leave.

"Liz?"

"Yes?"

"How are *you?* You've been through some pretty rough stuff lately."

"I'm okay."

"You sure?"

"I'm fine."

A week later I was sitting in a coffee shop in Central Square, finishing lunch and reading the papers. I was in the middle of a story about the upcoming elections when I sensed someone standing beside me. I glanced up expecting to see the waitress. It was Jack.

"Oh," I said, startled. "Oh. Hi."

He gave me a slight smile. "Hi."

We looked at each other.

"Would you like to sit down?" I said.

"For a minute." He took the chair opposite me. "I was passing by and saw you through the window, so I thought I'd just stop in and say hello."

"Oh," I said. "Well. Hello."

"Hello."

"How've you been?"

"Fine. And you?"

"Fine."

I dropped the paper on the seat behind me. "Would you like some coffee?"

"No, no thanks. I don't have the time."

"Okay."

He folded his hands on the tabletop. Behind the counter, the waitress hefted the coffeepot at me questioningly. I shook my head at her.

The tendons on the back of Jack's hands were prominent, I noticed.

"Liz—"

"What?"

He pressed his thumbs together. Then he unclasped his hands and let them lie flat. "I just ... I wanted to apologize."

"For what?"

He hesitated. "The things I said to you. That Sunday. The last time ..."

"Uh-huh."

"It was stupid, what I said. I was trying to make you feel bad."

"You succeeded."

"Liz ..."

"It's all right. Forget it."

"The thing was," he continued, "I was sure there was something going on between you and Marcus. It was starting to make me a little crazy."

"There wasn't, you know," I said. "There was nothing between us at all, at that point. He *did* try to start something once. I put a stop to it."

Jack inclined his head.

"Later," I said, "there was something. But it didn't begin until after you and I had ... come apart."

"I see."

"The reason I acted funny when I was with you was that I was keeping secrets from you. There were things Marcus didn't want me telling you. It was a very strange situation for me. Unnatural. I handled it badly, I suppose."

"I was going to write you a letter," Jack said. "And explain things. What was going on in *my* mind. I did start to write. Several times. Somehow, none of the letters ever got done."

I had nothing to reply to that.

"Anyhow," Jack concluded. "I'm sorry."

"Yeah," I said. "Me, too."

"Liz?"

"What?"

"Never mind."

I finished my coffee.

If I had never met Marcus, would the relationship with Jack have stayed intact? Or had it run its course anyway? Maybe Marcus hadn't been a cause but a symptom. Or, perhaps, a catalyst.

Eight years.

Jack and I had been through a lot together in that time. Together. That was the key word. The bad things that had happened to us had pushed us closer to each other, not pulled us apart. Certainly, we'd had disagreements and arguments. But never a break between us until now.

We probably could have repaired the break, but we hadn't. Instead, we'd let the estrangement grow. Why?

All of us had messed it up, trying to do what we saw as right: Tucker trying to hold on to what was left of his family; Marcus clinging to his daughter as the remnant of his; and Jack and me with our separate but intertwined lives, convinced that was the best way to lead them.

It wearied and confused me to think these thoughts.

And if I kept thinking them I'd get sucked down into a morass of emotions I desperately didn't want to feel.

I got up and paid my lunch check. Then I returned to the table to pick up my belongings. Jack rose. He followed me out of the coffee shop.

On the sidewalk we faced each other.

"Good to see you again," I said.

"You, too."

I held out my hand. After the shortest of pauses, he took it.

"Stay well," I said. I smiled and added the order I'd routinely issue him. "Behave yourself."

He seemed taken aback by that echo from times past. Then he responded in kind: "Got no option."

I freed my hand. " 'Bye."

" 'Bye."

I walked to the end of the block and stopped there to cross Mass. Ave. I glanced back at the coffee shop. He was standing there still. I waved to him. He waved back.

Eight years.

Not with a bang but a whimper.

A week after that I finished working for Marcus. I was twelve thousand dollars richer now than I had been when I'd first met him. And I'd picked up a few fairly well-paid free-lance assignments along the way. So I'd eat for a while.

I didn't stop the affair with Marcus. It continued for the next two months. The things we had seen, what we had heard, wrapped us in the bonds of a mutual understanding no one else could begin to comprehend.

And I did care for him.

* * *

A week before Marcus was due to return to Los Angeles, he asked me to go back there with him. To follow him, actually, after I'd gotten my business here straightened out and settled.

He asked me one night at the tail end of a dinner at my place.

I was finishing the last piece of fish when he spoke. I put down my fork and said, "What?"

He repeated himself.

"Griffin . . ."

"Wait a minute, wait a minute," he said. "Let me go on." He pushed his empty plate aside and set his elbows on the table. "I don't know how you feel about me. You've never said. I'm assuming . . . well, never mind. I know how I feel about you. I don't want this to end. I want us to be somewhere where we can be together."

"Griffin," I said. "You're married. Remember?"

He made an impatient gesture. "Gayle and I don't live together. Or do anything else together. We never will. It's over. The rest is just a formality."

I sighed and smiled. "What would I do in California?"

"The same thing you do here. Work."

"At what?"

"*Writing.* Jesus. There's all sorts of things you could do. Don't worry. I'll fix it up. I know a lot of people."

"I know you do."

"There are so many things you could get into. Television writing. That book I think you should start. Magazines. All the stuff you do now, only more and better."

"Where would I live?"

"Wherever you wanted." He hesitated. "By yourself.
With me."

"And after you got divorced? If that's what you intend to do?"

"Whatever's in the cards."

I nodded. "Griffin?"

"Yes?"

"Suppose I couldn't find work."

"You will."

"But suppose I don't?"

"That's not something to worry about. I'll help you."

Keep me, I thought.

I had a sudden ludicrous vision of me in a bikini,
anointed with seventy-five-dollar-a-bottle sunscreen, lounging by a pool, planning my day. Aerobics from ten to
eleven. From eleven to twelve a consultation with my personal astrologer. Then the fitness trainer. No lunch, because I had to stay as skinny as a nineteen-year-old. Then
a quick trip to Rodeo Drive. Then the hairdresser. Then
the nail salon. Then my herbalist or nutritionist. Then I
could fondle my crystals. An active life.

*Oh, don't be idiotic. That's not Marcus's world any
more than it is yours.*

"Griffin."

He was watching me expectantly.

"Griffin, I . . . no. I'm sorry. It's impossible. I can't."

His expression downshifted from expectation to in-
credulity. "Why the hell not? What's keeping you
here?"

"It's where I belong."

"Oh, shit. You belong where you go."

We went back and forth in that vein for another half
hour at least.

"Griffin," I said finally. "Listen to me."

"What?" He lit a cigarette.

I reached out and touched his free hand, then covered it with mine. "You're right," I said. "I *do* care about you. A lot. In some ways I'm closer to you than I've ever been to anyone. In some ways."

"So?"

"But I can't just rip up my whole life and transplant it. There are things here that I care about, too. And people. It's in my blood. I know. I was born in New York. But there are seven generations of New Englanders behind me here that . . . I guess I'm their product. This is where I belong."

He leaned back from the table as if to study me from a longer-range vantage point. "I don't understand a goddamn thing you're saying. I don't understand you. Do *you* understand you?"

"No," I said. "Not really. Not anymore."

He left in the late afternoon. He wasn't flying directly back to L.A. but to New York. There was some legal business about the production company that had to be conducted. I didn't go to the airport with him. It seemed like a bad idea.

We had a drink in the hotel bar. Marcus was subdued. So was I. He was still trying to get me to change my mind.

We were at the table that had become *our* table. The one where only tall New York–bred true-crime writers were allowed to sit. The bar was not busy. Outside the windows a nice mid-May day was in progress.

"You'll be alone," Marcus said abruptly.

I looked at him. Why did people always think that being alone was the worst thing that could happen? You were born alone and you died alone. What difference did it make if you spent some or part or bits or even all of the time in between that way?

And love? Who knew how long that lasted? Everybody wanted it to be forever. Everybody assumed it would be. But maybe it all came stamped with an expiration date on it, like a carton of milk.

There was nothing of this I could explain to Marcus. He wouldn't want to hear it.

"I'm all right, Griffin," I said. I bent forward and kissed his cheek.

He turned his head away from me. "You're a lot tougher than I am."

I smiled and shrugged. Probably I was, by his lights. To me I just seemed like me. "I think I should go now."

He nodded. "That probably would be the best thing."

"Well . . . goodbye."

"Yeah. 'Bye."

"Have a good trip home."

"Thanks."

I left the bar. At the door I turned and looked back at him. He was gesturing to the waitress for another drink.

ABOUT THE AUTHOR

Susan Kelly's first Liz Connors novel, *The Gemini Man,* was nominated by the World Mystery Convention for an Anthony Award for best first novel of 1985, and was one of the top ten books in the National Mystery Readers poll for the same year. She has a doctorate in medieval literature from the University of Edinburgh and has been a consultant to the Massachusetts Criminal Justice Training Council as well as a teacher of crime-report writing at the Cambridge, Massachusetts, Police Academy. She lives in Cambridge, and is at work on her next Liz Connors novel.